ROSE,

   ENJOY MY vision
OF BOHEMIAN SAN
FRANCISCO...

   CHEERS -

6-21-05

i

TRAPPED DOORS

ken janjigian

Pocol Press

POCOL PRESS

Published in the United States of America
by Pocol Press
6023 Pocol Drive
Clifton, VA 20124
www.pocolpress.com

© 2005 by ken janjigian

Publisher's Cataloguing-in-Publication

Janjigian, Ken.

Trapped doors / Ken Janjigian. – 1st ed. – Clifton, VA : Pocol
Press, 2005.

p. ; cm

Four novellas.
ISBN: 1-929763-20-4

1.   Self-actualization (Psychology)—Fiction.
2. Artists—California—San Francisco—Fiction.
3. San Francisco (Calif.)—Fiction. I. Title.

PS3610.A545 T73 2005
        813.6–dc22   0505

Dedication

For my mother, Alice Janjigian

In memory of my father, John Janjigian (1932-2003).

Acknowledgements

Eternal gratitude to Jeff Tinkham for his endless help with editing, ideas and cover designs since the book was first conceived.

Thank you to Mathilde Louys, who has been a constant source of belief and confidence in this book for the past four years. I would also like to thank Stephen Demirjian for his feedback and longtime support. Thanks also to Marjana Hotomski for her recent support and readership.

Thank you to J. Thomas Hetrick and Pocol Press for believing in the story and for your hard work, patience and flexibility while sculpting the book into its final state.

This book is also in memory of my uncle, Arthur Manasian (1931-2004).

Greil Marcus's book, *Lipstick Traces*, was an invaluable resource for the art history used in the novel.

Disclaimer

This is a work of fiction. All the characters and events of the story are a result of the imagination.

Table of Contents

i will wade out
        till my thighs are steeped in burning flowers

-ee cummings

henry fields
Boise Redux

I was on the bus on my way to my first day as a cabbie. The bus chortled down Haight Street. Two healthy looking twenty-somethings were panhandling on the corner of Clayton Street. Cloud Nine had a line out the door for breakfast. Seamus O'Brien was unlocking the door to his bar, The Gold Cane. A guy in white overalls was slopping soapy water on the windows of The Gap. A squeegee rested nearby. A guy twice my age, head slouched low, sat in front of me sucking on a brown-bagged bottle, the old born trying to go back.

I picked up a newspaper next to me. It was already open to the comics, horoscope, and crossword page. I read my horoscope. "You may be a little erratic today. Question the events that have recently taken place." That's me everyday, I thought. I looked at this day in history, "In 1933, the 20th amendment to the Constitution, the so-called 'lame-duck' amendment, was declared in effect." I looked at the Reflection for the day. "Love is what you've been through with someone. – James Thurber"

We passed the Ashbury sign. My old bookstore, Great Expectations, was on the left. The doors were locked. I had worked there for four years and quit two weeks ago. My wife was happy that I quit. She wasn't happy about my becoming a cabbie. I was thinking back to a conversation I never forgot. The conversation that got the wheels turning to this recent change in my life.

Nancy was sitting on the couch drinking coffee and holding one of our cats. I was at the kitchen table, sitting in front of my typewriter. I was about to start typing, to start writing. At that point I was working on a collection of sonnets about Rimbaud and Verlaine. Sonnets about their sordid, tragic relationship.

Nancy said, "Henry, can we talk before you begin?"

"Sure. It sounds serious."

"It is." She said.

I got up and sat on a rocking chair, diagonal to Nancy. Our other cat jumped on my lap.

"Henry, we've been in San Francisco six years and I'm tired. Henry, it's not working out the way we planned." Nancy said.

"Life is what happens when you're busy making other plans." I said, quoting John Lennon.

"I'm so tired of you using that quote. It's bunk."

"It's truth." I said.

"No, it's an excuse for missteps."

"Plans never go the way we want them. We aim and hope to come close to the target."

"We don't even have a target, Henry."

"What's not working?" I asked, knowing it was a ridiculous question.

"Everything."

"That's a lot."

"Are you going to continue this sarcastic avoidance?"

"You seem a bit tense." I said.

"I am."

"No one said it would be perfect, Nancy."

"No one said it would be this imperfect, Henry."

"Have you made a decision that I should know about?" I asked.

"Yes. Yes, I have. Listen, Henry, youth is over. It's time to quit. It's getting embarrassing. I can't live this life anymore."

"What life? Us?"

Nancy explained, "This life. Your life of poems in minor journals and half finished novels. Your life of screenplay ideas developed into nothing more than napkin notes. The whole art escape. It's got to change."

"Well, Nancy, I've been"

"Let me finish. I've got to change, too. My life tolerating your youth has to change. We're sadly, pathetically co-dependent in our malaise. I go to work. You kind of go to work. This isn't a life. It's a treadmill. It's time for a real job, Henry Fields. It's time to make some money. I want to have children and time is running out."

"How can you have any pudding if you don't eat your meat?"

Nancy rolled her eyes. "Henry, I need to tell you something."

I looked at her and forced my smile into serious expression.

"Yes." I said.

"This is real. We need a change. I want children, but not with you this way."

The thought of children was paralyzing except for the act of conception. At least we'd have sex, I thought to myself. I didn't invoke our lack of a sex life to Nancy at this moment because I had enough to handle with my lack of a career. My lack of money. My napkin novels. Of course, our asexuality could have been the cause of all the causes. What causes the cause that causes the previous cause? What was the first domino?

"Henry, this conversation is real."

"I know."

I didn't.

We'd had this conversation a few years back, but it was the genesis of many more like it. One of those moments in marriage that starts you on a permanent detour. It begins to slowly tarnish the original bliss. I bought some time after this by letting Nancy allow me to go to Grad school. I had told her I'd become a teacher by getting a MFA in Writing, which I did all the while working at the bookstore. My last semester Nancy and I worked hard putting together resumes and cover letters for teaching jobs. Nancy was so excited. She even thought our sex life would resume once I got an adult job. We talked about moving back to Boise where I could teach at Boise State. I had an old painter friend who could get me into the English Department. He was sleeping with the Dean...

"We'll have children and time with both our families that we've lost in youthful folly. I'm so excited to change our lives."

3

I took all those resumes and letters and dropped the possibility of change right in the trash on Haight St.

A few weeks after I graduated and with obviously no response from the unmailed resumes, I unveiled my plan.

"Honey, here's what I'm going to do. I'm going to take one more shot at it. I've been talking to Mike upstairs and he's got me convinced the cab could be my answer, my ticket."

"Henry. Everything's an answer for you. Answers. Always answers. Henry, kids look for goddamn answers. Adults realize there aren't any. Three and a half years getting a Masters and now your going to drive a damn cab!"

"I don't buy it. I mean, I do. I mean, I'm not looking for *the* answer. I'm just looking for my own little solution. I just feel I haven't let it all hang out. I wanted one grand shot at some art world success. Not this little underground niche I've been hiding in. Wallowing in. Mainstream success. If it fails, I'll get a professor job and we'll make decent money and buy a little house out in Santa Rosa or near Boise and garden together and have kids and live the years out peacefully."

"I don't know, sweetheart. I'm tired."

"I am too. I just need one more avenue to explore. Then, I'll be at peace with it and we'll slide gracefully into the life you want."

"I want?"

"We want." I said.

"And what's the cab got to do with it?"

"Mike says the cab is full of characters and plot, which is what I need. I can put the blood flow and flesh on, but it's the skeleton I lack. I've even started taking notes on Mike's experiences."

"You mean the backbone."

"What's that supposed to mean?"

"You have to ask?"

"Taking shots at me isn't going to help."

"I know, but I'm at the limit with our life. We've got nothing."

"It all depends on the method of measurement."

4

"Henry, I don't want to get into any philosophical discussions. We've got nothing and you know it, so cut the bullshit detours."

Nancy was very adept at sustaining my digressions. She had years of practice.

"This time, it feels right. It's not a detour. It feels right. I've been a fool in my own word folly. I know. I can handle anonymity, but it's un-attempted effort that eats me up. It's not success or major publishing. That's the veneer. The truth is it's a physical, almost biological need to accomplish a vision that I've had teasing and tormenting me since freshman year at Boise State. If I don't materialize the vision, it will materialize itself into the bitter later years. I don't want the bitterness. I want peace with you. I want you to be proud of me."

"I am sweetheart, but I don't want bitterness in my early thirties. You've got to wave the white flag at some point, Henry. You've already tried. Your Idaho novel got no takers. You put the vision down and you even had connections from the bookstore. You had your vision."

"My Idaho novel was visionless. It was youthful self-absorbed bullshit. It was a word exercise. Flawed. It was shit. The cab will get me into the lives of others. I'll just be this Cooper-like tenderfoot driver caught in the maelstrom of others running here and there. Everybody going and I'm in the same place."

"Hasn't it been done before?"

"Everybody going and I'm in the same place."

"It's been done before."

"Everybody going and I'm in the same place."

"Henry, Christ. Kill the mantra."

"I like the repetition of that. That's why I like simple, piercing poetry. A few more lines to that repeated verse and it'd tell what the novel would need three hundred pages to tell."

"It does speak volumes about us."

"Screw the Joneses. You never cared about that stuff when we met."

"When we met, I was 22. A decade has changed me, Henry. It should have changed you. You're almost forty!"

"Thirty-seven!"

"Like I said."

"One year's all I want. Six months to ride. Six months to churn the notes into a chiseled piece. Chiseled spontaneity. Let me be a footnote to history, but let me do it with a fight. I'm alive just thinking about it."

"Jesus, Henry another year. I don't think I can take it," Nancy sighed.

"You don't get it. We both win. I take a last stab at youthful dreams and we'll be getting more money than ever. Mike says I can take in $500 a week clean, which is fucking double what I'm pulling in at the damn bookstore setting up microphones for the overrated local literati. We'll put some money into some funds or CD's or whatever it is people do with money, so we'll be ready to get a house when I'm all done. We both win, Nancy."

"It doesn't feel like victory. It feels like more of the same, but fine, Mr. Fields, you've got it. One year, Henry. Then you start applying for teaching jobs while you try and publish. You're not expecting a best seller. You can teach and write like everyone else."

"It's a deal."

"I hope you appreciate this. No other sane wife would put up with this. You're on borrowed time."

"I wouldn't have married you had you been sane." I said.

"Likewise." Nancy responded with a hint of a smile.

"You'll see, honey. It's all going to work out. Spiritual and material peace will be in our grasp. The real truth will emerge, not some disguised lie."

Truth. Yellow Cab became my truth.

The bus crossed Market Street and I tried to recollect what Mike had told me about the system. Mike was as regular as they came. He'd been cabbing for twelve years. He said he made great money because he loved driving and he was American. Plenty of customers gave him a huge tip saying, "It's nice to ride with one of our own. One who speaks the same damn language." He lived upstairs from me and had two kids. His connection to the mind warp of San Francisco was his first wife. She was of the crystal, herb, and numerology mold. When she began dabbling in Haitian voodoo and consequently constructed dolls of her parents, Mike had had enough. Mike belonged in the suburbs amidst sports bars and strip malls, but he said that Haight St. and San Francisco had hooked him. "There's something about these fuck-ups that I like. Having them around is good scenery. Kind of keeps me balanced and content with the insignificance of my life. Everywhere else I'd be dull, but here my life seems exceptional in its dullness."

So Mike told me to tip the dispatcher, Delmore, to get my medallion, which I'd hand to the mechanic to get my cab for the day. A $2 fee would get a decent cab and $5 a "mint job". He said Delmore weighed about 400 pounds and was one fine asshole. If you didn't tip, or just a buck, you'd be breaking down twice a week, which is a cabbie's Achilles heel. "Screws the whole week up and you got to play catch up all week." A good bribe would give some precious airport runs as well, which is a "cabbie's bread and butter."

As I walked from the bus stop to Yellow, I remember having these strange, tragic epiphanies swaying my thoughts from gleeful to bleak extremes. It was suddenly crashing my senses that Mike had just offered my wishful thoughts another exit into self-absorption, romance of the self. The cab would give my failing thirties a revisit to my innocent twenties and the eventual crash would be so much harder than those of a decade ago. Back then it just seemed like necessary tragedy that I'd mold into a great and potent creation of salvation. A new way to hitting the winning shot in the state championship. This time, though, the stakes had changed. I'd lose my wife. My parachute would be off and the fall would be achingly lonely, harsh. Real. Simultaneously, I felt so aware of my flaws and past and self. The worry seemed so ridiculous. I could control the rip chord this time. I'd know when to pull out before Nancy would. This was the last chapter and its completion would lead into a new book. The old one would be forever closed. As I wavered from spiritual nothingness and mockery to the waves of wide-awakeness, I kept saying nothing mattered because Nancy would be there. Can't lose Nancy. Can't lose solid ground. Can't lose Nancy. I knew she'd be there. I knew one truth to be true. Nancy and I would ebb and flow, but we'd always end together. Can't lose Nancy.

"New driver, eh?" snorted a grossly rotund man behind bars and elevated above the floor of cabbies and mechanics. He had greasy black hair, thinning on top. Dark half moons hung under his eyes. Plumes of smoke were rising to his left. This was obviously Delmore.

"Yeah, first day."

"You ever cabbed before?"

"No, but Mike Shore has given me some prep on what to expect. I slid Delmore $2. I had planned on $5, but in the moment I didn't want to kiss his ass. I was feeling like a new kid in the 6th grade paying a bully with my milk money. In every job I've ever had, there's always been one asshole to make it unpleasant. I knew Delmore would play that role.

"Mike's one of the best," Delmore shouted.

"Yeah, so I hear."

"You do half as well as ole Mike and you'll be pullin' in some decent change."

I nodded, looking forward to the aloneness of my cab. Kind of my own boss for the first time in material existence.

"You seem too white for a cabbie."

"Didn't know there was a color requirement."

"Too educated, too."

I rolled my eyes and raised my shoulders not sure what I was trying to express.

Delmore looked me in the eyes. "What is this, some sociological research for some half-ass college, some college professor looking for recognition by researching the salt of the earth?"

"Not quite." I smiled and laughed realizing this guy was starting to turn me transparent.

"Or maybe you're some artist. What are you, professor or artist?"

"Does it matter?"

"You want a cab?"

He'd taken my $2, but my medallion was resting in his fat, sweaty palm beneath his curled fire-hydrant fingers. I immediately thought to lie, which I was never good at. Horrible, in fact. Truth always comes out of me, which has

8

made writing fiction no easy task. I wanted a lie, something I could pull off. Just once I wanted to undermine the ever-present asshole of my life. Out-do the prick before he got the upper hand on me.

"I sculpt." I mumbled. It wasn't quite the lie I wanted.

"Huh?"

"I sculpt."

"Really? You don't seem like a sculptor. Let me see your hands."

"What the hell is this? How 'bout a cab?"

My voice was rising.

"Hands first."

I put my hands up to the opening at the base of the cage. He grabbed my hands.

"You ain't no sculptor."

"How would you know? Who made you an expert?"

"I know two things, immigrants and artists, 'cause that's all we got here. I know third world accents and sculptors from musicians to writers. These ain't sculpting hands."

"They were."

"Why *were*?"

"I've stopped. Kind of a sculptor's block, so to speak. I'm hoping the cab frees me and puts a little money in my pockets."

"We got 'em all here. Every failure in art finds their way here. The immigrants, I respect. Artists, no. They're too fuckin' good to drive a cab. They're driving a cab because their so-called "muse" done got up and left 'em or the masses don't appreciate them. Muse, my ass. You should hear the shit that flies in here from the fuckin' artists. They're ahead of their time, post-mortem fame bullshit, Buddhist bullshit to get them through this lifetime. I've heard all the bullshit. You'd think artists would sling some good shit too, since their whole thing is based on twisting so-called reality. I'll take the Dominicans and Brazilians any day. The immigrants work for their family, but you artists lower yourself to work."

"Yeah, we artists are a terrible breed, but I'm a cab driver now, or at least I want to be if you'd give me my damn cab." I was beginning to loathe Delmore.

"You seem like a writer to me. I know a writer when I see 'em."

"I like clay and sometimes bronze, not words."

"What's your name?"

"Henry."

"Henry, I'm Delmore. Remember one thing, writer boy. Don't write about me. I'm telling you straight now because I've seen you writers come in here and use us lifers for your little hobby. Found some bastard's notebook in his cab and had pages and pages on a character based on me full of bullshit imaginations of my past and crappy fuckin' metaphors about me in the cage."

"I don't write. Maybe, I'll sculpt your cage, but no metaphors." I laughed a strained chuckle. This guy was all over me.

"Remember my warning. You better not use me for your pathetic efforts at art. I'll write my own novel, if I want. I ain't gonna be a part of someone else's. Take your medallion. Cab number 2874, see Hal, he'll take care of you."

"Thanks." I walked away, finally free. If every morning's like this, I'll quit by Friday. Delmore was the Cyclops of all previous assholes. He made the others look like Lilliputians.

"The funny thing though, is even if you do write about me, it will never see the light of day, because all you so called artists first, drivers second are here because it's the opposite. You're all failures. Fucking losers. You're cab drivers. Nothing more, nothing less." He laughed big and loud and cigarette stained. "Too good to be a cabbie, huh. Let's see how you fare. There's a pun for you writer boy. Farewell, cabbie. Just another cabbie. Mike I respect, you candy ass artists…"

And on and on he droned as I walked away. Mike never told me to expect this. Sad thing is, I agreed with just about everything he said. He knew me in less than thirty seconds. I spend thirty-seven years figuring myself out and he's got me in thirty fuckin' seconds.

I was walking toward this Hal guy and Delmore had spun some memories to my mind's forefront. My old man whipping my ass with his belt for the last time in good old fashioned, big sky Boise. His big, former farmer hands grabbed the back end of my neck and turned me around, but I glared at him and clenched my fist hard, blood blasting my face and my old man hesitated, then stopped. He put his belt back on through the loops and then looked me in the eyes and calmly walked out. I was ten and he'd never hit me again…Carrying a paint brush in one hand, a book in the other, painting the old halls of Boise State to pay my tuition. Delmore types, who were lifers painting the school over and over, given to their fate and I was envious and condescending toward them all at the same time. These Delmore types were always asking what I was reading and what I wrote about when I would stop to jot in my little dime store notebook I carried in the thigh pocket of my painter pants…All the while I was writing about them and their words and lives and complaints and quotidian feats…Selling Christmas trees…meeting Nancy…sportswriter for the Boise Press…thirty years old…married…San Francisco…Stuck …in San Francisco…bookstore…fighting with Nancy…little poems in little places…un-channeled visions and half-way ideas…Last chance in Yellow Cab…

"Hey, are you Henry?"

"Huh?"

"Are you Henry? The new guy. Cab 2874?" I looked at my medallion.

"Yeah, 2874, that's right. Are you Hal?"

"Yeah. Are you ok? You look, ahh, a little distracted."

"Yeah, yeah, I'm fine. First day, I guess I was trying to remember a few things my friend Mike Shore told me."

"Mike said you'd be in today. I was looking for you and I guessed right."

"It's that obvious?"

"Well, when Delmore reads someone the riot act and tries to get under their skin, I know it's a new guy. You should hear what he says about the immigrants. He just

11

turns the story upside down, elevating the artists and putting down foreigners."

Regardless, the speech still hit my core. "Yeah, no big deal. He's a caricature." I said, thinking maybe I was describing myself. "So what now, Hal?"

"You know how it works right? You went to the big Yellow seminar upstairs where the guys in ties tell the Yellow philosophy."

I nodded.

"Well, now all you got to do is drive. You know your zone?"

"Yeah, Haight and pan handle."

"Lucky you, hippies and punks, with no money, but plenty of needles. Never take them unless they show you green first."

"I know, thanks."

"Mike set you straight, probably."

I nodded.

"Well, you got a good cab. Purrs down the road. Here are the keys. You got any problems, call me or let me know when you return. You got the day shift, so it's really a piece of cake. Might get some speed queens finishing the night in the late AM and besides the foolish left-over hippies and punks, you'll get lots of businessmen going to the airport. The Haight's yuppified now."

"Times have changed."

"I'm glad. I'll take the Gap over some burnt-out phony protesters and angry youth above work."

"Thanks Hal."

"Don't sweat it."

Hal was a good guy, but I felt like a young kid being sent out into the trenches for the first time. I was thirty-seven and he couldn't have been more than twenty-eight. Delmore must have rattled me. He just hit those real spots inside that go untouched for so long, getting covered and masked and walled in like an old, medieval Italian city. I'd felt individualized, using the cab as a vehicle to right my life. I'd finally tapped into something like I'd wanted to so many times and he struck me down. He strung me together on a fragile thread with so many others in this ashbin for artists taxi universe. As I began to wallow in myself, I reminded myself to just drive. Shut up and drive. I talked too damn much to myself when all I have to do is let others talk to me. Hell, what better start could Delmore have been, considering my purpose? It's constant work trying to right the ship of my thoughts.

So I started up my yellow angel and went up the grimy, tire stained ramp leaving Hal, Delmore and the bleak taxi underworld behind and into a clear San Francisco blue sky day and my mind ceased digging within and everything seemed so open. I felt young. I felt something might happen that would lead all the detours and exits into their manifest destination.

So what the hell does a cabbie do in between fares? You either park at a hot spot like the airport or you ride around an assigned area. My area was my home. Nancy and I lived in Cole Valley, a couple blocks north of Haight St. It was a little more civilized than the Haight or lower Haight, which was full of kids and 20-something searchers. My neighborhood was full of former searchers worn into some role. There were quite a few professors, teachers, poet/writer/artist/teachers, literary revue owners. I put myself somewhere between South and North Haight. Not in the middle, because those were the true fuck ups or the exploiters of fuck ups, but some nether world not quite above nor below. The ground I walked on just never felt level. My identity often seemed like it was made out of Play-Doh. Ready to be undone and reshaped.

I had quite a few friends, but I didn't truly like many of them. Mostly I was just passing time in our conversations and looking forward to goodbye. One friend I actually liked was Samuel Connells. He worked at a café in my cozy, Cole Valley neighborhood. I figured I'd get a cup of coffee with an old friend I'd made during my $4.50 an hour bookstore days. Hit some level, familiar ground after Delmore's invasive assault. Sam had always come into Great Expectations to buy biographies of artists, from Judy Garland to F. Scott Fitzgerald.

On the way several hands were waving to get a lift, but I just ignored them. Their faces writhed with frustration upon seeing an empty cab whiz by them. I enjoyed the little semblance of control I had. Hell, this was my cab, and I was the boss. My own little private, mobile office. I could do whatever the hell I pleased.

"Henry, how are you, amigo mio?" Samuel asked from behind the counter of the Paris Commune, which was worker owned as its name implies. A Marxist café alive and well in San Francisco. Where else?

"What kind of watered down cocaine can I get you?" Sam asked.

"What's today's coffee of the day?"

"Kenyan dark roast."

"I'll take it."

"This will get your blood flowing. Are you pounding the keys or just thinking about it? It's always one or the other."

"Sam, today's my first day behind the wheel."

"Oh, shit, I forgot, and you were all nervous for a week and here I damn forgot. So what's the word of your new world?"

"Well, I haven't picked anyone up, but there's my little yellow angel out front."

"That thing's gonna give you some cash and some poems of everyday existence."

"That's what I told Nancy."

"She give you hell?"

"Not too much. We're at a crossroads right now. Kind of beyond it, looking back at it actually. I'm just still unsure which way we went. We'll figure it out. Something's happening or happened, I just don't know what. Anyway, if I were her, I would have left me long ago."

"Don't mourn what didn't happen. Just put it in verse and you'll figure it out. Get it out and the truth will stare right back at you with big relieved eyes."

"I told you I'm done with poems. They're dead. Prose is where I'm at. Good, solid capitalist writing. Make it up for money."

"Don't make it up, just let it out the way it is."

"No money in that. I don't want to get into it now, anyway."

"Fields, you're a Robert Lowell guy and you know it. Lyrically confess and you'll be true to yourself."

14

"Who's me, you or me?"

"Great question. Some days, I might be more you than yourself."

I took a deep breath. "René Descartes, can we change the subject?"

"To you or me?" Samuel unraveled a wry smile at me. "I love tweaking and twisting conversational consciousness, but change away amigo mio."

I looked around the Commune. "How's business?"

"Seeking a grounded, real dialogue Fields. Can't swing the philosophical swerve today, huh? You got it as much as I can give it. We're not killing each other here, getting an equal cut, and decent time off. Operational Marxism better than the real Paris Commune."

"What are you doing with your time off next week?" I asked.

"Reading, jotting down truths. Confessing the internal congress."

"Why don't you travel for a change? Get the hell out of here."

"Don't have the bourgeois wallet. Besides, traveling's bullshit. I'd rather read and travel inside. Real travel, not some roll of film bullshit. I don't need to take one step and I can travel thousands of miles and centuries of time. I got a ticket for the library."

"I think I'd take a beach for a week."

"Henry, you buying into that? Absolutely not you. Stupid humans lying on the sand trying to turn my color. All crowded together thinking they're having a good time. I don't buy it. I'm gonna continue with my truth trend. I'm in a healthy, self-destructive groove. Baudeliere, Rimbaud, Artaud, Modigliani, Plath, and now I'm into this white bread 50's cat, Ross Lockridge."

"What did he write? Ahh, that film with Liz Taylor, *Big*."

"Close. Same era and actress. *Raintree Country*. This Indiana guy writes a goddamn great American novel and kills himself the day before it hits the best seller list. They made him edit it for years after he'd taken years to get it out and then after it's sculpted and ready, he says that's it and buys the farm hours before fame. Had a wife and kids, the whole great big picture of tragedy. Some giant subconscious eruption moments before the world would have saluted him. Fame is deadly my friend. Be thankful of your anonymity. There's peace in it. And I'm also getting into this Japanese madman Mishima. Christ he was crazier than Manson, but a genius. He—"

"Don't you get depressed in this groove?"

"No, strangely exhilarated."

Samuel was about 6 foot 5 and weighed 250 pounds and he was a naturally chiseled mass of muscle and the kindest man I'd ever met, giving money to anyone he deemed in real need. His hair was in 70's style afro and he was the manager of this socialist experiment begun in the 70's with him and a few friends. He's the only one left and has no intentions of leaving. All the worker/owners pull in over 25k a year and he was proud of that and had no reason or want for more money. He's never had a car nor taken a vacation and he's lived in the same modest one bedroom above the café for twenty-five years.

"Coffee's great." I said.

"You feeling tortured."

"Huh?"

"Oh, you know subterranean artist life in a cab."

"You, too. Christ everyone's an analyst today."

"I'm impressed by it."

"I'm not. Maybe, I just want a goddamn job."

"Fields, my soulful San Francisco kinsman, the bullshit won't work with me. We're of the same spirit. Remember their hands."

"Whose hands?"

"Your future characters. Get their words, but remember their hands. The eyes can lie. Everybody thinks the eyes are the window, but it's the hands that hold everyone's spiritual neurosis. Observe the hands, Henry, and you get the soul. Watch them. It's like Homer in West's *Day of the Locust*. Whole novels exist in how one moves and rests their hands. Look at yours."

I did. My right hand was holding my left tightly. I let go.

"Fields, you're tense. You need to talk. You know where I am." Samuel said.

16

"Thanks. I'll be by."

"I want some taxi epiphanies."

"Maybe, I just want some fares."

"Epiphanies are why we are, Henry. Let 'em come. The hands, Henry. Neurosis has nowhere to extend after the hands. It's the last stop. It's all there. Trapped doors, Henry. We're all inside trapped doors."

I just nodded. I think I've got to get out of this loony city, I told myself. I'm starting to realize this city is too full of prophets hazing the periphery. I just might need the dull materialism of the rest of America.

"Let 'em come and then huff 'em back out like a roiling internal tornado." Samuel said as I was halfway out the door.

"I gotta go." I said trying to leave, but Samuel was still bellowing something about epic poems beyond color and into existence and something about Thomas Chatterton and arsenic and water cocktails. I remember thinking, "I hope my first fare's a plain old suit and tie insurance man, wife and kids, mortgage, retirement plan, and two weeks vacation 'til death do us part."

"Hey, 2874. That's you Fields." Delmore's low scratching voice came through the radio.

"I know my number."

"How are you doing out there?"

"Driving."

"Got an airport for you. Pick up at 1487 Fell between Clayton and Ashbury. Can you handle it, soft hands?"

Damn conspiracy and I'm the marionette on the 6th floor. "I'm on it."

"You know where SFO is?" Delmore laughed into a thick and liquidy cough that he must have directed completely into the microphone.

"Don't worry."

"Go get 'em professor and remember this isn't your little pottery wheel. It's a real job in a real world. This isn't pretend. Don't get lost."

"Thanks, Delmore, You're ahhh, ahhh, a real pal."

"The professor seems a bit…"

17

I turned down the volume. There's got to be a reason this guy's all over me. Some purpose, some response to his whole vaudeville act that will help me pass into the next level of Buddhist enlightenment. Or everything has no reason and he's just an out of orbit, free flowing prick.

I took a right onto Ashbury, down to the panhandle and circled around it via Oak and Masonic and then onto Fell. There was a pick up basketball game going on. I glimpsed at the players, both black and white. I ought to go play, I told myself, but I seem hell bent on recollecting events rather than living them. This cab could be considered a new turn at life or just another disguise, draped in trying to resurrect something that could only be recollected. Actually trying to reincarnate my failed twenties in an effort to re-do what's been done and lost to time. Little did I know that my lost twenties would soon be found.

My eyes then saw a small playground with some kids and mothers. Nearby, there was a bearded man in black martial arts attire doing Tai Chi or something similar. I also saw a young man playing Frisbee with his dog. Just before my pick up, I saw a big circle of Hare Krishna types, flaky flower children dancing in a crooked circle and assorted hippies surrounding the peace in. A group of well-dressed men and a few women were watching the flashback spectacle with some big video cameras and one guy, who had a clipboard, was looking at the group and making checks on his board. It looked like they were plotting a movie. San Francisco, real and re-imagined was happening and I was making my first pick up in my yellow angel.

I pulled up to a three story, semi-Victorian and leaned on the horn a couple of times. As I was waiting, I noticed a black woman on the second floor of the building next door. It was a drab, dirty, sky-blue, boxy post-Victorian with a tan fire escape front. She was sitting Indian style by the large bay window overlooking the busy four lanes of Fell Street. I tried to figure out what she was doing and had no idea, but her eyes were lazily looking downward and her hands slowly moving about. The sunlight shone on her dark face, large eyes, thin puckered mouth and small, narrow chin. She was terribly homely and upon my recognition of this, she looked up at the park and her eyes took in the gently wayward San Francisco life. She had no visible facial emotion other than the seemingly pained sadness permanently etched around and within her eyes. My voyeuristic moments were interrupted by a door closing loudly and I saw a woman descend concrete stairs. My fare. I looked back at the window woman when a big, black gate crashed shut and the fare approached my cab. She had red hair, long and shiny partly flowing down her back and the rest split and flowing evenly down the front of her shoulders. I immediately began thinking of Nancy. I thought of the old days when we kissed. Real kissing. Sexual kissing like youth draining its long fettered sexual energy. Not the kind of kisses that we had now. The kind of kisses reserved for aunts at holidays.

"Hi. I'm going to SFO, but you probably already know that." She said snapping my thoughts back.

"Yup. I'm on it." I said.

"My flight isn't until 11:30 AM. We've got plenty of time, so don't kill yourself."

"Ok. We'll go nice and steady." I told her, wondering why she said we, when I was just her cabbie and not traveling with her. Perhaps, it meant something. Perhaps, there was an attraction. After five years of virtual sexlessness, I was foolishly willing to hang my eunuch hat onto anything.

As I pulled from the curb during the break of rushing Fell street traffic, I took a last look at window woman and saw her holding a piece of something in the sunlight staring at it. It looked like a puzzle piece from a jigsaw.

After some silence, I uttered some unplanned words. "Actually, I'm glad we don't have to rush because it's my first day and I'm a little jittery."

"First day, really. You hide your nerves well."

I smiled into the rear view mirror. She was wearing a spaghetti strap yellow silk shirt that glided across her breasts. She had ivory white skin and green eyes under the red hair. She smiled back. Her beauty and attention catapulted my libido into desperation. Pathetically, I began sweating with desire. I remembered contempt for Nancy and our marriage and how it had reduced me to this teenage state. I blamed her, me, it. Perhaps most men would be the same way, happily married or not. However, I'd reached exaggerated proportions. This woman seemed to be receding in my mirror. She was drifting far away in my elongated mirage of a cab. I felt beads of sweat seeking rivulets along my temples and down my nose. Each time I looked back at her, avoiding eye contact, I saw her further and further away as if I were in some surreal stretch limousine. I took deep breaths, hoping my powerful inhalations would put my cab back to normal. I thought I was having a panic attack. High, dream-like anxiety. I couldn't feel the road. I was driving on melting tar. Christ. The thoughts of adultery were tunneling my neurons into absurdity. Why had she ceased talking? How long had it been? What was she doing? I looked back and she was fidgeting in her purse. Thrity-seven years old and I'm hopelessly pre-pubescent. God! I stared at her as she was preoccupied. Her breasts, shoulders, chin, all of her being, was melting me. She still seemed a mile away. Her collarbones were slightly visible. Her face was tender with a few freckles on her small, rounded nose. She had no accent of cheekbone, just soft, pillowy skin, all so unlike my wife. The more I looked at her face, the more it relaxed me and I started to breathe normally as my chest stopped demanding more air than my parched mouth could supply.

She sighed, then said with relief, "I thought I forgot my ticket."

I wiped my brow with a tissue from a box that Nancy had given me.

We caught eyes in the mirror. "Are you ok?" She asked.

"Yeah, yes, I'm fine. I had the heat on up here." I said, honestly.

"Yeah, it's a little hot back here, too."

I could see she had the ticket in hand, but regardless, I said. "You got it?"

"Yes." And she waved it slowly and closer to my mirror. I noticed her long fingers and finely manicured nails.

"Good."

"So," I started, "Where you headed?"

"I'm going to LA."

I nodded and recognized my cab had returned to normal size. Got to keep a conversation going and just look at her face, otherwise I feel like I imagine a mescaline trip would be.

"So, why'd you decide to drive a cab?" She asked.

"That's a good question."

"You don't seem like a cabbie."

"A lot of people have been saying that."

"You seem like this is a means for something else."

"Isn't every job?"

"Not all. So, what's this a means for?"

"I'm a sculptor." I said, sticking to my Delmore script.

"And the cab? Pays the bills, I presume."

"Well, I've been stuck creatively so I haven't sold anything for awhile. I'm hoping the driving loosens me up and sparks something as well as pays the rent." I was starting to like this sculptor stance. It wasn't much of a lie, so I could run with it.

"Really." She said without much of a surprise. San Francisco didn't produce the same effect as ole Boise. I missed old, slowed down, banal Boise. I missed a reaction of surprise toward my life. Attention. Feeling different.

"So what do you sculpt? Heads?" She said.

I was unprepared for any follow up. Delmore had seen through my lie and leapt past it.

"Ahhh, I sculpt my past, sometimes hands, I mean heads, not hands. Depends on the momentum, on how the past plays out within. Maybe, I should try hands though."

"Hands would be different. Well, that's interesting. At least you're not a writer writing about your cab experiences. That would be so trite."

"Yeah, done to death, but, well, it depends on the writer." I'm now willing to bet on a higher power conspiracy trying to mock my life. My own little celestial Dealey Plaza.

"That's true."

There was some silence. I wanted to talk about her and not me.

"So, how 'bout you. What's in LA?"

21

"Phonies, sunshine, tourists, beaches, Mickey Mouse."

"I take it you prefer northern California."

"Actually, I think the LA world is phony in a real sense, while here, people think they're hip to some truth or being, but it's all bullshit. In LA they're phony and aware of it without shame."

"We're all full of shit, I guess."

"Yes. So for me, in LA, there's business. I'm in real estate."

"Sales or rentals or—"

"Whatever they want, I'll do, but mostly sales. That's where the money is."

She was dressed well with nice jewelry and make up put on with class. Most of the women I'd been with were earthy, arty or cheap, none of which fit this lady.

"May I see some of your work?"

"Right now this is my work."

"You know what I mean."

"Well, let's talk about something else. My work is a sore spot right now."

"I only ask because, well, to be quite honest, I'd like to go deeper and further than just small talk."

"Huh?" Had she really said that?

"I'd like to know you better. Deeper and further." She giggled a bit, but not shyly. She was confident and sexy. "Am I being too candid, too quickly for you?"

"No, no. You just surprised me."

"We don't have a lot of time and I trust the energy I feel when I meet someone. I like our energy."

Was this payback for the Curse of Delmore? Was some balance suddenly entering my tilted, teetering life? Or would this be sheer imbalance?

I smiled into the rear view mirror. She was smiling back.

"We're almost there." I said.

Candlestick was on my left. I realized I hadn't seen a single Giants game during my San Francisco years, but I'd read poetry in a dimly lit, lesbian club on the periphery of North Beach. I needed balance. I needed this woman. I

22

wanted to say something bold. She had opened the door and the airport was minutes away.

"What airline are you?" was my bold response.

"US Air shuttle."

She was fidgeting in her bag again and leaning lower than before. I used every bit of my ocular muscles to keep my eyes above see level.

"Listen," she began, "I never got your name."

"Henry, Henry Fields."

"Well, Henry, I'd like to see your work when you're not feeling so down about it. Maybe I could lift your spirits. It would be a nice change from my real estate world."

"I'd like to show it to you, but, ahh, I'd rather just get to know you better, like you said, rather than just show you some of my hack sculptures."

"You're hypercritical of yourself."

"I've had help from others."

"Maybe that's why you can't get the momentum going. Maybe I can help you with your momentum, artistically and otherwise."

"I have a feeling you could help me a lot in some ways."

"I feel you could help me, too."

"I wish I'd started driving a cab ten years ago. That is, if I'd known my first customer would have been you."

"You're a very sweet man, Henry Fields. I can tell you've never cheated on your wife, but my sense tells me that's just what you need to do to get out of an unhappy marriage."

I looked at my wedding band on my hand that was steering. "Well, ahhh, you certainly have a knack for jumping ahead, but really, I'm not unhappy."

"Not happy and not unhappy."

"I don't like the word happy anyway. Peaceful is better."

"True peace or dull peace?" she asked.

"Not sure."

"That seems sure." She was good.

"Maybe."

"Maybe in need of some chaos."

"Controlled chaos, maybe." I played along.

"Oh, well, we can control it however we wish."

"You're killing me."

"I'm trying to do the opposite."

"You know, I don't blame my wife."

"I don't either. There's not always blame to be given. I operate on instincts Henry and they are rarely wrong. Here. I don't want to miss my flight."

She gave me $100 for a $22 fare.

"Please, this is too generous." I said.

"It's just good luck for your first day."

"No, really, I—"

"How 'bout you keep the money for dinner tonight with me. I'll need a cab at 9 o'clock and then we can go out to eat."

"I finish at 6:00"

"Do you have a car?"

"Yes."

"Than call it a cab, just for tonight. Tell your wife something creative. You're a creative man, Henry."

"Of course. I'm not thinking too straight here. It's not often something like this happens to me. I'm a bit jittery."

"It makes you more attractive. See you at 9:00."

"Yes."

I got out of the car to get her bags, but realized she didn't have any bags. So, I opened her door. She got out and kissed me softly on the lips. She put her hand on my cheek and pulled me tighter into her mouth. Her tongue moved sensually into my mouth. Slow and graceful. Erotic. Then she stopped. She whispered, "This was our first date" and she walked through a revolving glass door. I stood there, watching the door spin around and around. It must have been one hundred revolutions.

Perhaps, this whole cab affair… my desire to take this job… move into the apartment below a cabbie and thus be inspired to leave my dead-end, book store job surrounded by the adventures of others…lives being lived…to quit sports writing…to have met Nancy while working three menial, tough-skinned, poet-souled jobs – painter, Christmas tree salesmen in the windy, dry, cold Boise Decembers, and

24

sidewalk scrubber – while keeping Verlaine in one hand and Rimbaud in the other…to have taken ten years to finish college…to have set ablaze all the journals, poems, lyrics, stories, confessional novellas, every form in which we've caged the written word…an ego sacrifice near the ending of a great ego in Ketchum…A big blaze in the Spring twilight, watching the smoke twirl night ward as if new openings would be burrowed free by torching my failed past releases and the misalliances of my inspirations and incinerating my youth, misdirection…If I hadn't ended my relationship with Arlene Murdoch…if I hadn't gotten hung up in 70's hedonism, anti-ideology, the middle class bourgeois life is the bane of modern life with friends like Elgyn Simmons penning metaphorical sci-fi stories only to end up a LA bell hop hated by Nancy for his feckless ways…past symmetry knotting and confounding the present…It all rests on Nancy, got to get us back, sexual, together, coming, touching, or is Nancy false and the desire real?…and this woman, whose name I never got. This new, strange tantalizing woman.

More fares and maybe more temptations. More stories and more Delmore accosting my existence in its transparent armor. Penetrating my shaky, spiritual core. Maybe all these things going further were the catalyst to something I wasn't wholly aware of. Thirty-seven years haven't taught me much, but I constantly remind myself that the present is never really what it seems to be. The moment is quicksand. There's so much more going on. The subconscious reigns the palace infinite. But, just maybe, this time I was on to something. Further awareness. Further knowledge that would penetrate the veneer of the comic kingdom I've so painstakingly been creating.

I had a notebook and pen for between fares time. I jotted some things down after L.A. Woman left, recording some dialogue untrusting of my memory or muse to recollect it right. I was off to a novel start. I was beginning to realize the cab was going to confront my paper-mache present and force action. Perhaps, the novel would never be, but my life might. What I hadn't known was that this yellow angel would drag my past and its great regret into the backseat.

That night I was waiting at the airport. I told Nancy I had a rescheduled therapy session. L.A. Woman was waiting for me when I pulled up. We chatted in the car for a while. This time she was in the front seat. I tried to concentrate on what was happening in the moment.

"I never got your name." I told her.

"Eve Hastings."

"Henry Fields."

"I know," she reminded me.

She reached out and we shook hands.

"A pleasure, Henry"

"Eve Hastings. How appropriate." I smiled.

"How so?"

"Metaphorically. A biblical hurry. You know, Eve, this isn't easy for me."

"Because of your marriage?"

"Of course. Otherwise, there'd be nothing stopping me from kissing you immediately."

"Is a bad marriage worthy of fidelity?" Eve asked as we left the airport in my Ford Escort.

"Yes and no."

"That means no, if I may be presumptuous."

"Maybe."

"Are you in love with her or the boundaries of the vows?"

"I don't think I'll know unless it ends and I can see it from the outside. I need a new perspective"

"Henry, we've known each other for less than an hour, but I feel comfortable asking you anything. Do you mind?"

"No."

"How's the sex?"

"There isn't." I said, feeling like I was at the make believe therapy session.

"None?"

"No. Not for five years."

Eve, this stranger, took my hand with both of hers as she leaned towards me. She slowly caressed my fingers and then held my hand between her palms. She moved our hands until she pressed mine along her breast, moving it slowly over and down its firm slope, over and up, several times along the thin silk covering. She then moved my hand down her leg and up her skirt. This game continued for most of the ride. There was no conversation, just the sounds of heavy, on the verge, breathing.

We arrived at her house.

"Come up. I want to change and then we can go to dinner," she said.

I tried to think with my brain.

"We'll never make it to dinner."

"Not such a bad thing. Dinner after."

"Ahhh, I don't know."

"Henry, your resistance is making me want you more. You actually respect your sexless marriage enough to hesitate."

"Strange, huh?" I said, exhaling and inhaling heavily.

"Sweet and so out of male character, especially for an artist in this lost city."

"How 'bout tomorrow?" I asked.

"For?"

"To see each other. Let me sleep and think and do the right thing."

"You're a good boy, Henry Fields."

"I wouldn't go that far. It's not as if I've stopped this snowball from rolling towards inevitability. I'm here, now, tonight, touching."

"It is inevitable. I feel it, too. Henry, don't think I do this often. I haven't felt an instant ease and attraction to a man in ages like I feel with you. My instincts are directing this theatre."

"What time tomorrow?" I asked.

"Four o'clock. The Delta gate. I'm taking the shuttle again to LA."

"Why don't you stay the night?"

"It's not home."

"Ok. Four o'clock it is, Eve."

She left without a kiss. I heard the black gate crash shut. I turned towards the sound and Eve blew me a kiss and turned away quickly before I could return it.

I felt equal parts hero and lout.

27

I drove away and thought to myself, "How can you have any pudding, if you don't eat your meat?"

On my way home I tried to channel my sexual energies resurrected by Eve into desire for Nancy. I considered relieving myself of the pelvic tempest at a construction sight port-o-potty, but decided to dam the flow and save it for Nancy. Besides, I'm too Boise, and not enough Bukowski. Wish I were more prodigal deviant like the L.A. poet scoundrel, but it just isn't me. Samuel would have agreed. Just isn't me.

"So how was your first day? You haven't told me details." Nancy asked as I settled myself on the couch. She was feeding our cats, Billy and Tyler.

"Ahh, not so bad. Of course, there's the requisite asshole, but that's no surprise. I had some interesting fares, a few stories, and made some good tips."

"Lots of jerks out there?"

"Sure are."

"How much did you make?"

"Well, after the $50 for the cab's use I took in about $150."

"You're kidding."

"No. I told you, more money and my last shot in one mobile package."

"Jesus, Henry, that might be $600 take-home, $750 if you worked the same five-day week as everyone else."

"I told you, one day for my last shot, and four for money. That'll leave us with some weekend time together. I'm not a five day week guy."

"I know."

Instant tension began. We had enough skeletons to fill the closets of Versailles.

She let it go. "Anyway, that's more than double your best salary here. Maybe, we can actually take a vacation this year, besides visiting family in Boise." Nancy said with hope in her voice.

"I like it. Maybe, a nice week driving Route 1 and Southern California, too."

"Yes, let's do something," she said.

We rarely dreamed, even little dreams.

"How 'bout a plane to an island in the Pacific and just sitting on some sand. We've never done it?" she said.

"Well, if we could just get the credit cards down." I said stupidly. I was great at self-sabotage.

"That fifth day would take care of it. Do you realize you're losing $600 a month by working four days a week? Hell, we'd have a vacation and zero balance in less than a year."

"Nancy, let it rest. Let me write the damn book and then I'll work six days a week and we'll take two vacations and do all the other crap that money buys."

Whenever we had these conversations, I remember how Nancy fell in love with the notion of me as the young poet trying to sidestep society. The notion of seeking internal sanctuary, rather than external trappings. No traps and new paths. She didn't see through my pose and nor had I. We ran on that for several years. Now she'd gone from idyllic romantic affection to bourgeois beach vacations and I'd seen so far through myself that I was trying to prose my way out of it for redemption. Still, despite my transparency, I couldn't look at myself in the mirror and see a Cab driver, just like Delmore had said. Seven hundred fifty dollars a week wasn't enough. Zero balances weren't enough. Island sunshine meant nothing. Delmore was right. One day in the cab and I was indulging in epiphanies and peeling away poses. I just had to get it right with Nancy. The rest would follow. I loved her. Can't lose Nancy.

"You know, honey, driving gives me a lot of time and I was thinking today, it's not about credit cards or vacations or Boise trips or any of those accessories. It's about renewal."

"Of what?"

"Us."

"Is this about change? About you leaving me?"

"I said renewal. It's about sex. Jesus Christ Nancy, I want to make love to you. I want to screw like we'd screwed before. Angry, passionate, as if it were the only thing worthwhile in life. It's the only goddamn chance to get out of this sorry world, if only momentarily. We can't go on without it. How did five years go by?"

"No Henry. You're wrong. It's about material comfort and peace. We had passionate sex. Where did it get us? Our marriage has changed sex. I think everyone's does. No one says it, but very few are doing it. And those that do are just going through the motions. I don't want us deceiving each other. Fake orgasms, lying pleasure."

"Why the hell does it have to be fake and lies! If I don't turn you on, say it directly. It's bullshit. We're deceiving ourselves if we think a sexless marriage can endure."

"Why, all of the sudden, are you so horny?"

"Five fucking years Nancy!"

"What happened at the therapy tonight or in the cab today?

"It's got nothing to do with tonight's therapy. This has been building for a half of a decade and maybe, the time in the cab just crystallized it. You don't think our dead sex life is an issue? You don't think about it?"

"No, I've accepted it. I think maybe it'll return when your life is together. When we have a house, a normal life, some kids, stability."

"How the hell can we have kids? The immaculate conception?"

Nancy rolled her eyes at my sarcasm. "When we're finally settled. When you get your art fix saturated and accept its course as secondary and our life and future as primary. I think about it, but within reality. Henry, I'm convinced our sexual troubles are related to your juvenile writing need."

"Juvenile! What the fuck are you talking about?"

"Your vulgarity is obnoxious. Keep it on paper."

"It used to turn you on."

"On paper and I was twenty-three years old, Henry. You see, you can't get over twenty-three. It's like this giant hurdle and you just trip every time. No, you don't even jump, you go around and around, without ever going ahead. The cab's another fantasy."

"Nancy, you're the one going around with periphery bullshit. Vacations and good-on-the-outside jobs. So you can tell your family and friends that your husband's not a cab driver, bookstore clerk, failed poet, but a teacher or professor. That's acceptable failure to you and others. To me, it's waving the white flag. I'm not sidestepping anything with us. Maybe, with life I've been, but I'm waking up now. We agreed, one last year. But with us, damn it, I want to rip your clothes off and give you pleasure. That's not going around. That's straight ahead. You on the other—"

"I don't feel it, Henry. I can't just manufacture passion—"

"No, but if we try, maybe it'll happen."

"It's bullshit. Our problems are larger than sex."

"I think are problems begin with sex."

"Henry, wake up! It's a result, a symptom of the big picture. I want you to change and evolve from juvenile art whims into adulthood. I'm tired and sex won't relieve the fatigue."

"What will?"

"Haven't you been listening?"

"Too much."

There was some silence. This argument, although more heated than others in recent memory, would drift away as usual with no climactic end, no resolution. It would be superficially forgotten, but kept within, interred, but lurking. We always ended with dignity, but I felt we needed depth, finality, danger. Dignity was getting us nowhere.

After a few minutes of silence, Nancy asked, "So, what about dinner? What should we do?"

"We should finish our fight and not dance around the hurdle."

"What else is there to say other than time will tell?"

"Why can't you make love to me?"

"Let it go, Henry."

"Nancy, make love to me. Let me make love to you."

"Honey, I'm touched by your desire, but I can't force it. We decided to let it return naturally. I just don't have the energy for it. It's not there for me and maybe you're just kidding yourself. It will resurrect itself beautifully one day in the future. I believe that."

"Nature's taking too damn long, honey."

"Henry, concentrate on the cab and your book. Get it done for me, so we can move on, wherever that leads. I don't give a shit about friends. I want to be proud of you. We need to bury our twenties. You're almost forty. It's time to shed the delusions of the twenties."

"Right now the twenties don't feel so bad. I feel caged. Then, I felt wide open."

"See, you've never gotten through to the reality that life is a cage. Just let it go Henry. It's not as good as you think it should be. The cage isn't as bad as you think."

"You know, if I were an outsider, listening to us, I'd swear you're trying to change me and using the possibility of future sex as bait. As a lure."

"You're not an outsider. You're right here."

"Am I right?"

"You're paranoid, but if it would snap you ahead, I'd do it."

"I know what will snap me ahead."

I kissed Nancy softly. I touched her shoulders, arms, and breasts. I wasn't deluded. I became aroused immediately. I took her hand. She didn't resist. She followed me to the bedroom.

"I'm sorry."

I heard her, but continued.

"Henry, stop. It's not going to work. It hurts. I tried because I do still love you. My mind's not ready. It won't work."

I had tried fingers, tongue, my penis, words, everything. Nothing.

"So," I began, "It's really dead. Hopeless."

"I prefer suspended."

"Do you believe that? That it'll all just come back when I mold myself to what you want."

"I'm not trying to mold you. Or maybe I am, but I believe it's for the better. It's not some Orwellian mind trap where I'm the puppeteer, like you're implying. I just want a normal life. I've been patient. I can't be anymore. I'm trying to mold a married life, not you. Oh, Henry, I don't know anymore."

She began to cry and I withdrew.

"You're right honey. It's time for me to evolve." I said hoping to erase some tears.

I held Nancy and then we held each other and slept. It was as if the attempt at sex was enough to knock us out like sex used to.

I woke up at 2 a.m., fixed something to eat, and sat at our small kitchen table next to the window that let in a brilliant, star brightened black night. It was September. The summer in San Francisco. Halfway through my sandwich, thoughts of a different scenario with Nancy interrupted my appetite for food. I tried, but I couldn't even imagine it. Our sex life had reached such a nadir that erotic solitude couldn't even conjure consummation. The roadblock melted into Eve. Thoughtlessly, I went within and indulged myself, easily, naturally.

After I finished, I tossed the rest of my sandwich in the trash. Scribbled a quick note to Nancy in case she woke up, got in our little Honda and headed into the September night to the Bay Bridge.

I remembered sitting there just after Nancy and I arrived young and alive in San Francisco and sought Hart Crane-like inspiration 3,000 miles away from HIS bridge. I was jealous of Crane. I should have been gay. I should have had real conflict with my old man, not some unsaid, invisible emptiness between us. Tangible pain. Homosexuality. Real dissidence, not some posed existential melancholy void of foundation. The queers got to be the guts of the underbelly with an achingly real need to express rather than just being stuck in some netherworld of frustration...Why do I get into these thought patterns? What I should have been doing was marveling at the bridge itself. So many flock to the Golden Gate and its undeniably majestic qualities. Its royal, red carpet exit to the end of the west, to the precipice of a disjointed utopian hallucination. Yet, it's the Bay Bridge that lies in the shadow of the golden royalty. The Bay Bridge is all power, testosterone, all simple blue-collar strength extending across the great expanse of America's last bay. It's a mighty, silver iron behemoth piercing the center island, Treasure Island, like a medieval sword only to begin again connecting east and west. It's this bridge that merits

33

the awe and wonder, while the Golden Gate is an imposter, illusion, fool's gold. I know if my father ever came here, he'd agree. He'd appreciate the Bay Bridge and see it the way I've seen it since the first day Nancy and I crossed it.

"So you're back for day two, Mr. Sculptor, writer, artist or whatever it is you THINK you are." Delmore said to me as I gave him my $2 bribe.

"Did you have doubts?"

"No, I figure you're some month or two cabbie. Once you realize you ain't getting' no kick here and nothing comes from it except the money, you'll move on or back to wherever you were last. You guys are all looking to go backward anyway."

"We'll see. How 'bout the medallion?"

"You don't like talking to me, Mr. Sculptor?"

"Oh no, Delmore, I just regret we didn't begin these morning talks long ago."

He let out a loud, hearty, cigarette-hacking laugh.

"Hey, Fields, I got you a special fare today. Old lady McCabe. Every Tuesday morning, she's a 9:30 pick up, 1872 Fillmore St. She goes to Safeway, then the Chinese Tea garden in the Park, then down to Ocean Beach and back. Meter's running all the time. It's an easy C-Note."

"Japanese Tea Garden, not Chinese," I said, pushing my luck.

"Big fuckin' difference, Mr. Poet. You want it?"

"Sure."

"Good. Mr. Poseur."

For a moment I liked Delmore in some strange, veracious way. He provided boundaries, recognizable lines that are too often blurred by those we know.

"I'm a caged-bird and you're a cabbie. Get used to it Fields."

I nodded semi-affirmatively. "We could do worse."

"Horse #3762. Old Lady McCabe hates tardy artists."

I got to Old Lady McCabe's at 9:29. She was waiting on her porch, standing with the aid of a tripod metal cane, and wearing an old zipper back, polyester dress. I

34

wondered how she got the zipper up because I assumed she lived alone. She lived on the first floor of a beautiful, bright, recently-restored Victorian. It's one of the famed four postcard Victorians next to each other on Fillmore with the city's skyline lying peacefully behind.

I, myself, was far from pacific thoughts. I was thinking about Eve, feeling the momentum of adultery weighing my thoughts. I had tried so hard with Nancy last night. We needed an orgasm and I tried so goddamn hard. She rationalized everything and now I was witnessing my own internal chain reaction flowing into infidelity. The justifications were in a rising well from which I started to drink heavily.

I saw Old Lady McCabe begin her slow approach to my cab and I got out to help her. She was all bone and sagging, withered skin. Her crooked, bony arms and hands were covered with large, purple green veins rising and falling like the hills of Alameda County.

"Ma'am, let me help you."

She didn't look at me, but she did say, "You're a new one, young man."

"Yes, ma'am, it's my second day on the job."

"Did Mr. Oliver tell you the route I go?" Delmore, I thought, as I held her feathery arm.

"Yes, I've got it."

Thereafter, Miss McCabe shared segments of her eighty-plus years on the planet. She was from a tiny town in Iowa and grew up on a farm during the Depression, dust bowl years. She reminisced about hiding between great stalks of corn reading Jack London novels. She'd sit reading turn of the century, California adventure stories until her father got suspicious and yelled at her for slacking off. She'd put the book in a plastic bag and bury it underground. She'd resume harvesting or planting between paternal screams and dreaming of the sea and mysterious lands. She had to quit school after the 8th grade because that's what girls did in Bucaine, Iowa back in those days. "The Roaring Twenties never hit Bucaine," she said.

The oral autobiography spun along Ocean Beach Drive, where Nancy and I often walked during our early dreamy San Francisco days gone by. Her nostalgic words filled the cab. We drove by the coarse, brown sand and solemn brown water energized by scattered surfers, artists, and teens smoking. They sat along the three-foot cement beach wall randomly adorned with skilled and unskilled graffiti. This was my windshield vision, while my internal sights were woven with the movie of Eve and I undressing tonight. I could not envision Nancy and I sexually. We'd become siblings. Another love had grown, but not the one of forever. A diametric love, wanton and sensual, seemed inevitable tonight. I tried to escape what some hyped-up therapist may call the virgin-whore syndrome and instead turned my thoughts to the history pouring out of my back seat. I was here to escape myself and absorb the tales of others, wasn't I? I wanted to outwit my own repulsive desires. I didn't want to cheat on Nancy. I wanted to cheat on Nancy.

"I got hitched, as we said back then, at twenty-one, like a tiller to an ox. It was awful, life that is. I was damned to a dead, servant life. The only difference between me and the farm animals was that I slept inside. I remember those years, all my years with frightening clarity. My hair and skin have been beaten by the years, but my memory is always in a state of spring, if I may be poetic."

"You most certainly may," I said.

"We stayed married for ten years. Ten long, sad years. Oh, he never beat me or physically injured me, but it was me. I wanted more out of life. My friends thought I was crazy and selfish when I dreamt aloud of running away to the West, but I couldn't get it out of my daily thoughts. Those soil stained, London novels had permanently disheveled my soul. You see, the way I thought then, was my whole town had resigned itself to a life of waiting for the tombstone, while the world outside of Bucaine was spinning with life and adventure. It was a different time. Mystery existed. You know what I did? I laughed at the tombstone and put on the coat of the black sheep, the prodigal daughter in the 1940's, twenty-five years before the foolish hippies. One friend and I plotted our escape. A run into the night on a train into the mystery of the West."

I was thinking only in a San Francisco cab could one hear a female forerunner of Jack Kerouac speaking poetically of possibility. Only here could a seemingly crabby, almost dead, old lonely woman bury the secret treasure of escape in her heart. Or perhaps, it was only here that one would let it out.

Secret goddamn treasures of escapes. Mine was a candy-ass caper of the twenty something soul gone awry. I should have paid my dues covering Varsity softball games for the East Boise Press, so that today I'd have a decent, respectable journalist career. Nancy was Right. Instead, I took the exit for too many secret treasures, which I'd assumed would reveal themselves through the low, strange, fringe road. These alleged treasures within, that I'd staked a life on, never existed. It was all some sad, Halloween costume, worn all year, whispering a lingering mockery of adolescence. Tell me more Old Lady McCabe. Take me out of me.

She continued her cryptic heart vignettes as I tried to listen purely. We cut a swerving swath through the seven miles of Golden Gate Park. Colorful flowers, powerful trees, green grass, and blue and yellow above. I knew why she wanted to drive along the vast Pacific and into the Park's verdant path. I tried to unhinge myself of me and see, truly see the natural panorama unfolding in front of me and hear, truly hear, the oral history unraveling behind me.

Her friend convinced her to hop a freight going west during WWII, at a time when newspapers were discussing the potential of a German Europe. America hadn't entered yet. It was around late 1940, but there were jobs aplenty for women, as men began to train for the inevitable. The two soon-to-be Rosie Riveters stashed a little money away for a couple of months. The night they were going to leave her friend got cold feet.

"'You should've gotten cold feet your wedding day, not today,'" I told her, but she didn't listen to me. So what did I do? I went anyway, all alone on an evening train for $11 one-way and I haven't been back since. I left a note for my husband and I'm sure he just replaced me. It wouldn't have been difficult, like hiring a maid."

She had some glory years alive and free along the elevated ebb of youth before the flow settled and dissipated the surge of severance. She worked in a factory and danced with sailors during the war. She romanced more than one of them as she put it. Peace brought the end of work and short-term romances.

"I was a single woman in my late thirties in the post-war euphoria and I couldn't have been sadder. My whole family and life was a half a country away. Yet, I refused to return. Those moments of life during war kept me going and I knew what awaited me in the Midwest. I put my personal sadness aside as San Francisco and the rest of the country began to rise up after the victory and, young man, anything seemed possible then, unlike now."

She had more romances, all with sailors, but soon they lost interest in her. She took a job at AT&T as an operator in 1947 and stayed there until 1985. Several times she almost went back to Bucaine. Her parents' deaths almost got her back, but she never returned. She'd divorced Iowa and never saw another person from her past. She married a Filipino man, who was involved in real estate, but his true passion was alcohol. They had a daughter in November of 1963. Old lady McCabe's voice flattened like a sail suddenly without wind. She spoke but a few minutes about her divorce and daughter, who had a child. The father disappeared during pregnancy. The three of them shared the apartment where I'd picked her up. Generational mimicry is virtually inevitable. Apples rolling near their trees. Cantankerous, talking Oz trees.

There was silence. My wife, Eve, and my life began filling the spaces. What was I repeating from the past? What was my mimicry driving this cab? Or was I unconsciously trying to redirect the flow of my earthly time? Those questions were too big. I had a decision about Eve ominously dangling ahead. It was my own little Genesis in a cab. What I really needed was clean and precise suspension of my thoughts. Let instincts take over.

"What does your daughter do?" I asked.

"She's a nurse at Kaiser."

"That's a good job. She's done all right for herself."

"She's made mistakes, but so have I. Her boy needs a father. We're not enough. It's sad how things happen again. No matter how far from Iowa I am, Iowa never leaves. Maybe, it's God's way to say my way was wrong. Running's never the answer."

"Maybe not, but it's irresistible at times. I ran and I might run again."

"Young man, I suggest the opposite. Look your problems square in the face and go at 'em head on. I regret running. It took me decades to realize it, but I see my mistake every time I look in my daughter's eyes. It has ruined my daughter and grandson and me. It caught up to me. Do you have kids?"

"No."

"Well, running is still wrong, but at least you bear your own cross."

"Yes." I said, while I thought, keeping your orbit small is the answer.

"Young man, can you pull over at the Japanese Tea Garden?"

"Yes, Miss McCabe."

"I'll be back in ten minutes."

"Take your time."

"That's good for you," she said looking at the meter.

"No, no. I'll turn it off." I pulled the red arm down and the little purr of money and time clicked off.

"You don't have to," she said as she exited the car.

Miss McCabe sat at a bench in the Tea Garden. I sat in the cab and momentarily pondered what she could be thinking—I concocted images of Bucaine, her ex-family, her marriage, divorce, daughter, grandson, Navy men days. I thought of the ephemeral, cosmic rush of her Jack London, escape years. I thought of the sad, earthly eternity of her AT&T years. It didn't last long. All roads led back to Eve, of course, and the coming reality that my marriage, or the growing falsehood that it was becoming, was going to end tonight when I had sex with this woman I'd just met. There was no question that McCabe, Delmore, the Cab, were all face-slapping signs of life change. It wouldn't take some metaphysical, warped San Francisco twirp to point out that our life is dotted with a clear path. We've just got to open our eyes and water down the misled energy. We pursue or we stand still. Every epiphany of this week led to pursuit.

Morality and fidelity to a lost cause were static. My reasoning even convinced me it would be better for Nancy if I chose Eve. A kinetic choice would circulate so much energy in both our lives that had simply grounded to a scarily transparent, empty halt.

Beyond this, my life as a poet had been a sham. I'd belittled my passions and been deaf to internal voices for far too long. It's as if my very existence has been to debunk my very existence. I've been like the designated rabbit runner setting the pace early on and then drifting to last, a pawn for the others. I got struck hard by Whitman's youthful cries and then drifted passively in the very face of their call. This weekend I'd pen some fruitless poem about an old lady and her past, have it picked up by some local journal, feel a minute moment of redemption, and slither onward until Nancy finally left me. But this time, there'll be no poem. There will be life. There will be lyrical penetration with another woman. A new world. Not make believe.

McCabe was still bench-bound and my watch read 3:30 p.m. I was supposed to pick up Eve at the airport soon. I couldn't wait any longer. The giant contradiction of myself rolled onward. I played picaresque poet-manque, except I drank only two beers a night, never cheated on my wife, had no sex at all, no pain, and no boils burned off my adolescent body by some insane, Christian witch doctor aunt. I was Exley without the nut house and the booze. Lukewarm and all watered down. I was jealous of pain. I had none. I had no right to pose as a poet. I had a right to create some pain. I had to see Eve, so I could look back on all the ennui and see it for the pain that it has been. Visions of sex and explosive word flow became my horizon.

"Ok, young man, I'm ready."

"Do you need a hand?"

"No, No," she said, getting in the cab.

My Bartleby-like-'I prefer not to tonight' wife had snowballed me into a delirium of Eve. I had a five-year orgasm mounting, blue balls with the blueprints of a skyscraper. I could think of nothing else. I was dazed and delusional. I loved it.

"Young man, slow down." McCabe said. I looked at the speedometer I was going sixty in the twenty mph park drive.

"Sorry, I got a little carried away."

"What's the rush all of the sudden, young man?"

"No rush, I'm just trying to get you home. Are you tired?"

"Do you need to be somewhere?"

"Actually, I have an appointment."

"Delmore said you have the dayshift?"

"Yes, well, I promised an old friend I'd meet her at the airport pretty soon. I don't want to be late." I couldn't even lie about the gender.

"Who's your old friend, if an old, bored lady may be so intrusive?"

"Just an old friend from Idaho, which is where I am from."

We didn't talk for a while. I zipped out of the park, down Fillmore and towards the four Victorians. I pulled over at her house, trying to disguise my haste for efficiency. I got her groceries out of the trunk and put them at her front door. I went back to help her.

"Young man, I'm all set. My daughter's home and she can help me with the groceries."

"Are you sure? I don't mind."

"I don't want you to be late for your appointment."

"I won't be."

"Please. I'm all set," she said, slightly irritably.

"Ok, Miss McCabe. You have a good day and it was quite nice meeting you and talking." I turned down the stairs and headed off to my destiny.

"Do you want some money?"

"Oh, I completely forgot. Let me check the meter."

"Here, don't bother."

She handed me a crisp $100 bill.

I was about to politely refuse, but she cut me off.

"You're not special. Every driver gets this and I'm sure they told you as much. Now get to the airport and do whatever it is you have to do."

She looked quite deeply into my eyes with a mysterious, half smile and a glare that seemed to say more than thank you.

"Thank you, young man."

"You're very welcome. By the way Miss McCabe, I'm not so young."

"Sure you are." She said and unlocked her door.

"Money and material." Fat man's voice bellowed from the radio as I left the four Victorians.

"Huh?"

"Good money and old lady's life to write about. Oh I forgot, you're a sculptor," he said with hacking laughter punctuating his mockery.

"So, what did you try, stories from behind the cage?" I asked.

"I just watch failures. I wouldn't make things worse by thinking I'm more than I am, like you types."

"Did you get anywhere? What was your title? Behind the Cage?"

"Going on the offensive, professor. What's up out there?"

"I'm just trying to get a little more out of you to add some depth to my sculpture when the block ends. I think your ridicule might break the wall."

"You're a bad liar, Fields. Try being a cabbie, and get off your self-imposed importance."

"Delmore, you ought to be a therapist, except you've got the touch of a grizzly bear."

"How's old lady McCabe? She take care of you?"

"Oh yeah."

"You're welcome," and he clicked off before I could say thanks.

Just maybe, Fat man was cracking the wall between me and my life. I was beginning to realize the reality of my marriage. I was standing outside of myself and starting to see what was actually happening.

My marriage was over.

In my haste to get to Eve, I arrived early. I parked near all the other cabs waiting for their bread and butter run.

42

Fat man was calling out various cabs for pick-ups and I ignored his calls for me. I had time to kill. The giant step I was about to take settled in my thoughts tranquilly. The only anxiety I felt was lust sensing its desired conclusion. I was the dealer of my own tarot cards contingent on my whims and wants, not some antiquated mystery disconnected from reality.

Except this giant step suddenly changed direction. Somebody decided to throw a new card on the table.

A woman approached my cab looking right at me with a slight, nervous smile. It wasn't Eve. The lie I had just told Old lady McCabe had come true. An old friend from Idaho was entering my cab. Nothing had really happened to me in five years. Now in a few days, events of the past, present and future were rattling around like conspiring stars in my cabbie galaxy.

I rolled down the passenger window.

"Hi, Henry."

"Arlene." My jaw landed in my lap.

"It's been a while."

"Yes."

"Are you busy?"

"Ahh, no, not really."

"Can I sit down?"

"Sure." I leaned over and opened the door then changed my mind. "How 'bout if we sit outside? I've been in here for hours."

"Ok."

We sat at a bench near the possessed cab with the sounds of cars, planes and people on the move all around us.

The future was offering sexual salvation. The past arrived, confronting me with the one lost relationship I'd never gotten over. My present was crystallizing its lost cause truth. Where to go?

I'd devastated Arlene in our mid-twenties between my University of Idaho and Boise State years. I was so full of the arrogant force of youth and potential poetry brewing and simmering within. I left her and returned to her whimsically for five years. I'd caused and received her tears. She loved me and I loved her, but it was masked,

43

protected, feared. Things have been coming to light. Everything has been clouded in the endless mirage of artistic escapes. She was one of the sweetest women in Boise and I was one of the biggest fools.

"Well, Henry, I'm somewhat surprised to see you here in a cab. I thought you'd be famous or close to it by now."

"Not yet. Still working on that." I said.

"Maybe, you should stop."

"Yes, yes, yes, I know."

"Heard that before."

I looked at her and smiled.

"I always thought you were stubborn enough to persist long after reality gave you the message." She said.

"I've never been good at seeing what's right in front of me."

"So how long you been driving?"

"Less than a week."

"Really?"

"Yes, another exit."

"And the goal? The reason for the exit?"

"I guess the same as all the others."

"You seem nervous, Henry. Relax, I don't hate you anymore. I hate what you did, but that was a long time ago, and I'm over it now. The feelings have evolved. I understand you, thanks to some help."

"Therapy?"

"Yes, it helped. I should say, helps."

"I agree."

"Has it helped you?" Arlene asked.

"Yes, but maybe not as much as you. I probably wouldn't be in this cab, if it had."

"Why are you in the cab?"

"Words. One last try at words. This is my last shot. Otherwise, it's the middle of the road."

"What's the middle of the road for you?"

"Teaching, maybe back in Boise at the College of Southern Idaho. My brother's coaching hoops there. I just got my MFA, so maybe the unpretentious College of Southern Idaho would let me in."

"So you'd be back home."

"Yeah, too many academics here. Plenty of those who can't, teaching. I'm still seeing if I can."

"Can't you do both simultaneously?"

"Yes, yes."

"Your wife says that."

"Yes."

"Henry I figured us out, but not you. You just don't fit the art-driven soul. No tortured childhood. So regular. It never added up to me. Your anti-money stance never went away."

"I'm not anti-money. I'm non-money. I have none and I couldn't care less about it. And who says the artist has to be bred from one set of circumstances."

"You're right. It's just something that ran in my head many times before."

"Before?"

"Mostly." Arlene said, a hint of red filling her cheeks.

"Well, if you don't mind I'm quite tired of analysis, mine and everyone else's. I'm actually in the moment of an awakening and dragging my self along logical paths is probably going to fuck up the epiphany."

"What epiphany?"

"Explaining it would probably fuck it up too. Let's just say I'm on the verge of knowing exactly what I'm gonna do with my life. How 'bout your life? Any epiphanies besides realizing I was just an immature asshole not worthy of your grief?"

"I wouldn't put it quite so crudely, but it's more or less accurate. I'm not too into epiphanies. I leave those to the poets and priests, but I'm doing pretty well."

"I'm happy to hear that. Did you finish school?"

"Yes."

"And what are you doing?"

"Well, here's the short version. I got my degree and kept working for my father. I was doing the bookkeeping, but it got old fast, being a quasi-accountant. I never liked numbers, anyway. "

"I remember lying in bed with you listening to you complain about being a dead end numbers cruncher and begging me to read you Collette."

"That was my therapy from spending eight hours punching a calculator and hearing the receipt churning onward."

"You loved it when we took turns reading aloud to each other."

"After you left, I was, well, you know how I was. I went to therapy and went forward amidst our ruins. Therapy saved me, so I went back to school to be a psychologist. I got my degree and now I'm practicing. That's why I'm here. For a conference, that is."

"That's great. Congratulations. I bet you're great at what you do."

"Thanks. I like what I do," she said with a smile.

"You got on with your life pretty good after me."

"It took time."

"Arlene, someone's trying to tell me something. I mean I gave up marrying you to be a down-and-out cabbie. Think of all the free therapy sessions. God knows I could use them."

"Who knows what would have happened? With you, I may not have become a therapist, I just would have relied on seeing one."

We both laughed. The air had gone soft and easy.

"Did you marry?" I asked her.

"I'm going to."

"When?"

"Next summer. We met in school. He's a therapist, too."

"Oh God! What a pair. I don't think that's very healthy Arlene. Endless analysis."

"We actually barely speak about it. We try to keep it separate."

"That was your analysis."

"Yes, the end analysis."

"So…ahh…you know, Arlene, I really screwed up."

"How so?"

"With you."

"You did, but let's not get into it."

"I was such a jerk. So young, so foolish, but the sad thing is I haven't changed much. I mean, I feel like I've changed more this week than in ten years. God, the whole noble pursuit of word bullshit has sucked me dry. It should have been the noble pursuit of us, and words secondarily, but I, you know, I've been self-analyzing myself into clarity lately. Somehow, I construed peace and normalcy as malignant, as a liability. The whole suffering artist crap extorted and manipulated me. I don't know the first goddamn thing about suffering. I'd like to wipe out the last ten years. The time since I left you."

"If I may offer one piece of advice."

"Please do."

"Think ahead, not behind."

"Yes, yes. You're right. Arlene, this is insane, but I have to ask you something."

"What, Henry?"

"What if I said give me one more chance?"

"What!" she shrieked.

"I know. It's crazy. It's out there, but talking to you now, looking at you, listening to you, I see my whole flawed road was from the end of us. With you, I finished school, got some minor fame in Boise poetry circles. Without you, I've been anemic. I want to go ahead again with us."

"Henry, stop now. You're desperate and acting on a miracle cure by lunging without processing anything. What about your wife?"

"We're dead. Playing the game. It's over. That much I know. I just truly realized it."

"The epiphany?"

"Yes, one of them. Another is us. I mean, why did I get this cab job? First, the dispatcher woke me up that my whole art existence is a mask, then the artifices just began melting. My marriage was next. Now you. I don't believe in God, but I believe in some mad kinetic energy connecting actions through alleged coincidences. This ain't no coincidence. You'll never guess why I'm here."

Arlene was shaking her head. "For a fare," she mumbled.

"So to speak. For an affair."

"Huh?"

"Seriously, I met a woman yesterday and I am supposed to pick her up in ahh, ten minutes. Don't think less of me, but my marriage is over. It's been sexless for five years. I've been too loyal. The best thing I can do for Nancy is leave her. I know I could leave first, but this will speed the process. Anyway, that's another issue, morality, whatever. The irony is I see you at this moment."

"Henry, you are all over the place. You need help."

"I know. It's just that, seeing you has, hmmm, well, it's letting me pour all this out into the world."

"Henry, this is more than I can handle. It's bringing back some painful years that you put upon me and more importantly, that I let you put upon me. My life is in another realm than yours. I'm actually happy."

"Could you be more happy if we were together and committed?"

"I don't think I can answer that and maybe I don't even want to know."

"Because if you do, it might be yes?"

"Yes, but the devastation and cataclysm would be brutal to get to that yes."

"Let's get in my cab and drive to Mexico."

"Mexico! You're insane." She laughed and shook her head. "Henry, this isn't happening. I'm not taking it seriously and I won't hold it against you in the future."

"A week together. I'm serious. We'll go to Zihuatanejo in Mexico. Stare out into the Pacific and rescue the memory."

"Henry, maybe you ought to find that other woman."

"Arlene, the fact that you say 'maybe' means deep down you're interested. There is still something there for me."

"Henry, I loved you, but how do I know this isn't some offspring of a wild emotional ride that you're on. Surely, it is. I've got a conference in Marin. Why don't you drive me there? Forget the affair. End your marriage and begin your life. I'm flattered by the insanity of Mexico and would have done it ten years ago, but not now. Why don't we keep in touch as friends and who knows?"

"Meaning?"

"Meaning, I'm not married yet. That's all. I don't want to discuss it anymore. I care about you and want your life better, but don't take foolish steps to grow. Responsibility isn't so boring."

We got in the cab and drove by the Delta gate. I saw Eve. She caught my eyes. I tried to say 'sorry' with my look. I believe she thought I was choosing marriage. I wanted to thank her for helping me choose divorce.

The inevitable end of Nancy and me didn't quite go as planned. While I was taking some days to figure out how to tell her, I came home to a note in an empty apartment. She'd taken everything and left a note apologizing for the cowardice of her departure, but she felt our conversations had always railroaded her pursuits. She explained what I already knew about us and then said there was someone else, which I hadn't known. She took everything and left me the car. She figured that was fair, since our furniture probably added up to the value of the car. Despite knowing it was over, I felt as if everything had been sucked out of me. Gravity was stronger than me. I felt like collapsing. My veins were empty of blood, my bones hollow.

I was made of air.

I never saw Eve again, but Arlene let me turn to her. I knocked on her hotel door one night and collapsed into her arms and wept ten years worth of tears. I unloaded all the pain in tears and words. Arlene took it for me. We talked and talked. Or rather, I talked and talked and she listened, tender and true, to my cuckold blues. We made love the last night. It was surreal and beautiful. The first woman I'd entered in five years. The first woman besides Nancy in over ten years. She left, but we agreed not to resurrect the past again. I tried Mexico one last time, but she just laughed and said, "Henry you don't need Mexico. You just need your self." I wanted to marry her, but I let her go that night. I wanted to respect Arlene. I wanted to love her.

I wanted her to love me.

A few months later I was still driving the cab, had a roommate, and spent my evenings after work by the great bridge. I'd sit on a bench South of Market Street. I was actually below the giant concrete ramp that began the bridge. With the sound of cars loudly hissing by above and the footsteps of the financial district folk behind me, I feverishly wrote down the experiences of those first few days, intertwining past and present, Boise and San Francisco, the inimitable Delmore, Nancy, Eve, the Haight, everyone and everything of those first few days. I was channeling every unfettered vision in an uninterrupted flow to the page. I could almost feel the words coming out of my fingertips. When I was almost done, I typed a page that said, FOR ARLENE. I didn't have an ending, but I knew I would. I put the 400 pages in a satchel and stared out into the bay below the bridge. I couldn't see anything, but a few scattered ship lights and pure blackness. I didn't know how much time I had sat there. It must have been hours of peaceful nothingness. The greatest peace I'd ever felt. No, not the greatest. The truest. I was about to take action, but I wasn't sure exactly what. I knew it would come to me. I would let it and then run full force with it.

A few nights later, my roommate set up a reading for me at a lesbian club in North Beach. Some of her friends had seen a few of my poems in the Haight-Ashbury Literary Journal and had inquired about me. I wasn't ready to read Bay Bridge Visions in public. I chose to read a poem called Class Reunion, which was about my ten year high school reunion. Arlene had been there with me. Before I got but a few lines out, I knew the ending of my story. Its obvious clarity disintegrated the walls I had constructed. Melted wax. Losing so many of my years was too painful, so I fell into a clarion fit of protective laughter. The lesbians kept applauding me. I was laughing and they were clapping. Perhaps, they thought my madness was planned. Part of the show. A little riposte at art. A comic undermining of meaning's uselessness. Naked art, cheesy nihilism or a tepid, Henry Miller gob of spit anti-credo, credo. Something other than what it was.

Only in San Francisco.

I dropped my poem and left the stage, laughing myself into tears. The lesbians applauded more and more. They were chanting, "Encore". I got in the car and took off with nothing but the pages of Bay Bridge Visions resting in the passenger seat.

I could see the conspiracy in its purity. The last ten years had their purpose. To bring me back to Arlene. I would never return to San Francisco. I would live the rest of

50

my life in Boise, married to Arlene. I would go home again. You can go home again. I would prove that and let the escape of San Francisco slip into my wake.

Field's Wake.

Now, I just had to convince her.

stoker caudwell
The Spectacle

Each year in school my classes slipped more and more into the avant-garde. My political science classes were taught by unwaveringly ideological Marxists. Literature classes were European symbolist or American beat. Art classes were Dada and Surrealism. Film classes made the above look conservative. It was 1988. The Berlin Wall was still up and so was mine. Everything was escape. The trappings of the excessive left were an umbrella under which I hid.

I didn't want to feel the rain.

During the madness and folly of the higher-ed loony bin, Lyra entered my life like a vernal thunderstorm. Her beauty wasn't quick and immediate to the impatient male eye. However, its depth was planted deeply within me. It grew strong and potent with eternal reckonings.

She was my classmate in most of the same mad, reality-jolting classes. We were swept into the same mind bazaar. Psychic lemmings. Our hearts would follow like lost sheep. I fell in love with her more and more with each passing, spiritually seductive class. Soon she was all I thought about.

All the time.

I began to make plans of communication. As befits obsession, I developed the plans with the detail of a great thief, who analyzes every possible event to insure success. However, I was no great thief. I was the timid, bumbling wannabe crook, who always backed out at the 11th hour.

That all changed near the end of senior year in a post-WWII film class taught by a Greek neo-beatnik, Nick Karcinogenas. Nick wore all the requisite ornaments of the downtrodden soul searcher. He was thin, had droopy, life's-too-heavy shoulders and always dressed in black. His salt and pepper bushy hair was an anarchy of waves and curls. He lectured once a week at the Worcester Public Library in connection with the university. He was appropriately placed off campus.

Quarantine the madness.

Nick allowed his outcast brethren of the Worcester streets to attend class. They were mostly homeless, harmless local quacks. Together they mixed with the elitist college kids who sampled sadness and pain like new clothes. Of course, I was one up on the superficial, soulless elites. My life wouldn't be mapped out and monetary. It would be open, spontaneous. Surreal. I knew what I was doing by not knowing what I was doing.

Youth.

Professor Nick fit right in. His agenda was to give life to the dead societies of subterranean, star-crossed cabals. Men and women of the European cafe underworld. Nick trumpeted those hallowed, footnote to history movements like a troubadour. There was the occasional modern art show or dusty, barely read tomes that outlined the transcendent manifestos of blind visionaries. "A secular divinity is what they and all of us seek, consciously or unconsciously," Nick would meekly bellow from time to time. Each week he would launch a monologue and show a film about these movements. The connection was often invisible.

All the better he probably thought. Surrealism.

I finally met Lyra while Nick was quoting words of Dada offspring movements crawling the war worn streets of Europe. A doomed setting I left unconsidered. Lyra's glow had altered my vision. Nick provided the audio of sensory derangement, sowing my madness pure.

"Ahh, yes, they, these two, Dada and Surrealism, are quite known among those in the know, so to speak, but what of those under them, more powerful, more headfirst and reckless in thought, fragmented, ahhh, under their own loftiness of sky-pointed, tainted heaven goals? Yes, the Situationalists and Lettrist International. They'd claim a week should be six days not seven. Rupture the calendar. Start anew. Always new. Time was a wasted, disturbed concoction restricting us. But time was only enemy number two. The great thief of the soul was art. Art was the great lie disguised as truth. Art was a beast in sheep's skin. Art tried to transcend time and all our useless assertions of ordered evolution in the most tepid of ways. All sheep and lemmings framed. Art entrusted the hope of change and transcendence into a frame to be gazed at and forgotten. These two movements wanted to implode the hypocrisy of art, be it paint or word or film or whatever the insulated escalation of feeling might be. Hanging it on a wall to be seen or printed to be read was the lie of art. Art was sucked into moneyed upper crust manipulation. Hmmmm, ahhhh and perverted and adulterated into tepid existence from its real, raw form, which was the impulse. Art is impulse flowing not impulse ended.

The impulse was ripped-off and, ahhhh, yes, stolen from the maker, us. The impulse to relive, change, evolve, devolve, turn the whole thing upside down, find the hidden city where it's all going, the elusive road, the true temple of wisdom. Ahem, ahh, so the Situationist International and Lettrist International were a whisper that tried to scream from the primal core only to end up hung up or covered or shown in a dark room to an audience. Concretely, they aimed at artists who sold their works. These were the true liars complacently selling their impulse to those in power. Their complicity put them in the nest of the status quo. The urge of art should be to rupture the status quo. Art became grotesque burlesque belittlement of the impulse founded on change. Picasso, Miro, Van Gogh, Gorky, Gauguin, all of them. All of them frauds, so spoke Situationists and Lettrists. Their question was 'What if the impulse is concentrated, unified, retained in its purity and incarnated?' Their works of anti-art were never sold and only attempted to spread the impulse. They even mapped cities geographically drawn to make daily life the impulse that went into art.

So, they fought and lost to the spectacle that overran this century into the Michael Jackson world of today. Art had become a pop spectacle and they pleaded to destroy art because it turned pain and atrocity into a likeable, acceptable, huggable object. Art has become a cabbage patch doll. Deadly cute. This was murder of a mystical, gnostic new world vision. A poem was rape of the poet. They were seeing things completely inside out, which to them was outside in. Isidore Isou comes and forms the L.I. elevating the artist to divinity if outside the world of currency. He, ahhheeemm, tried to reduce words into letters because with letters you have infinite truths and realm and origin, but words just restrict and trap and ahh, so he sought the origin and high art would reinspire language out of its quagmire of gloom, repitition, monotony and then it will lead to an economy of elegance without coins, but full of spirits no longer mummified by art's decay."

I didn't ponder Nick's galloping prattle too much. I considered it strangely lucid. I think I thought I got it. I wanted to let it seep into subconscious terrain. It didn't matter too much though. Reinventing art took a backseat to my hunger to meet Lyra, to learn Lyra.

She sat near me on the bus back to campus after that class and like all the other times I plotted the right way to enter her world. However, her glow had become so strong and deified to me, I would always weaken. The energy was overwhelming. Dozens of times I had the attempt planned and then we'd get off the bus. She went her way and I stood the fool. The meek will inherit the earth, but not Lyra.

As I waited for the arrival of a fearless moment that would never come, Lyra came to me on the bus.

"It's a little unsettling, isn't it?" she asked me.

"Yes." Thinking she was referring to my trepid self.

"I mean we're here to think and if you think about it, their vision is less insane than the spectacle ahead of us."

"Huh?"

"Are you ok?"

"Yes."

"You look a little surprised."

"I am."

"Why?"

"I've been trying to think of a way to talk to you and now I'm talking to you." I confessed surprising myself.

"What have you been waiting for?"

"I guess for you to talk to me."

56

"I think I had that feeling. We're in a lot of classes together and sometimes I'd see you staring in my direction, but not directly at me. I just had the strange vibe that you might have been thinking of me. I know it sounds conceited, but that was the vibe."

"Caught." I put my hands up. "It was no conceit. I was obvious."

"Don't worry. I'm happy I was right, otherwise I'd be the fool."

"Instead, I am."

"Yeah, but it becomes you."

"Is that a compliment?"

We laughed and the glow had lost its barrier and now became a force pulling me towards her.

Lyra began, "Anyway, I've wanted to talk to you about all this mad stuff that Nick goes on and on about. I need to talk to someone. I feel like my insides have been sucked out of me by all his talks."

"It's hard to describe, but the future is certainly emptier looking, listening to him."

"It's all hollowed out and vacant," Lyra concurred.

"He kind of spreads an ugliness to anything accepted."

"It's really hitting a nerve. Tapping into some hidden level I don't know about."

"I can connect to it. A bit scary, don't you think?" Lyra agreed.

"It actually just makes me want to go."

"Yeah, I get that feeling too."

"I mean I've always tended towards a bleak outlook, but now, my bleakness is strangely energized. I feel like I'm in a hurry to do everything. Impulse and whim suddenly seem so pure, rather than foolish. Buried whispers are starting to scream."

"Kind of like the whole terrain has become quicksand and—"

"And if we stand still, we'll sink with the rest," Lyra said.

"Yes, and the rest seems like such a tragic reality."

"Comically tragic."

"Tragically comic."

57

"Tragicomedy."

"Like seeing everything through funhouse mirrors."

"Reality turned rubber."

"Yes, yes, a thousand yeses," she said softly laughing and staring deeply into my eyes. I was more in love with each second that passed.

Soon we started meeting after class for drinks. We helped each other process the unhinged doors that Nick let loose. Our talks took on the full-blown bloom of escape, of what to do next, where to go and how to avoid the vacuum of the ominous spectacle secretly giggling ahead.

In my room one night, Lyra initiated another Nick-inspired talk.

"I'm starting to get truly troubled by the spectacle."

"Me too, and we should be, don't you think?" I asked.

"Yeah, to think otherwise would be false."

"What to do about it is the problem." I said.

"I like what they imagined to do, Stoker"

"I don't know about that. Once you disintegrate money, then religion, then society, and finally art, what the fuck is left? Lyra, I don't even understand what they imagined to do."

"I don't think they did either. They were shaping impulse. Impulse is indefinable."

"I'd like to define it."

"Not everything is verbal."

I said nothing.

Lyra continued.

"Sometimes, it's feeling or impulse then to let its flow proceed unimpeded. Maybe we can't get it because we're too locked into the spectacle chain. We think we're on the outside looking in, but we're really not. Imagine if everyone were off track, or at least the giant majority were, and so few were clued in."

"And these guys were clued in?" I asked.

"Maybe, maybe not. Who can say? But maybe they left the impulse and Nick has passed it to those open to it."

"Us?"

She nodded.

"I need more definition. It's all vague and confounding," I said.

"Men are so pragmatic. You need to relax, unhinge a little yourself," She urged.

"I'm trying."

"I know how to help," Lyra said with a mischievous grin.

She unbuttoned her cotton dress and let it drop to her ankles. Most of our talks ended this way, which was another reason I looked forward to our flighty conversations. She was very uninhibited sexually. We had made love the first night we hung out together. I stood up and finished undressing her and then lifted her smooth, petite body and put her on my desk sitting where one would write. I then pushed all the books and papers onto the floor. She took off my shirt and I got out of my jeans. I turned her body so her legs hung off the side of the desk and then gently pushed her down onto the desk, caressing her everywhere with my fingertips, lips, and tongue, engaging all the senses. Then I entered with my tongue and got her closer and closer, holding her wrists with gentle force. Just before she came, I entered her completely and as her head fell off the end of the desk I came like I had never before. She came moments after I had finished.

Each time we made love it was different. Each time it followed a natural path with no awkward moments and it was never verbal. I had believed Lyra's glow was our spiritual connection. Literally, the result of our chemistry. We talked about it and she agreed. Our talks, our coitus was beyond what I ever imagined possible. As our love climbed sexually and spiritually, filling every pore with fulfillment, Nick did his best every week to excavate all that had been assumed and taunt the new vacancy.

"So Isadore Isou proclaimed the non-existence of youth was a sickness. It was not an age, nor a billboard of the spectacle, but a feeling and it was being hog-tied like a hapless, helpless calf in a sad, robotic rodeo; chased, overwhelmed, roped and then cheered as an entity of the spectacle. As he said, 'Let youth cease to become the consumer of its own élan.' This was all before it became a

60's cliché. Before it became a spectacle within the spectacle as the 60's had been. The great lie decade. Hmmm, now our elan, our vigor to be, is usurped. Just turn on MTV and watch energy unraveled, cremated and stored in cellophane. So they, Isou and his covert cavalry of midnight ideas, begged to start over, remove God from the language, God was a semantic weight. New letters, then new words, then new language, new ideas, ahh, ahhem, new cities, then new systems, then, ahhh, the brave new world…new, all new, new, new, new. It was a chant, a plea for new, an eternal mantra imploring eternity. And the connection that Greil Marcus makes in the section of our book for today's class is this desire, this desperation leapfrogged from the cafe society to some down-and-out kids called the Sex Pistols who tried to disseminate their desperation and all the while being conned by a guy named Malcolm McLaren. Another usurper who sought to market the desperation and possess the élan for a buck. So tonight's film is the Great Rock 'n' Roll Swindle."

    Lyra and I lay naked in bed. I was still inside her. Our bodies were still interlocked and moist with each other. We had fallen asleep immediately after. I gently pushed her off of me and sat up. I grabbed a tissue from the nightstand to dry off. She didn't wake up.

    I was staring at her room and taking in the material extensions of her personality, waiting for her to wake up. We had been spending all our time together and we always went back to her single after Nick's class and made love. The lectures and films with Nick continued to seep inside us. Some elites mocked the words, didn't listen, considered it way out there, illogical babble of a 60's burnout who'd had too many trips inside the kaleidoscope. We knew it was certainly way out there. That's what we liked about it. It was logically cosmic. Cosmological. We brought the right internal chemistry to absorb and brew external potions. The loneliness was deeply existential. The earth had become a trampoline. The future a trapdoor. Our physical love gave some breath and energy to the Satrean nothingness.

    We had spent so much time making love and talking about everything and trying to form senselessness into sense, that I had never really looked at her room in detail. She had several cameras beside her desk. She was a photography major. On her wall, she had about two dozen or so framed black and white photographs, most of which she had taken. Most of them were from Maine where Lyra was from. Several were beautiful landscapes, typical copies of Ansel Adams. There were several photos of people, seemingly candid shots. The people photos were all cut-ups. That is, the photo was three, or sometimes four photos taken to produced one picture. The various shots were then placed next to each other as a triangle or square to connect the broken images into one. There was probably a term for this in the photography art world. Cut-ups seemed to work for me. I liked them. They represented the various selves in one self. However, three or four seemed insufficient.

On her desk were several texts on photography. There were also several novels stacked with the binding facing me. The top three were Thomas Wolfe novels, *Look Homeward Angel*, *The Web and the Rock*, and a giant mother of all novels, *Of Time and the River*. There were some other books stacked on the top shelf of her desk, but I didn't bother to read the titles.

There was also a family picture in the corner of her desk. I could see Lyra and a brother and sister, as well as her parents. It was an old picture. Lyra looked about ten or eleven. I smiled back at her giant, young girl's smile.

The current Lyra started rustling in bed and she put her arm around me very tightly as she began awakening. I kissed her. After a few minutes of silence, Lyra began. Her voice and eyes were troubled.

"You know I feel emptied out inside." Lyra whispered.

"Me, too." I winked and I kissed her.

"Yes, sexually too, but I mean spiritually. I feel simultaneously empty and energized. This strange conflict inside, spiritually undone. How can I describe it? The only image that comes to mind is a novice on a sailboat. Catching the wind sometimes and going and then messing up the rudder and direction and stalling. Going and stalling with no consistency."

"Don't take it too seriously. The guy's just a strange, retro cat trying to peel off some layers of our vision." I said in my best mock 50's hipster speak. "Probably just the flipside of a Jim Baker evangelist or one of the religious con men traveling around with constructed miracles done for the money."

"It's working. I'm ready to run out into the world and live and simultaneously crawl under a rock and hide. I can't control how I take it. It's taking me."

"It's nihilism. I bet if we investigated these Euro Café guys, they all came from tortured youths and rather than confront their own agony, they railed at society for distraction."

"Everything is distraction anyway. Besides, who cares about their youth? The path they took doesn't negate the philosophy formed. It doesn't undermine their construction."

"You mean destruction."

"Whatever, everything ahead is a mockery. The more you really ponder it, the more the future looks like a fucking spectacle of spoken, unrealized reality. Everyone slipping off some cliff and accepting the fall."

"That's Nick talk. Let's not fall into his chasm. I don't know. I'm not too broken up about the whole damn spectacle mess because their nihilism led to us. I'm crazy about you. I'll walk off the cliff and do it gladly if it's with you."

"Will you walk away from the cliff with me? I mean look down from the edge and turn your back at it."

"With you, the direction is irrelevant."

Nick began. "Ahh, ahem, so Europe is always decades ahead of us in most things, good or bad. These sub-underground shadow movements crept anonymously, save for some minor, back-page skirmishes trying to throw upheaval at the spectacle and its unwitting followers, such as the assault on Notre Dame. However, they were heard across the Atlantic. They were felt unconsciously. Their thoughts were seized because nothing dies, nothing is for not, every thought drifts tangibly despite its invisibility. Nihilism is a lie. The American beats turned nihilism and existentialism into beauty. Beatitude. Of course, they were maligned, misinterpreted, consumed and ridiculed by the spectacle, or moloch, as Ginsberg would label it. The difference between them and Isou's movements was great and small. Great, in that they, the Beats, were truly American. They, ahh, ahem, cast stones and yelped at the iniquities and absurdities of Moloch, but were also suffused with our uniquely American positive naiveté. Our land, unadulterated with so few wars and so little history of insouciant disruption and distortion, is a tender kitten to Europe's tired, old lion. Kerouac and his felaheen kinfolk were beatific to Europe's beaten. So this hopeless, destructive, existential, anti-material force crossed the Atlantic and turned optimistic, dreamy, alive, zealous, exuberant existentialism—childlike in hope—innocent enough to merge Atheism, Catholicism, and Buddhism. Yes, Kerouac of our nearby Lowell looked at beaten, ravaged, drugged and drunk pariahs of modernity and saw divinity and hidden angels swelling with interred spiritualism unable to sidestep the spectacle thereby imploding into mad internal passages and external chaos. The bridge, the ticket across the spectacle wasn't as political as the Situationalist and L.I., but purely art. Art was the bridge to eternity, not some concocted, Christian church bullshit morality, but heaven was open for those of the written word or colored brush willing to trespass themselves. Jesus would be an artist today. They sought personal edens through friendship, sex, love, words, jazz, externalizing suffering. To be alive from 1945 to 1950 was a spiritual high when youth could taste experience before film, TV, and pop culture mocked the endeavor, ripped it of its purity and usurped its élan to advertise the newest dishwashing detergent during a thirty-minute spectacle of disenchanted youth starring Gilligan as mock beat, Dobie Gillis. Again the spectacle won. Beatitude became a twenty-two minute useless sitcom."

Nick paused. He rubbed his hands together.

"Tonight we are going to see a film, Heartbeat, which was based on Neal Cassady's wife's writing about the beats. It's a rare woman's perspective of a largely male club. First to patch up the great flaws of this tepid

63

Hollywood film, let's listen to some purity through Kerouac's saxophone soul. This is from *October in the Railroad Earth*. Nick pressed play on an old reel tape recorder. The machine hissed and scratched its way into voice:

> There was little alley in S.F. back of the
> Southern Pacific Station at third and Townsend
> in redbrick of drowsy lazy afternoons with
> everybody at work in their offices in the air you
> feel the impending rush of their commuter
> frenzy…truck drivers and even the poor grime-
> bemarked third street of lost bums even negroes
> so hopeless and long left East and meanings of
> responsibility and try that now all they do is
> stand there spitting in the broken glass
> sometimes 50 in one afternoon against one wall
> at 3rd and howard and here's all these Millbrae
> and San Carlos neat-necktied producers and
> commuters of American and steel civilization
> rushing by with SF chronicles and green call
> bulletins not even enough time to be disdainful,
> they've got to catch 130, 132, 134, 136 all the
> way up to 146 till the time of evening supper in
> homes of the railroad earth when high in the sky
> the magic stars ride above the following hotshot
> freight trains – It's all in California, it's all a sea,
> I swim out of it in afternoons of sun hot
> meditation in my jeans with head on
> handkerchief on brakeman's lantern or on books,
> I look up at blue sky of perfect lost purity and
> feel the warp of woop of old america beneath me
> and have insane conversations with negroes in
> several story windows above and everything is
> pouring in, the switching moves of boxcars in
> that little alley which is so much like the alleys
> of lowell and hear far off in the sense of coming
> night that engine calling our mountains.
> Harrumph!

The scratch and churn of the tape continued and Nick just sat on his stool and a minute passed. He seemed to be in a meditative state. He slowly stood up.

"One shouldn't just hear those words. One should absorb and digest them. Osmotically listen. One should let each word flow into the bloodstream. Poetry should not be heard. It must be felt. Kerouac was trying to verbalize the instinct that the SI and LI wanted to capture into daily existence, post-destruction of the present. Kerouac may have considered it possible, but only on a lonely, individual level of salvation. He sought the flow of language from a deep internal unknown oasis he wanted to feel and disseminate to others. Like those who try to go too far, he was crucified. Instead of the church we have the spectacle doing the dirty work. Instead of Pontius Pilate washing his hands, we have MTV."

Nick pointed upstairs to the overhanging projection room where the same, unknown young man ran the projector. He was only seen at the end of class when he and Nick left together. The lights went out and the film began.

Lyra and I continued our odyssey through Nick's orbit. The lectures that disjointed alleged actualities. The taste of the vacant. The films darkening the regular and blessing the avant-garde. In between, we made passionate love and had long, soulful talks about life after graduation. Spring was coming. It was the middle of March and the end of our four-year term was fast approaching. Parties were more and more prevalent with weekends starting on Wednesdays, but Lyra and I had lost our friends. It was just us and we didn't care. Time with friends seemed empty. All conversations were dull away from her. Other relationships seem pretend when a real one is found.

We spent many nights in the Astronomy Lab where Lyra had her work-study job. We'd stay long after closing with the lights out, so the campus police wouldn't know. Under an observatory sky-light, black sky and white stars above, we'd make love and talk and make love again and talk. An inevitable crescendo arrived. The irresistible risk inherent in the amalgam of Nick, us, and youth long smoldering, finally caught a flame of direction.

Our conversations, our relationship, had been building to this dialogue. It was often after sex, when my thoughts were momentarily cloaked in peace that Lyra began deep, troubled conversations about the void. I had little trouble with the void, spectacle, Moloch, emptiness, nothingness, at this moment. I was madly in love with Lyra. All the trappings of existentialism were positive and attractive to me. It was the void that brought Lyra and I together. How could the spectacle be scary to me? Nothingness brought me everything.

Before meeting Lyra, I had confronted the void with some art therapy. I usually wrote every morning with a cup of coffee by my side. It was spontaneous writing about anything that came to mind. I rarely had blocks or moments of hesitation. There was plenty of bullshit within that needed to get out. Anyone with a family has a wealth of bullshit to express. I had a family.

I had bullshit.

I had words.

In the couple months with Lyra, I rarely wrote. She encouraged me occasionally. She even read some of my spontaneous scribbles, which I rarely did. She wanted to collect and edit them. I didn't care.

With Lyra the bullshit had dispersed, like a good massage unties muscular knots. I was in love. Who needed art?

On the other hand, art was everything for Lyra. Photography was her art, but she also painted and sculpted. She said many times, "When you kill God and embrace existentialism, what's left? Not everything, just art."

"And love." I would say.

"My romantic hero." She would say, kissing me and laughing.

In the observatory one night we had the conversation that had been fermenting for months. It was April 22. We were lying supine on the floor staring up at the night sky. The word game began.

"Let's go," Lyra nearly shouted.

"Where?" I asked.

"Just go."

"Go?"

"Yeah, go."

"Where's go?" I asked.

"Anywhere we want it to be, but not here. There's no go here," she said, half-smiling.

"What the hell is so good about go, anyway? Maybe it's overrated. Maybe we should stop. I've been liking stop if that's what we've got."

"You don't have the urge? You're not feeling a particular momentum?" she said surprised.

"Yes, between us and with us I'm going everywhere I want."

"Me, too, but I'm tasting more. That is, I want to taste more."

"That says something about us."

"No it doesn't because without you it would be worthless. With you, it becomes an adventure together. Hasn't this been our evolution since the bus anyway? We met while going somewhere." She smiled.

"Yes, from one end of town to another."

"Well, let's go from one end of the country to another."

"This summer? Get the diploma and run west."

"Let's go see the country and then the world. It's that simple. We'll slip out sly and unbeknownst in the dead of night alive." Lyra said, eyes and smile wide.

"Maybe you've had too much Nick for your own good. I don't want to be a cliché traveling around the country like wannabe Kerouacs. Just the people he despised. That's all so tainted now. It's all been done, then done again, and then redone. We'd be mocking ourselves."

"That's because the spectacle has mocked it and you've bought the mockery. We'll make it original. It won't be some romp for a few months getting drunk in many cities and passing out in cheap motels until we get home to mommy and daddy to start the real world of resumes and cover letters. I've got a plan."

"Why don't we wait until graduation?"

"That's just the cliché we should avoid. It's not honest. It has no instinct. I want to unravel our instincts and follow their course."

"So you're a Situationalist now?"

"Why not? It's time."

"I don't know sweetheart. We're dealing with European absurdist, utopian movements. Sometimes, I think they were just miserable fucks venting madness."

"Why are you so concerned about them? This is about us. I think there's more to them than you say, although I don't deny that element. What I'm seizing is the energy, the flow towards some unpenetrated horizon. A horizon we can only taste now. Poetry in life, at least for a while. Think of all the robotic gray ahead of us."

"It's romantic, it's picaresque, it's—"

"Why is the soul so mocked?" Lyra questioned, a bit perturbed now rather than playful. "If someone says I'm going to find myself, it's considered foolish and for fucked-up losers. The ones ridiculing are the future middle class alcoholics, wife beaters, and divorcees. Husbands playing golf endlessly and wives bitching about their husbands. The dreaded dull class doomed never to know a thing about themselves, which to me is inferno. I know I'm talking about my parents, but they aren't the only ones. They are just peas in a pretend pod."

"Sweetheart, I understand what you are saying. I've got parents too, sliding along the molded road. I just want to know what the hell we're going to do and how we can get to where you want to be."

"Photography and words. The camera's a truth gun and your words will deepen the truth. Here's a chance to experiment. We'll make a novel of words and photos. We'll live it and then create it. We'll get inside ourselves through art and travel and love before it's too late."

"A truth gun, huh?"

She nodded and smiled.

"When?"

"Tomorrow."

I gave her a kiss and we laughed and rolled around as one on the floor.

Lyra gave some specifics to her plan.

"Lately, I've been obsessed with railroads. I've been reading so much Thomas Wolfe. I had to read *Look Homeward Angel* for a class and now all I'm doing is reading everything he wrote and there are these amazing passages about the railroad in America. I've always wanted one theme to photograph and now I've got it. The dying railroads. I want to take pictures across the country of railroads. We'll travel by train and stop at a bunch of cities to photograph the stations. Capture the old world disappearing. While I do this, you'll be putting down the words."

"It's a good focus. Beautiful. It has a clear end. The West." I told her.

"It doesn't have to end, Uncle Sam."

"Sam I am."

"Sam you are. I mean, the west shouldn't be the end."

"Then what?" I asked. "We go from trains to boats."

"I can't stand some of the language we use. Sam needs to let go of focus, ends, purpose. It's just so damn dated. Like forty years from now it will be laughed at. I just want to go, period and capture the soul of the dying railroad. I just want to hear the sound of the train. I can't think of anything more intoxicatingly peaceful than the steel churning on steel amidst open prairies and unfettered fields. The contrast kills me."

"Sweetheart, this is your show. I'm just going to follow your instinct. When do we leave?"

"At dawn tomorrow."

"Huh?"

"Mañana, at sunrise."

"Why? I thought you were kidding."

"I told you why."

"The impulse?"

"It'll give some adrenalin to our muses. Make it run. Leaving after graduation would be so depressing, so trite, just like you said. Dawn tomorrow unravels the instinct without plans, focus, goals, time!"

"This is crazy."

"You haven't even heard the crazy part."

I fell back onto the bed and put my arms out and began laughing. I couldn't have been happier despite my meek protest. I was so gone with love that Lyra could have asked me to do anything and I would have done it. She leaned over me and kissed my face and my neck tightened from laughter.

"What about money?" I asked as we packed. It was 3 a.m. and we had finished gathering her stuff. Whatever we didn't take, we put in a big garbage bag and would drop it off at the Salvation Army. No possessions, but what we could carry. Divest to progress. We were bohemian soldiers seeking visions, not possessions. I was certainly the reluctant bohemian, but I'd play the game as long as Lyra led the way. There was just something right about the whole thing. Logical in its absurdity.

So I thought.

"I've got a few thousand saved and a credit card. I don't care what you have. We'll put it together and it'll get us to California. We can max the card out and screw our credit. It's not like we'll be applying for mortgages or anything. Besides, we'll be overseas by the time collection agencies come around."

"Overseas?"

"That's the second part."

"This go thing's got you gone. When do we stop? When we get back from around the damn world?"

"Sweetheart, let's not burden ourselves with when and where. They are depressing words."

"Ok, it's all go, go, go then."

"Precisely, but there is a plan so your male control neurons can straighten out. My sister teaches English in Thailand. We can go around the world teaching, all the while keeping the words and photos. There are railroads everywhere. They will give a setting to my eye and your words. Give us a focus. I'm not all scattered. The result is that there doesn't have to be an end, just a next."

"I only have $300."

"Fine."

"Yes, but can you promise me one thing? Just one." I wanted to cut to the chase of my anxiety.

"Anything."

"Be with me for a long, long time. Don't leave me anytime soon. I don't want to say forever because that would be too much weight, too unreal, too much societal bullshit hopping on fantasy. Just let's make us work as well as the art."

"I want nothing more than you and us."

"Do you promise?"

"I promise. A long, long time. As long as long can go. As long as the instinct takes us," she said.

"Lyra?"

"Yes."

"I love you."

"I love you, too."

She jumped into my arms. We laughed and kissed.

It was 4 in the morning. There was a three quarter moon and the night was as clear as it was cool under low, spring stars. We were in Lyra's '78 Plymouth Reliant K car, which she had inherited from her recently deceased grandmother. I was driving and I saw the university fade in the rear view mirror.

"I think this may be the most boring car ever made." I said.

"Even the names are abysmally dull. K car and Reliant." Lyra concurred.

"Very communist. We're talking practical. Perfect for us. Dropping out of school moments before the diploma is in our hands."

"I know you're a little hung up about it."

"Yes, but I feel the urgency and I'm excited about the energy of the unplanned. I'll relax. Art and love on the run. What better time than right now."

"We're getting out all the angst and putting in the truth. Do you know how many lives are lived without a single moment of truth?"

"Too many. We're accumulating moment after moment."

"But, you know, what we're doing isn't all that impractical, practically speaking."

"Tell me one level-headed thing we're doing."

"Well, I'll give you two. First, you don't even need a stupid diploma to get a job. Nobody ever asks for it. You put it on your resume and everybody assumes. Everybody I know has never once shown their degree. Second, the banks will never process our school loans because we haven't graduated. They kick in six months after graduation. As long as we're in academic limbo, the banks think we're still in school."

"Sweetheart, you've been thinking about this for a while."

"Vague plans that were never formalized until I met you."

Lyra lapsed into talking about the spectacle, Situaltionalists, Nickspeak. I tuned out the words and just watched her. I followed the angular, yet soft curves of her face. Her skin was ivory with a gentle reddish hue and her auburn hair complimented the coloring as it flowed with slight waves to her shoulders. I was in deep.

She continued.

Alive, liberated, and on the run inside and out.

"Tell me more about this teaching English."

"There are a million schools around the world. Everybody wants to learn our language and we automatically qualify by virtue of our tongue and imaginary diploma."

"Where would you want to go?"

"It's more like where wouldn't I want to go, which is almost nowhere."

"Where do we start?"

"Boston."

Lyra explained.

"I want the first pictures to be in Allston, just off Storrow Drive. There's this overpass above railroad tracks twisting and intersecting, all rusted and the wood is old and eaten. We'll begin with decay, death."

"Better to begin than end that way."

"Yeah, we'll get it out of the way; unburden ourselves with its heavy notion."

"We should be there by sunrise."

"What better way to capture death. I've had this picture in my mind for so long. Every time I drive back to school after a break I pass by it on the Mass Pike. I've wanted to take the picture, but only at sunrise. We can take a walk along the tracks and you can put your words down while I take the picture. Both forms of creativity happening simultaneously. You can get out all the things you're not telling me," Lyra said.

"I want to tell you everything."

"You will, sweetheart. Everything will be put forth between us. Pure intimacy. The only thing between us will be our skin."

"I couldn't imagine our exit any better than it is right now."

Lyra leaned over and kissed me.

"I have only one stop we must make."

"I thought it was about go."

"It is with one stop along go. White Sulphur Springs. It's a little city just over the Virginia border in West Virginia in the Alleghany Mountains. I don't know much about it, which is the way I like it, except that Alex Clarkson lives there. At least, last I heard he did."

"Really?" I often wondered what had happened to him. We hung out a bit. An honest college bohemian who didn't seem to be on the pose for four years. He loved booze, drugs, and Karl Marx. Bohemian to the bone, but somehow dignified. We were in a couple of political economy classes together. He gave this perversely lucid presentation on how to restructure the world. The whole goddamn world, economy, politics, everything.

"What's he up to?" I asked.

"Last I heard, he was writing a dissertation called Marxism After the End of Marxism. He got into West Virginia on a scholarship. He went down to a farm in this town near the school to study and live off the land, literally."

"What farm? I mean whose is it?"

"His. He inherited it from his family."

"Typically Marxist. Land owning, family supported ideology."

"Well, regardless, Clarkson's life is interesting and would be a great photo. It's right off the train. He wrote me and told me he can hear the train from his house.

"I thought it was all about spontaneity and unplanned photos."

"Are you jealous?"

"Probably."

"You needn't be."

"You know, my last image of Clarkson is one of those odd indelible visions that never leave you. You have a zillion damn moments in your life, but probably less than, say, 1,000 recur. I see him standing in front of that Freud monument outside Jackson Hall saying, 'Well, I've finished and after four years I haven't got one single fucking marketable skill,' and then he let out a great big cackle."

"He was always a bit *off*, but at times so *on*. One of those super intelligent dope smoking derelicts you might find in some isolated place in the Pacific trying to recreate the world one island at a time."

"A future Kurtz or Kazinsky."

"Yeah, but not so evil."

"Yeah, not now, but evil needs time to evolve. The ideology doesn't pan out and the heart grows dark."

"Well, at least he's not one of those sell-outs. Those yuppies in film class taking advantage of an easy three credits by kissing Nick's ass in journals, but mocking him behind his back. I mean here's a Marxist sticking to his ideology—"

"Now, that's scary."

"No, I don't think he's rigid with his plans. I think he's trying to evolve them as the walls come tumblin' down."

"It's pretty goddamn arrogant to think you can figure out the whole historically mad mess."

"Arrogant or ambitious?"

"He's definitely bright. Perhaps, a savant. He had some plan in Moss's class about income ceilings and capital redistribution and no more national boundaries and a new French Revolution as a result of the income gap in the U.S. Then there was something about baseball and sports triggering the end to the beginning because of the average Joe realizing the scam of fawning over multi-million dollar athletes."

"Revolting against the spectacle." Lyra said.

We stopped in Allston, which is a student area of Boston. Lyra went off with her camera and I found a quiet spot along the dead tracks. I took out my black and white speckled notebook and began the spontaneous flow at this moment in this place. It wasn't hard. I just gave myself to the internal visions and verbalized them uncritically. It was often spiritually peaceful by the end. Time stopped. Ego diluted. Painting daydreams into words.

Buddhism embracing Surrealism.

The process usually lasted a ½ hour. Lyra was done before me but she didn't disturb me. When I was done, I recorded the date and place of the expression. We had decided not to read the words or develop the visions until leaving America. We would never look back at the creativity of one country until we were in another.

We decided to sell the K car. We wanted to have freedom during the motion of our travels. We would take the train, of course. Our place of expression would be at every stop without driving to look for it. It was too obvious. We'd surrender further to fate.

We found a used car dealership and got $600 for the car on the spot. Lyra signed over title and in minutes we shed the metal. Divestment can be rapid. We were like spiritual strippers on the move, shedding everything we could. We bought one way tickets to California. We could get off at any stop along the way and get back on for no charge. White Sulphur Springs sure enough was one of the stops.

"Right now I couldn't imagine us apart." Lyra said as we settled into our seats, which would be our beds as well.

"Now?"

"I want to think and feel in the moment."

"And after the moment?"

"Don't think about after the moment."

For the first time I felt a strange, almost tangible distance between us emanating from our Clarkson, Marxist discussion. We were away from the sheltering sanctuary of the campus for the first time. It must be that I told myself. We were free, alive, creating memories. She was right. The moment is everything now. If you taste it right, the whole of the body and soul melds seamlessly and painlessly. I had to let go of the control that crept along my thoughts regarding

Lyra. I closed my eyes. I breathed deeply into my abdomen. I tried to think of nothing.

Lyra interrupted me with a gentle kiss on my temple.

"Yeah." I said.

"Let's make love right here."

"Where?"

"In a bathroom."

Everything was easy for Lyra. I told myself to adopt her unburdened ways. She believed everything was possible. I was beginning to believe.

After we got dressed, we smoked and drank beers in the dining car. We looked out the window at New England fields on the verge of verdant spring. Lyra took pictures at different shutter speeds and millimeters consciously trying to create the surreal. The empty fields suddenly became a cemetery and Lyra took pictures of austere, New England graves made of mostly flat stones.

"I love cemeteries," Lyra said. "They make me feel peaceful."

I smiled at her. "I'm not surprised."

"You're getting to know me so well that you can predict what I haven't unveiled."

"I think so. Hell, death is peaceful and everyone's got apprehension about it. It's life that's really terrifying. Something like that is what you're thinking."

Lyra smiled at me and returned to the world of her lens.

By lunch we had sped briefly through Connecticut and were in New York State nearing the great city. She spoke about different photo techniques like overlaying surreal photos into one teasing image and triangular and quadrangular shots pieced together into a puzzle like the ones on her dorm wall. She went on about the merging of her photos and my words into a book and how beautiful and pure it was. We were expanding and overhauling travel into new parameters and motives.

We bantered on and on about the project. Lyra wanted all her photos to be used regardless of their quality. I mocked her beat ethos of preserving everything and disregarding selectivity. She agreed with the beat belief that not using something would be turning your back on something sacred, divine, genuine. I reminded her that Kerouac's best work needed to be rewritten over and over by himself and editors. Following the dogma of everything coming from above was an offshoot of too much speed and pot-rotting perceptions of clarity. She told me to let go of analysis. She said there was no place for science in poetry. We discussed approaches and possibilities during most of the travel time until she fell asleep with her head resting on my shoulder and her body curled up in her seat in fetal position. I stared at the land passing by and the city in the distance. We were heading into Grand Central Station.

In Manhattan, we walked along the train tracks until Lyra found a spot that encompassed views of Manhattan in the background. Lyra said she felt that she was discovering her eye with each shot and no class could ever do what travel was doing now. She said the thrill came from the fact that they were living the story and had no idea what the next chapter would bring. We walked to the base of the Brooklyn Bridge. Lyra decided to add bridges to the themes. "Just fits," she said.

We had dinner at an Italian restaurant in Little Italy. We drank a liter of cheap house red wine and ate a simple spaghetti dinner and salad. We decided to find a hotel to get some real rest before boarding the train again. We found a squalid hotel in Chinatown. It was dump, but we crashed on the dirty sheets and lumpy bed surrounded by cracked wallpaper and cockroaches scurrying below.

When I woke up, I saw Lyra wrapped in a white, hotel towel. Her wet, auburn hair dripped water slowly down her shoulders into rivulets descending between her breasts that rose firmly above the tightly wrapped towel.

"Waking up to this sight is like going into a dream rather than out of one," I said.

"Shall we enter the dream fully?"

"It's your dream, amore."

"Leave the towel on."

"Ok."

"Sit next to me." I said.

I sat up waking fast to the driving adrenalin of the libido. I ran my tongue above the towel licking the water off her clean skin and rubbing my cheeks and whole face within the firmness of her towel-pressed breasts. She lifted my face and caressed my lips inside and out with her fingers. Then, she pushed me down on my back and took off my shorts and got on top of me, while I pressed myself along her moistened outside.

She was now in charge.

She slowly unwrapped the towel and then wound it into rope form. She tied my wrists tightly with it. She rode on top of me for a while drawing me close several times and pulling away, until she finally took me inside and I quickly came. She continued back and forth until she came. We fell back to sleep together, still exhausted from all forms of escape.

"Wake up." Lyra whispered, nudging me out of a deep sleep.

"Will you leave soon?" she asked.

"Will I leave where? You mean will we leave soon?" I mumbled sleepily.

"No, will you leave me?"

"Why do you ask something so ridiculous?"

"Just answer it."

"No. It's a stupid question. I'm yours. I'm in love with you, Lyra."

"I love you too, but it can go as quickly as it comes."

"Who says?"

"It can. All of history says so."

"Well, mine's not going anywhere except further into you."

"What the hell do we know about love?"

"Right now, I'm living it. What else is there to know?" I said sounding like her. We were changing hats.

"I'm just a little tense, worried about something coming between us, something stopping our trip, our life together."

"Sweetheart, we are our destiny."

"I'm afraid, Stoker."

"Don't be. I'm not. I love you."

78

Later on the train heading to Clarkson subterranean farm, I panicked about money and expressed my concerns to Lyra.

"They're not paying for school. You are. It's your loan and your life," she said adamantly.

"Yes and no. I don't know if I've got the balls to live in a vacuum."

"We're twenty-two. I don't think we've got to worry about our parents. If yours are anything like mine, they're probably a lot more fucked than we are, stuck in some stationary doldrums. We've got movement, motion, newness."

"I want to talk about money. I'm not calling them from fucking Omaha saying I need help like the damn Neil Young song."

"It won't happen. Just pretend they don't exist for a while. It's cruel, but healthy. True separation is needed in families for each individual, I think. So, let go. Excise yourself and see what will occur."

"Oh yes, and then the truest of all truths will appear, peacefully ever after."

"I didn't say that, but who knows?" Lyra said, winking at me.

"I'm not too concerned about the umbilical cord and philosophical ideals right now. Are you listening? I'm concerned about the money and the eventual embarrassment it can cause."

"Mundanity. It's a nice rhyme for insanity. We have no time for mundanity now, but if you insist. I told you I've got about $1500 and a credit card with Five K max. So we've got almost seven thousand. I think we can swing it across the country with that. Hell, we could even stay in goddamn Marriott's if we wanted. Yuppie beatniks."

"Doesn't it trouble you that the money's yours and barely nothing is coming from me?"

"I don't even feel like it's coming from me. I have no discernible connection to money. Mine doesn't feel like mine. I really don't feel anything with money. Mine is yours and yours is mine. Why count?"

That night in a motel, we were lying in bed watching TV and drinking a bottle of red wine. We needed some time away from the train and a night without motion. Lyra broke the stasis. "I want to do something to you."

"By all means."

Lyra took my shirt off and then got on my back as I lay down in massage position.

She began talking about Chakras, synapses, and neurons as she seductively and soothingly pressed her thin, but strong fingers into my skin.

Softly, she began stroking my skin at the Asian points of dammed energy. She held my hand and caressed the tender, forgotten flesh between my thumb and index finger stimulating the sensors. She applied pressure to the tiny, ignored muscles and tendons.

"Close your eyes and let them roll backwards into your head and force no thoughts. Take in peace and release everything else. Just feel the sensations I'm bringing to your hands," Lyra said sensually.

She continued from that point to my inner elbow area, shoulder, behind my ears, jaw, under my chest, between the hip and genitals, behind the knee, ankle and soles of my feet, all the while soothingly speaking tender words designed to mentally slow my thought processes, while her hands took care of the physical. I was nearly asleep as her lips touched mine. Her lips proceeded down my neck and chest until she began orally massaging the one area she hadn't touched.

Lyra paid the bill for the motel, while I drank coffee sitting on the curb in Coalstone, Pennsylvania. I was feeling unabashedly alive and noticing that I hadn't noticed the sky for a long time. I mean really noticed. I took in all the contours of the clouds and the surrounding endless azure. It was as if I'd simply forgotten the natural canvas above us.

I wanted this to go on forever. Our companionship, the sex, mining the core together with creativity. Mundanity was forgotten. A waste of energy. I was indifferent to seeing Clarkson. One quick visit to the past shouldn't be disruptive. After Clarkson, we could head South instead of West, perhaps. Newness might be a key to the elixir, like the mad Situationalists of Nick's class, always seeking novelty. We could go South right through Texas into Mexico and Central America. Exotic, little countries like Belize and Honduras were more new than Utah or Colorado. That's done over and over, driven into cliché. We could go all the way to the Southern tip of South America. Stand on the edge of Cape Horn. We could stop in each country, teach some English and move on. From there the Orient, Europe, and Africa, always one step ahead of yesterday headfirst into art, masks dissolving into gleeful form and after—

"You ready?" Lyra asked.

"Huh."

"Where were you?" Lyra said smiling.

"On our way."

"To go?"

"Yeah, good ole go. The astronomy lab seems eons ago."

"Did it ever exist?" Lyra mused.

"Inasmuch as our inception."

"Really, though, what was running through your thoughts?"

"It all started with the sky. I just kind of got ahead of myself. Everything's just too good. My head is wandering without walls. I've got all this space to fill, all this possibility to consume. So many things left unrecognized to actually envision, as everywhere and obvious as the sky. I ignored the sky for a long time. What a shame. What a sham."

"So many shameless shams ahead, Stoker, but we'll sidestep them, my love."

We drank coffee in the dining car and smiled and kissed each other all the way to West Virginia. We barely spoke until we got off the train and made our way to Clarkson's farm.

"I don't know which house it is," Lyra said as we arrived at a street she believed to be Clarkson's. "I don't see any numbers and he didn't give me a number anyway."

"We'll just knock on one of them. There aren't many and everybody probably knows everybody so they'll tell us where the mad Marxist is."

"Does he bother you?" Lyra asked.

"No, actually, I kind of admire him. A friendly, good-looking, athletic Marxist is a rarity. Usually, they are soft bellied and wan as if they have been sedentary all their life with the only light hitting them halogen. He's one of those rare leftists who doesn't seem to be using theory to blanket the psychic wounds of youth."

"The psychic wounds of youth," Lyra repeated dramatically.

"So, should we try this one?"

"I don't see why not."

We headed up a dirt driveway with an old, Dodge pick-up truck.

"I don't see a front door," Lyra said.

"Let's go around back."

We approached a window on the side of the large, old farmhouse.

"I hear some voices. It sounds like Alex's and a woman's." Lyra said quietly in the voice of someone trespassing.

"Let's listen for a second to make sure."

We bent down and knelt near the window in a position of maximum audibility and no visibility.

"It's time. I've had it," said the male voice. "Let's just end the bloody thing once and for all. I never wanted it in the first place."

"You're right, I know, but sometimes, it feels so good to escape into it, but moderation hasn't worked. You were right," said the female voice.

"We'll never get to where we imagine to be with it. Let's kill it."

"What the hell's going on?" I whispered to Lyra.

"It sounds like Alex."

"What the hell is *it*?" I asked.

"I don't know."

"I take it back; his psychic wounds are coming out." The voices began again.

"We've got to do something." The male said.

"So let the sacrifice begin.'

"Once it's dead, more is possible."

"Depth. The deep drop of depth." The woman said.

They were giggling slightly now.

"We might find nada down there," the man said.

"Then we confirm it's the same as here."

Lyra looked at me and mouthed, "What the fuck is going on?"

I responded silently, "I don't fucking know."

"For Nietzsche!" the male said histrionically.

"For a youth of truth unfiltered by big brother!" she responded in a wild voice.

"To rescue the subconscious."

"Ready?"

"Ready!"

We heard a click and cock like that of a shotgun and then the same sound again.

I looked at Lyra and she nodded her head upward at me to get me to stand up and stop whatever the hell was about to happen. My heart was racing.

"Stop!" I screamed leaping up into visibility.

I saw Alex and a woman, both armed with shotguns, and they turned to me smiling and surprised. I saw the guns now pointing at me and I collapsed to the ground like an elevator having snapped free of its steel wires.

"Stoker! My god, what a surprise," Clarkson said.

"What the hell are you doing?" I said, still on the ground.

"What the hell does it look like?" Clarkson said.

"It looks and sounds like you going to fucking kill someone. What the hell should it look like?"

"It looks like we're about to kill something, not someone."

Lyra stood up beside me clutching my hand. I saw Clarkson's eyes notice our hands and he then said, "Lyra. Another even more beautiful surprise."

"Well?" I said irritated.

"A TV."

"What?" Both Lyra and I said.

"A TV. Denise here and I were ready to free ourselves of television and we got a little dramatic. Just some theatrical fun. Sorry to scare you, but you should've knocked. Hell, we could've killed you."

"No, shit. Can't you just give it away?"

"That wouldn't be so ceremonial. Hell, look what the ceremony brought us. I never believed Native Americans could summon rain or what have you with dance and ceremony, but who knows now. I mean we set out to kill the brainwashing box and human friends arrive. Unbelievable."

Denise looked at Clarkson and said. "Maybe you're a shaman sweetheart." They laughed.

We didn't.

"Why don't you come inside? What a great surprise."

"So, you guys quit school on a moonlit whim moments before graduation?" Clarkson began as we sat at a big oak table drinking red wine and eating turkey sandwiches prepared by Clarkson's girlfriend, Denise.

"Not quite moments." I said.

"More or less." Lyra said.

"Do you have regrets, Stoker?" Clarkson asked.

"No, I was just clarifying some facts."

"Well, facts get in the way of romance," Clarkson said, behind a wry smile. I wasn't sure if he was being sarcastic.

"Facts and facts and facts and more facts. A factual pile of lies," Denise said.

"Well, well, the whole escapade is a courageous leap into the unknown. A snub at the groomed, easy life. Unless, of course, it's a little detour, prior to getting the nest egg started." Clarkson said. Denise laughed.

"It's no detour." I said. "We're in it for the long haul, sans resume, Alex."

"How respectfully disrespectful. I salute you. I'll tell you this, no eternal reward will forgive us now for wasting the dawn, and you've gone headfirst into the dawn. Great secular miracles. Anyone trying to benumb their senses into future truth can stay with me and Denise as long as they want, right sweetheart."

"We love the dawn," she said.

"Sunrise has truth," Clarkson said.

"You know we never killed it," Denise said, looking at the TV.

"That's right. They're tough to remove. They slide by firing squads like Dostoevsky with some last minute news. It's a Russian TV. We'll kill it after dinner."

"Lyra, why are you so quiet?" Clarkson asked.

"Ahh, I don't know, a little tired, coming down a bit from our escape."

"Well, don't come down too much in my house. How can I, we bring you up?"

"Yes, anything Lyra, you name it," Denise said, putting her arm around Clarkson.

I interrupted. "Well, what's your plan here, Clarkson? Reworking Marxism while Gorbachev brings it down."

"Shall we get into that now? I'd rather find out what's bothering Lyra."

"Actually, what's bothering me is fatigue," Lyra said. "We've been on a rush for, what 72 hours, and now it's hitting me. So, before you explain the errors in the history of the world and the corrections, I think I'll take a nap. I'm beat."

"Here, follow me, Lyra. We have an extra bedroom with a big bed for both of you," Denise said, taking Lyra by the hand upstairs to a loft that was partially bisected by a wall, one side of which was the extra bedroom. The other must have been the bedroom of Clarkson and Denise.

Lyra gave me a kiss, finished her glass of wine with a big gulp, and followed Denise upstairs.

"So, tell me what you're up to," I asked Clarkson while we continued eating and drinking.

"Farming."

"You're really living off the land."

"That Turkey was ours. Killed it a few days ago. Fresh and free of government chemicals. There's nothing better than sinking your fingers into mother earth and nourishing yourself from your own efforts. Real connective, my friend."

I looked behind me out the window seeing the extensive land with farm animals grazing.

"It's all ours. We grow or kill everything we eat. We only eat meat once every week or two. Maybe, more in the winter. Keeps you warm. We grow our own vegetables, including the magical variety of fungi. Everything, my friend, including the wine, is homegrown and CIA, FDA, and Uncle Sam free. More organic than organic."

"The wine's pretty good." I said filling my glass and topping off Clarkson's. I noticed the bottle had no label.

"We freeze, bottle and preserve a lot for the winter. Rice and pasta and things of that sort we go to an organic store in town. I'm simply removing all that is affiliated with exterior sources and living within my creations and needs. It's not permanent, I don't think, but simply cathartic. Let's call it an experiment. A before and after. It's my little homage to the 18th century Transcendalists, Alcott and the other utopian New England mad, queer folk."

"I thought you were down here at WVU getting a PhD. in Marxist rhetoric or something like that."

"Not quite rhetoric," he said winking at me. "I was. I was teaching a class, a discussion group really, for a political economy class. I was on a stipend for the program and had to be a Teaching Assistant. So, we were discussing Franz Fanon's *The Wretched of the Earth*, and I got hit hard. Smashed into awakening. "

"How so?"

"I was in the middle of class facilitating the phony fucking verbal tennis, so damn fake. The freshmen were waxing guiltily about the first world exploitation of the third, or in other words, their parents' BMW compared to some sorry soul in Burkina Faso whose whole life's earnings wouldn't add up to the value of the damn CD player of said BMW and the epiphany exploded."

"The world ain't fair?" I said sardonically.

"Ole Professor Moss and Marxism were a folly. I mean the whole system, his whole tenured gig was never re-examined because had it been, he may have stumbled onto the reality that the system he had pasted together was infernally flawed. But the epiphany wasn't that. It was him doing fucking sit-ups in the gym at school. I saw him out of the classroom one time in the gym working out in boring sweat pants and a white v-neck undershirt. Still playing the role. And that's what it was. All a role. The image was indelible, but interred until that moment."

"What did you do?"

86

"I walked out in the middle of the discussion group, muttering 'I'm done' to myself. Over and over again. 'I'm done, I'm done, I'm done.'

"A clear exit full of conviction," Denise said.

"I left the whole Marxist, neo-Marxist need for a father crap behind. Didn't think twice. Haven't since. Then I meet Denise and she hooks me into the Alcott scene. Here we are. Flirting with purity and individual utopia. The only kind that can be. Scaling it down to see if it can work on any level. Imagine trying to make it work in an entire country. Human hubris is mind-boggling. I'll stick to two people and go from there. Groups cause problems."

"Is it Utopia?"

"I don't like that word. It's like happiness. Flawed words. Those words have no place in the reality lexicon. They're like the rabbit at the dog track. The dog is dying to get it, rarely does, and those rare times he does, it's fake."

"What words do you like?"

"It's liberating, but slowly. I feel as if each day I take a step out of myself, heading toward something new. Kind of like unzipping a wet suit and climbing out. Unlearning all the spoon-fed crap from day one."

"So are we in a way."

"Really?"

"Getting away, on the run, you know." I almost brought up our artistic endeavor, but caught myself thinking it was our secret, our treasure that shouldn't be tainted with words to others.

"What's your game?"

"Same as yours, I guess with motion thrown in."

Clarkson smiled at me knowing I was holding out.

"You know, Stoker, Denise and I do things differently around here. How long are you going to stay so you can really play our game? You say yours is the same, but no two games are ever the same."

"Just a night, I think. Like I said, we're into movement now."

There was some silence. Clarkson poured some more wine and our conversation eventually got into things he was interested in. We talked about his opinion that the Nation-State was coming to an end. He envisioned the death

87

of country, patriotism, nationalism, a new world free of borders and immigration agents, and the fall out would be a world government. He jumped back and forth in time tracing it as far back as Greek city-states and quickly through the age of Empires and the emptiness of religion, up through the French Revolution, the Paris Commune, Taiwanese Capitalism at the shores of Chinese colossal communism, the socialized, watered down capitalism of Europe and into the un-watered down, almost pure capitalism of Reagan, which was putting us on the brink of revolution according to Clarkson. He truly believed within decades the U.S. would be in the throes of major revolution from below, anti-intellectual. He believed the Soviets and the West would fall, not far apart.

"It's like a puzzle, synthesizing the events of history, like weaving a blanket. The end product will be the flawed future, unlike Marx's version where his ego blinded him to himself thinking he could pull down heaven onto our wounded planet.

I got bored.

"Well, this stuff is a little heavy for me. Lyra and I prefer the run away fools in love thing to a panoramic analysis of history."

"I tend to go overboard. I told you I'm stepping out slowly. I still get lost in the rhetoric and professorial bullshit. I'm trying to get into my microcosm here with Denise, but old selves die slowly. In fact, they probably just fade away without dying, to coin a phrase. Kind of perpetually linger and poke at you from time to time eternally."

I nodded sipping my wine.

"So, how do you stay totally self-sufficient on this land? You have no job? How do you buy stuff from that organic store you mentioned?"

"Denise and I work the land, live off the fruits and vegetables, we kill our own animals, drink our own wine, like I said. The grapes are imported from Italy. I wish I could have a vineyard, but the soil and temperature of West Virginia won't permit it. I'd like to head out to Sonoma or Napa someday, but the land is too expensive. For money we sell some of our excess at a farmer's market on Friday mornings."

"Good ole down to earth capitalism." I said.

"It's great at the level of the local store and the farmer's market, but any higher and I'm still repulsed. Marxism was a sad, deplorable detour, but it doesn't mean I'm sold on what we've got."

"It's all we've got."

"For now, for now. Something will give. I'm just tired of looking for it. Small levels and small steps now. When it gives, let it happen naturally. Let it come to me. Racing after anything never gets you to it."

"I agree."

"Are you sure?"

"Yes," I said.

He nodded, but I took it as a patronizing nod.

After some silence, Clarkson casually asked, "So, are you two really in love?"

"Yeah." I said quickly.

"Absolutely?"

"Are you in love?" I asked him.

"With Denise?"

"Yeah. Are there others?"

"Not now, but you never know. Ahhh, no, I'm not, but love is very cagey, tough to pinpoint your definition. I have feelings of love for her, but in love seems derivative, impure. It's like we've decided to put ourselves in a zoo, while the animals are going around fucking naturally, laughing at us. We've concluded that monogamy is ridiculous. Husbands running around screwing, wives with vibrators, it's a mad, mad world spinning amok in that alleged monogamy universe, Stoker."

Just then there was some noise at the door. There was someone mumbling indistinctly.

Clarkson said, "That's my Marxist friend. You'll get a kick out of him. He's in a different stage. Or perhaps, on a different stage."

Clarkson let him in. The guest was short and had curly, greasy brown hair receding and thinning. His cheeks were ruby red. He didn't so much as walk as stumbled ahead.

89

"Surplus profit, surplus profit," he wailed. "I tell you I'm going to solve that riddle and then the gates of egalitarianism will swing open so hard it'll knock ten CEO's over like duckpins. Surplus profit will be the big ball down the capitalist ally and those two percenters will fall by the wayside like pins. Oh, I like that metaphor. Yes, Alex, it's like I always say there are many ways to skin a cat. Ole Uncle Karl'll be proud once the surplus profit dilemma will be taken of his shoulders. He's tired, He's—"

"Maple, we've got a guest."

Maple seemed to come into focus, registering where he was. "Oh, my manners are gone when I'm thinking out loud. Excuse me, I'm Marcus Edburg, but everyone calls me Maple. Before you ask, that's because I use maple syrup like others use ketchup. I just want to clear that up right away. Yes, my father used to razz me on that for so long. He hated maple syrup and he'd hide it on me. Oh, just the first of a lifetime of things we didn't see eye to eye on, but you can skin a cat many ways. "

"Hi, nice to meet you," I said. My eyes couldn't help but roll.

"That's Stoker Caudwell, an old friend of mine from school. He's here with his love, passing through," Clarkson added.

"Hmmm, passing through, oh, why don't you stick around, join the group?"

"Well, we're traveling. Thanks, though."

"Surplus profit dilemma needs heads. What do you think of the problem?"

"I wouldn't know where to begin. It does ring a bell from some of Moss's classes," I said to Clarkson.

"Surplus Profit!" Maple shouted. "Surplus Profit is the damn reason Uncle Karl can't rest in peace. It's why Stalin put an ice pick through Trotsky's skull. It's why Vladimir Ilich's dream failed. It's why Chairman Mao slaughtered his own. It's why Marxism is a mockery in the West. Had the Paris Commune just been given more time to elasticize, stretch into its own being, had, oh, skin the cat another way, the Marxian map is only a map, it needs time to breathe, let the compass find the right magnetic cord. You should have seen those red neck bastards today. They spit on me. Right in my face." Maple's face turned red and seemed to distend with anger.

Clarkson intervened. "Surplus profit is the money beyond which we need. The money that must be funneled back into the state to spread to those who can't work or students or—"

"You mean taxes," I said.

"No, taxes are a capitalist word of oppression," Maple said.

"You know I really don't feel like talking about this," I said.

"So be it," Clarkson said. "Why don't we have dessert? I'm done with Marxism, too, Stoker. It's dead. Killed itself. Historical suicide."

Maple let out a giant sigh, then inhaled deeply and exhaled. He was almost panting like a tired, old dog just sitting down in the shade on a hot, summer day.

"Denise, how 'bout some dessert?"

"Sure," she said from the kitchen. "You can get some fruit from downstairs."

"We've got wonderful preserves from last summer's peaches, apricots, pears, all different kinds. Goes great with brandy."

Clarkson left the room.

"So, Mr. Stoker, did I tell you the damn kids were spitting on me?" Maple began.

"You mentioned it."

"I'm handing out flyers for a meeting and these kids start calling me pinko and heckling me. I felt like I was back teaching high school in New York when the kids were animals back in the 70's. They threatened to kill me. So this one hippy hater comes real close and just spits in my face. Why? Can you tell me WHY?" Blood poured into Maple's face.

"You disturb the equilibrium," Clarkson said on his way downstairs.

"They're threatened with the realization that our existence, our parents' existence is deeply flawed and one day Uncle Karl will reign when all this attempted forced communism falls into the ashbin of historical forces and ultimate communism, or positive humanism as Uncle Engles called it, rises and 5,000 years of religion and greed dissolve. This damn soil was communist to begin with long before Uncle Karl put it to paper. The natives were communist. Natural communism. Not some ascribed failure. All throughout The Americas until Columbus and his henchmen started the American Genocide."

"You know, Maple, I hope you're right, but right now I'm going to check on my girlfriend," I said, enjoying the sound of the word girlfriend and the end of Maple ranting.

"Listen, Stoker, if you get any ideas on the surplus profit dilemma, share them. This is not about venting. This is about humanity's detour steered by less than two percent because they own the damn means of production. Surplus profit can and will redirect the flow. We will undermine the tragically stolen means of production. The meek shall inherit the earth. Scripture isn't all bad, just the bloody church ripping off yet another revolutionary Jew. Many ways to skin a cat."

"You bet," I said ascending an old wooden staircase to the loft that hung above the living room and kitchen.

Lyra was sleeping soundly upstairs in an old wooden bed covered by a thick, soft quilt that had probably been stitched by hand. I sat next to her and gently caressed her cheek with the back of my hand. It was the amalgam of peace and excitement that made me know she was the one. What I was doing right now was what made her special. There was softness and tenderness that ran along my hand, but inside I felt the fire of my sexual attraction to Lyra. The blend of these connective energies was all I could ever imagine a relationship with a woman to be. This was the harmony that Clarkson and the genius fool Maple sought, but would never find. I found it.

This was love.

Lyra was feeling weak and tired. Perhaps, she had caught a bug, she told me. She would get plenty of rest so we could head out early in the morning. I was happy she was resting and getting her strength after the rolling madness of our escape had come to stillness here in West Virginia. I was happier that we would be alone and moving in whatever direction we wanted tomorrow.

I left her alone.

Clarkson did the dishes, while Denise, Maple, and I sat outside. It was an unseasonably warm April evening. The first whisper of summer. Denise sat in an old rocking chair and was sketching in a big artist's pad. Maple sat on a wooden swing with big, thick twisting ropes ascending to the peeling green, metal crossbar. I sat staring at the half moon and the pure blackness between the stars. I wasn't very interested in talking to either person, but if I had the choice it would have been Denise.

Maple began. "So, where you guys heading?"

I could hear the sounds of the dishes clattering beneath running water inside.

"Ahh, We don't truly know, but probably South."

"Ohh, New Orleans is South. My old man used to take me there every year. Yup, Willy Loman, my old man. He was a shoe salesman and every year we'd go down to New Orleans and it was the greatest time of my life. We'd go into Bourbon St. bars and my father would give me half glasses of his beer and I was the happiest kid in the world. Then that all changed. All of it. You know how? You know why?"

"No."

"My father was a right wing McCarthy-ite. Worst move we ever made was firing MacArthur and not bombing the Gooks to oblivion. He thought Truman was a Commie! That he had been infected by the red plague. So I come home one day from high school and asked him all sorts of questions about Vietnam and why Marxism was so bad if it just wanted equality. It seemed like common sense, I told him. That was it. He went crazy." Maple's eyes widened and the blood blasted into every capillary in his face as the memories sought escape.

"Maple, adolescence is tough, man. Your father sounds unreasonable."

"Sounded."

"Sorry."

"Ahh, Christ, what's the difference. New Orleans is a great city. You know what, though, why don't you stay here? We need voices. You see Clarkson and I are really different. I believe Uncle Karl was so close if not for the surplus profit dilemma, but Clarkson thinks less of dear Uncle Karl. He's into widely varied dialectics. He's more into the social oppression and sexual dysfunction causing economic evils. He's more cynical at twenty-four thinking society is a hopeless, hapless mass and so he's given up already. He's stuck in small stuff. Thinks only about implementing on individual or small group levels. Nineteenth century transcendalism, Fourierism, and all that. It doesn't fly now."

"I know, he told me," I was, still looking at the blackness between the stars.

"I'm vice versa. Social pathology is a fallout of the economic mess of an inegalitarian system. Clarkson thinks about Freud and Reich and sexual psychology now instead of the bigger picture. Means of production is much more cataclysmic than wanting to sleep with your mother or imperfect orgasms. You know Reich?"

"Heard of him. Yeah. Orgasm theory."

"Yes. You know your stuff. Well, it's all interconnected and we approach it differently, but it's out of that difference that gold can be spun from straw. There are many ways to skin a cat. Why don't you throw your spoon into the dialectic pot? Throw some honest hope into the future and avoid the greedy run from life. It's all one big Pyrrhic victory otherwise."

"Maple." Denise said looking up from her sketch pad. "You don't see what's in front of you. You just keep harping on your economic uncles and paternal created theories, but just look into the man's eyes."

"What?" Maple said suddenly slack-jawed and droopy-eyed.

"He's in love. He doesn't give a southern hoot about your Uncle Karl or dialectic stew. His soul is happy, alive in the only true way."

"I didn't say he couldn't be in love to join the cabal."

"He doesn't need the cabal. And what cabal, anyway? The one among your various selves?"

Maple gave her a dirty look.

94

"To tell you the truth I'm not interested in any groups, real or otherwise. Denise is right. Lyra and I are in love and we're going to travel a little recklessly for a while and then I imagine settling down and being boring. I have no idea what I'm going to do, but I just know it's going to be with her."

"Are you sure?" Denise asked.

"Yes. Why do you ask?" I said.

"Why did you come here?"

"Lyra wanted to check this place out. She's into photography and thought it would flow with our artistic project. And she's an old friend of Clarkson. And I am, too."

"She hasn't been taking many photos."

"We're not here to just take photos. She's feeling sick, anyway. What's your point?"

"We can join them or we can let it unnerve us. I've gotten used to it. At first, I reacted traditionally, but I've transcended it. It's just sex and togetherness. Who says it has to be monopolized by only two bodies, two hearts? It's the oldest myth of the human condition."

"What the hell are you talking about?"

"Do you hear any dishes?"

Denise put her pad down so I could see it. She had sketched Lyra and Clarkson naked and in bed in a sexual position.

I was speechless.

"My version of art therapy." Denise said with a little giggle.

Maple laughed like a snorting pig then said, "I don't get the need to imprison sex either. We don't own what we should, so we try to own what we shouldn't."

"Why don't you react naturally rather than the way we've been conditioned to react?" Denise said.

Maple said, "She's right. You can overcome jealously."

"Shut the hell up you Marxist clown!" I finally screamed.

I went inside to disprove the sketch and the cataclysmic image rolling around my head. Clarkson wasn't in sight. My eyes roamed the expansive one room kitchen, dining and living room. I noticed the TV still there, unscathed. I heard my breathing all short and gasping like a wounded animal. I thought I heard soft human sounds upstairs, but I couldn't be sure that it wasn't the product of the sketch battering my thoughts. The images in my head voicing themselves.

I went upstairs. The possibly imaginary sounds of the sketch ceased. I came to the top where the thin pine wall divided the loft into two bedrooms. I went to the right where Lyra had been sleeping.

I saw the sketch.

They separated. They both looked up.

"Stoker, don't rush to the end. We're not in love. It doesn't have to affect you." Clarkson said as Lyra lay next to him partially covered by the sheets.

My lips begin to mouth words, but my breath barely existed. What little air going in was used for my lungs to function. Language wasn't physically possibly as I stared at Lyra and Clarkson in bed together. My entire being had been severed and my organs were hanging on to what was left.

"We didn't mean for you to find out this way. These things sometimes just evolve without plan. She still loves you." Clarkson said.

Lyra said "I do, Stoker. I have feelings for Clarkson, too. Why should I repress them for us? Later it will just haunt us in different ways. This could actually make us better, stronger."

I stood there shaking my head slowly in disbelief that my lover was in bed with someone else and that they were treating it as a bohemian philosophy lesson.

"Fuck you!" I said as loudly as I could, which was a whisper.

"Stoker, she's right. Maybe this isn't the time to discuss it, but tenderness doesn't need to go unexpressed. I feel it for you, too. The physical shouldn't be ignored. Otherwise, violence—"

Lyra interrupted. "Stop, Alex. It's not the right time. We're being insensitive. Let him take in one thing at a time. It's too overwhelming. We should have explained it, rather than shown it."

My disbelief slid into frustration at not acting out. I wanted to grab Clarkson, let loose my fists in a barrage, but my body wasn't in control. I wanted to be Mike Tyson, but instead I was Charlie Brown. My mind had traversed elsewhere and the body stayed. I felt far away from myself. My hands felt yards away from my eyes. I even looked down to see if I could see them.

More words filled the air.

"Stoker," a female voice went on. "Just relax and think about the beauty of sharing physical love without the bonds we're told we must have. You could be with Denise and we don't have to have hate and jealousy. We can reach a new level. We can still travel, honey. I love you. We're not over. We're just more encompassing. More real. We're leaving suburbia fully not superficially. Let me help you lie down. I'll stay with you. Clarkson can leave until you truly digest our reality and its evolving truth."

"Yes, I'll go downstairs. You take my place Stoker." A male voice.

Clarkson began to get up. I had one instinct in my disconnected body. To run. I turned and headed down the stairs.

"Wait honey!" Lyra shouted.

As I ran, I felt my body reconnecting with the strides. The need for escape gathered my senses.

"Don't react this way. It's not even your reaction. It's the reaction you've been told to have." Clarkson said from upstairs.

Maple shouted coming in from the porch. "Stoker, just take it easy. We don't have boundaries here. What's their use?"

I saw Lyra's wallet on the table. Maple watched my eyes and followed them. I instinctively decided to take it with me. As my hand reached out, Maple's hand beat me to it.

"Just hang on, Stoker, don't be hasty. You've got that runaway spirit. It wasn't just Lyra. There's something in you that senses the enormous madness we've all been draped in. Uncle Karl saw it and paved the way for people like us. Join our cabal. We can use you. You haven't lost Lyra. You've gained us. We're in it together."

97

"Give it to me." I said.

"Just wait." Clarkson said from the loft.

"Fuck you!" I said, air and body returning.

"Look at yourself. You're like a puppet. Your reaction is completely contrived. Peel it off. Skin the robotic cat." Maple said. "You don't want to end up like my father spreading misery. We know what's wrong. Let's find out what's right."

"Shut up!"

I pulled my arm back, clenched my fist, and hit Maple with a right cross squarely on the jaw. As I was winding up and then uncoiling, I remember Maple staring at my fist about to crash on his face. He didn't flinch. Maple's frumpy body tumbled to the floor. The wallet fell. I grabbed it and headed to the door. Lyra and Clarkson ran after me half dressed. I ran and ran and the footsteps behind me went silent.

I made it to the train station. I slumped against a wall. My heart battered my ribs. My breath was short. I didn't know what was happening to me physically. It was as if I literally had a broken heart. I now had two thumping bloody masses of muscle aching. I understood broken heart for the first time. I never wanted to understand it again. I understood why my aunt never remarried. Don't get back on the damn horse. My chest hurt so much. I had to breathe. I tried deep breaths. Long and slow inhalations and the same style exhalations. I wondered if I was having a heart attack. I started crying. Weeping like a baby. A woman approached me and asked if I needed help. I shook my head. She ignored my response. She sat down next to me. She held my hand. I fell into her shoulder and cried and cried and cried.

When the tears stopped, I apologized. I was embarrassed. Humiliated. She was in her forties. She must have known real pain. She told me to explain what had happened. I told her the whole story. She listened. She just listened.

My heart was still beating wildly. She continued holding my hand and put her other hand over my heart.

"What are you going to do?" she said at the end of my explanation.

I thought about it for one second. "I'm going to continue going west," I said.

"Good for you. Good decision," she said softly. "Do what you set out to do. Do it for yourself and she'll fade into the past."

I nodded. I'm going to San Francisco with her money I thought. I'm going to write my way out of the pain. Finish the journey undeterred.

I was breathing easier. I hugged the woman. I had told her everything, but I don't truly remember telling her anything. Those moments were a blur except for the warmth this stranger gave me. All I can remember is the feeling. I don't remember what she looked like. Specifics don't exist. I got on the train with the ticket Lyra and I had bought. The woman gave me her card. I hugged her again. I told her I would never forget what she did for me.

I wrote spontaneously all the way across America. I got off the train at certain points daily. I took walks into the town, found a spot to eat and described the moments. I sought the subconscious, but consciously tried to keep Lyra out of the verbal exhalations. I didn't want to pine over her. I wanted to leave her and us behind. It hadn't been real. It didn't belong in my memory though I knew it would remain eternally. I wasn't able to lie to myself completely.

When the train pulled into San Francisco, this is what I had. A notebook full of adventures, observations, unknowns, dreamy conversations, verbal cubism, magnetic fields, all Bretonian spontaneity.

Cars all piled up upon cars. It was this massive junkyard of dead cars and a sign read "Entering Dragon Falls – The city with the most junked cars." These piled colors of metal car sandwiches with a giant crane magnet hanging screaming metaphors above driving youth ready to pick up more dead cars to add to metal mountain and the road was strewn with road kill – squirrels, birds, raccoons, cats, dogs – more so than had ever noticed before. Then stopping at a tiny nowhere diner eating a BLT then smoking cigarettes and watching the townies talking about sports and a couple of stooped over cooks cooking the dead – and into motel memories of her strong – and a mighty migraine emerging rendering supine and madly lonely for her with phone imagining ringing and considering returning and dumping the whole absurd idea and confessing some crime to someone…some crime I hadn't done and here it is coach, one more try on the mound like it was done alone in my own universe so perfectly concocted with a masking tape square on the garage door and a tennis ball whapping the paint off speck by speck – finally it recedes a bit, so off to the lobby. It was small and peaceful if sad and sitting down watching the young girl behind the counter making small talk, but not beyond, just small, small talk between cigarettes then off to a bar nearby full of unsuccessful businessmen in bad insurances salesman suits, piano music, chatter, lots of chatter, voices, perhaps I had a fever and was a bit delirious. Someone asked if I was ok and I felt little beads of sweat on my forehead, yes, yes, just drinking my chilled straight Stoli that tastes so great wishing I was in the KGB…wishing I was a cosmonaut…Back to the room after a quick smile at lobby girl and laying in bed realizing everything was really hilarious, really funny in the monstrous microcosms floating everywhere and the silly exaggerated anthem of love lost for Lyra was all part of the indulgence, but the indulgence could be expurgated like sticking a hose in your colon and hydrically flushing out all the residue until it came clean. Here's a big wave to the new and the little cities in every city I'll see and this girl in the lobby was…

Pouring rain of Nashville at midnight in a little pub and a lonely 23rd birthday celebrating the romance of movement and flow, of new cities everyday and dawns and twilights angling new visions all conspiring bright shaded possibility if the mood and moment were freed to run. Couples talking quietly and watching TV and nothing happening, but friendly southern small talk. Looking over at two young lovers not talking, but imagining something, imagining going to go…thoughts of the friends who would try to create creativity as the motivating moment of everyday days, but that falsehood wasn't the springboard of this all.

Must be some sort of lost unity severed unknown along the way and whose secret, strange loss rerouted all inclinations higher and more potent than the unrequited love of a constructed angel gone down right before one's eyes...and a café on the fringe of Vanderbilt with students and blue collar types ate big American breakfasts of butter soaked eggs and flapjack meals with their isolated groups. Sounds of cracking eggs plopping on the black griddle and spatulas scraping the surface and bacon sizzling and coffee splashing into mugs...and across Tennessee over its eponymous river into Memphis and a blues club at night soothing the ennui of miles and miles alone...and the darkness, music and cold beer blanketing the foolish fears of pilgrimages done over and over and over again always thinking this one will lead anew, when the true and only real anew would be the taste of a woman, but not a woman besides those lost to the past knitted visibly in memory in sight so conversation begins with a neighboring stool, who begins his story, or was it imagined by me...So I transferred here from Michigan. I got so tired of friends and family going through the stages, I hate the stages, the so-called biological stages, goddamn transgressions, intransigent transgressions, I like to call them. Boom. You finish your school and go out a few years settling to a job and then marriage and buying a house and a kid and the holidays become a relentless talk of the transgressions from job, to wife, to property, to kids, to investments I imagine and kids lives, and it all recedes. It just shuts down. So I turned my back on it all, transferred out of my goddamn city and came here to Memphis with the same job. I sit in a cubicle and play with people's money, money market mutual funds shit, but the beauty is I only need a few hours a day, so I can play computer games and I listen to music and at night I just come home and play video games. Dates? They're rare, but when I have, I screw it up or come on too strong or too soft and can't seem to get it just right...just end up back in the virtual world. It's all just transgressions that cast a sticky web over everything...that was the gist of what I think I heard while drinking away and staring at any beauty I could find in some blues supported Memphis honesty and what I honestly needed was the honesty of a woman's body without any entanglements. It'

101

*been too long, the next stop's got to have at least the vision
of a woman's body in all its honesty...*

*Many miles alone into Amarillo and another motel
room whispering too much to stay in silence. After a few
banal bars without talk beyond, I found a strip bar with less
than 5 people sitting at tables and a beautiful woman
dancing on a protruding stage replete with the stripper's
pole. She was thin and Asian with hair short and silk-like
shining under the dusty light surrounding her. I was
drinking chilled straight vodkas between beers and drinking
fast trying to stem the pathetic loneliness from developing
into mad lust, but of course the booze only fomented the
desire...A guy at a table next to me slides his chair over
starts gushing about how this woman was beyond sexual, in
another stratosphere and that he had to have her. He's been
coming in every Monday for months just to see her and he
wanted to be with her, but he didn't have balls to go beyond
money in the G string...She walked off the center stage and
moved to a go-go stage to the right close to us dancing
behind the bars all alone while the tiny Monday crowd
watched the next act on the main stage. The next woman
was larger, full bodied in a cowboy hat and holster with
blonde hair. The Texan type, while the sultry, small Asian
seemed unnoticed, except by me and my neighbor. She was
wearing a yellow G-string and quietly dancing lost amidst
the lust for the American woman. My new drinking and lust
stricken partner kept going on and on about Akeio as he said
she was called and I was drinking faster and smoking more
trying to quell the mountainous loneliness from the miles and
motels alone and from everything for that matter which
became maddeningly lucid when confronted with beauty so
nakedly near and Gus kept saying how most of the men
wanted the big, blonde Texans, but not him. This Asian was
an angel, more than beautiful, more than sexual, even
mystical. She had an aura, a golden aura.*

*"Do something about it Gus." I told him. "Money
works, she's no angel, she's a stripper."*

*"Yes, yes, I know, but it's more, I've elevated her or
she's elevated me about her. The attraction is pure. Paying
would corrupt the myth."*

"Please, Gus."

"I know, I know, I'm a fool all caught up in some perverse, irrational, poetic momentum."

Gus, was well dressed and had a goatee with messy bohemian brown hair with a couple of earrings in his left ear. Poetic momentum? Yes, the momentum of the unspoken and untried. Well, seize it. Just then a tall man sat at our table and asked to join us. You like her don't you, he said to Gus. $100 and she's yours for the night if you treat her right. Gus got up and left. He said nothing and left fast. How 'bout you college boy, you wanna get your rocks off like they never been before. I took 5 twenties out of my wallet and handed them to him under the table. He nodded at Akeio and she left the stage going in back. You got a car he asked me. Yes, I told him. Wait in the parking lot, she'll be there in 5. That will be the best $100 you've ever spent and there are more like her, kid. An hour later I was alone in my motel room and was even lonelier and strangely I felt like I'd betrayed Gus and I began to miss Lyra more than ever. The alleged antidote served to sharpen and spread the runaway of melancholy. More than anyone, though, more than any self-indulgent blues, I thought of Gus wondering why honest poetic sensations were so pathetic.

The sun splintered into dusty rivulets through the tattered curtain of a cheap Amarillo hotel room. Checked the bed in a surreal, sleepy stupor touching for my Asian whore. The trick had been turned and the commodity paid for. I thought of Lyra. I thought of her place in the world. I thought back to my angelic whore. I thought of her lips, skin, breasts, hair and then back to Lyra and replayed the cataclysmic night with Lyra...I sped for the New Mexican border zealous and satiated from the night and morning. What if I'd gone to South America? What if I were in a cubicle or in a meeting....Johnson we need more analysis of the cost trends of an extra large drink included in the special as compared to a medium or for that matter the deal with the cinema. What's happening? Did you get the package deal of two tickets with every second meal. Movies and meals. Dinner and the movies. They go together. People work all week. They need to go out to eat and then to the movies. It's a lock. They win. We win. You win. I win. We all win. Get a phrase. Lock it up. Ok, Johnson, remember, you're the

103

best, positivitly...What if...no, what will be will be. Che sera, sera...California alone, new and novel friends, anarchists and artists, anything else is concession. Everything bright and changeable on a capricious notion only fenced in by currency, which despite the lament of the self indulged anarchist or artists remains a needed frame around too many amorphous possibilities. A pursuit gently pursued. Passed through Northern New Mexico and the red clay earth and various Indian Reservations – fenced in societies bound by currency, culture, history, pain, humiliation, pride; dark, deep souled people with heavy shoulders tense and tight. It's in the musculature. That's the gateway. Wandering groups tied to sky and earth now chained to poverty, drugs, alcohol...so say the cozy profs in air conditioned offices...maybe the fences were sanctuary from a money maddened hollow people going back and forth, back and forth, back and forth, why back? Sanctuaries beckoning everywhere like an old college friend's mad thumping inkling for a secret creative society founded on an art journal that would propel and attract youthful winds into temporary eternities...And on through Mosquero, over the Logan river, Ute Creek, through Tucamcari, all this via Route 40, a straight shot on open New Mexican land. Finally, heading North of 40 through the Adobe City of Santa Fe and lunch in the Indian Farmer's market, buying some Indian beads and jewelry on the road and up into Los Alamos and a tour of the first Atomic explosion so poignantly juxtaposed to the native's fences. Here's irony so ironic it'll make you ill. Little biopics of Einstein, Oppenheimer, Fermi, and those who severed the past and began a new era of human history, 1945! Finally, up to Taos across the Rio Grande and a steak, black bean and rice dinner in a college town before a memorable New Mexican sunset in front of a little motel in the center of town.

A clean and simple room with all the essentials, a bed, a night table, bible on top, a desk, chair and a window. No TV, clock, or paintings. I sat by the window smoking and peering into the cool April twilight, magnificent orange purple horizon kissing the red, Midwestern earth. Remember Isaac MacAuley's call for manipulating facts into untruths thereby unwittingly arriving at truth. One must lie

*into truth. Bullshit. Truth that is. Unraveling is the
essence. The outcome is alleged truth. The outcome is
irrelevant and thus truth is an abstraction, da-da-da-
da...Catch the now and let it go, not falling prey to the
midnight why.*

*I pulled into Reno. It was the last stop on the way to
SF, where I'd exhale the whole trip into words in the midst
of inexorable youth offering the slippery peace of a gnostic.
I found a motel across the street from one of the large
casinos and took $300 from my stash, which I'd use for the
nights festivities. Tomorrow I'd be in SF and staying with
Xeno and planning the journal of which I was not truly
interested, but was interested in Reno and gambling and
seeing what my final night across America would bring to be
vividly remembered in early morning solitude in an unknown
apartment. Unknown.*

*I was walking around the $5 tables looking for a one
that seemed to have the right setting when a young, blonde
dealer smiled at me. This was the setting, I thought. A
woman's body is the real slippery peace and this time
without paying for it. She was very young, maybe 18, with
some slight acne and blonde hair, but a shy, seductive smile
that made her more attractive than she really was. I sat
down and asked for $50 in chips. I started playing $5 hands
and after 20 minutes the table was empty. She had a
diamond on her finger. Soon, I started winning hands that I
had actually lost. I smiled every time she cheated in my
favor.*

*"You don't have to do that. Aren't they watching
you?"*

*"I don't care. They don't mess around with the $5
bets. This is trivial for them. They can't watch all the tapes.
A little help here and there won't be noticed. Can we stop
talking about it?" She whispered.*

"Sure."

*"So you're from, sir?" She said in a welcome-to-
Reno tone.*

"Boston."

"Hmmm."

"And you."

"Right here."

105

"And you're married." I said looking at her finger.

"Oh this." She said looking at the ring.

"Yeah."

"Oh no, this for the other men."

"What other men?"

"The other men besides men like you."

"You don't know me."

"I'd like to."

"Likewise."

"See, the other men wouldn't use that word, likewise. It's a beautiful word. I really like words, words like likewise, where two words become one. Isn't that a beautiful thing. Two words becoming one. Two things becoming one. Two becoming one." She said softly laughing through her words.

"Throughout, widespread, hereafter."

"Oh, yes, beautiful words."

"I like words, too. Words are, ahh, words have openings."

"Yes, words open us, but in the wrong hands, they are abused. You see the dealer over there." She motioned with her eyes. "You know what she did to me."

"No."

"Play one more hand and then leave. Can you meet me at the restaurant on the top floor? You could buy me a drink, maybe something to eat."

"Sure."

I put up a $10 bet. She widened her eyes and nodded more. I put up 4 more $10 chips. She hesitated. I put up $50 more. She dealt the cards and I had 10 and she had 7 showing.

"Sir, would you like to double?"

"Yes."

She dealt me one card. An ace.

She opened. "Dealer has 17. Nice work, sir."

"Thank you."

I had won $200 all together. I left a $10 chip as a tip thinking if I left more it would be too suspicious.

"Have a good night."

"Thanks."

106

We sat in a revolving restaurant high above Reno. I was drinking brandy. She was drinking a screwdriver.

"What nationality are you?" She asked.

"Same as you."

"How do you know?"

"What's the difference?"

"None."

"So we're the same, then."

"You're very sweet. How long will you be in my little sad city?"

"Don't really know, day or two. Who knows?"

"You know what she did to me?"

"Who?"

"The dealer I pointed out to you."

"No, tell me."

"She started working here a couple months ago. She was real shy, quiet, repressed. She told me she took the job to try and change herself. Open up her personality. Helped her relax and let the true self out. We drank and she tried drugs with me for the first time. Just easy stuff like marijuana, a little coke, Quaaludes, but no major stuff. Just enough to let her taste the other side, you know."

"Go on." I said motioning for refills to the waiter.

"So she starts dressing different, gets her hair done, you know drops the nerdy nun image that she had. Starts wearing black and tight things, you now all the clichés like freaking Olivia Newton John in Grease. It was kind of funny. Ridiculous, but guys started looking. So, she was living with her dead computer programmer boyfriend and wanted out now that she was coming out. She hadn't had real mind blowing sex in her life and he was a real drip. She was full of anxiety about it. Couldn't stand him anymore, so I tell her to move in with me and my brother."

"You really went out on the limb for her."

"You said it. So, she's hanging out with me, my brother and my boyfriend a lot. Then I come home from work a few nights ago and -"

"Your boyfriend?"

"Yes, I should have seen it coming, like you just did."

"Well, hindsight and an outside eye makes it easy."

"Well, I was a fool. My boyfriend, I mean ex-boyfriend, had the leather jacket, motorcycle, just what Robin needed, wanted. A little danger. Screw that type. I've had it. They're full of shit." She said finishing her drink.

"What type isn't?"

"They're all full of shit, but how do you avoid a type. We can't."

"You're right." I said

"What type are you?" She asked.

"Since meeting you, a very happy type."

"You're just saying that 'cause I let you win a bit."

"Wouldn't have mattered."

"I hate my own type. I like to change it."

"How?"

"With these."

She reached into her purse and pulled out a little plastic container and shook it so I could hear the sounds of pills clattering.

"They're homemade. It's got a little ground peyote, Quaalude, coke, and other stuff I can't remember. My brother made it. He's a drug expert. He's studying pharmacology."

"I don't know. The ingredients don't sound all that university like to me."

"Don't fret my new friend."

"Will it kill?" I asked

"No. It's not a new one. I've had it. It's only got a touch of sedative so you can mix it with alcohol."

We took the green and purple pill and toasted.

"To your brother." I said.

"To new types."

"To new types." I repeated.

"I think the restaurant is spinning a little faster."

"Can you believe Robin?"

"Maybe she did you a favor, getting rid of biker boy."

"You're right. I just can't stand the sight of her face."

"Did I say thanks for letting me win $200?"

"My pleasure. You're a sweet man."

108

"You ex-boyfriend's crazy for letting you go."

"You're sweet."

"Should we go somewhere? Like to my room."

"No, because if someone sees us, I'll get in trouble. A drink is one thing, but the room is another. Maybe, they'll check the video. Maybe, this is dangerous. Maybe, I'm going to get in trouble."

"You're getting paranoid."

"I'm not. I'm just aware of what a fool I've been."

"Take it easy. This concoction is making you edgy."

"If someone's sees me drinking with you and they knew you were at my table and won, they can put 2 and 2 together. Christ."

"Let's leave."

"I've got to leave alone."

"Well, give me your address and I'll come to your place."

"Shit, I'm an idiot."

"Just calm down."

"I need this job. You don't understand. What the hell do you care? You're just traveling through, looking to get laid."

I was about to say her name, but realized I didn't know it or I'd forgotten it.

"I don't even know your name."

"Good. Listen, I want to pretend this didn't happen. I need my job. And I'm not going to lose it to give you a piece of my ass to remember so you can tell your friends about in wherever the hell you're going and whatever the hell you're doing."

"San Francisco to the first question and as for the second question it would require a lot of time to truly answer and I get the feeling time is something you and I don't have."

"You couldn't be more right. I'm gone. Thanks for the drinks."

"No, thank you for –"

"Shut up. Don't you get it?"

She left and I said nothing watching her. I accused her of paranoia, but it was really just sudden prescience and she jumped of the game we were playing. I decided to save

the $180 I'd made after drinks and take off for San
Francisco now. The whole city was depressing me after this
woman's instant metamorphosis that left me alone again and
the drug was starting to freak me out. What the hell did I
just take? Got to get out of here is all I kept saying to myself
like a mantra through the waves of this ridiculous drug
thumping my heart and blood pounding in my veins. I went
to my room, threw my stuff in the bag and paid my bill. I
sped out of Reno into the Sierra Nevadas.

Everything was soft and melting very slowly. This
wasn't a wise move driving with this unspeakable concoction
in the system. Take it slowly. I saw a sign that said
Welcome To California and pulled over to the side of the
road just before the words and looked at them for a while
drifting into the places past and imagined...I was out of the
car following words I think I thought I heard coming from
the other side of the hill. It was a cold March evening and
the sun was slipping down the coming clear night behind a
distant mountain. I traversed a small hill tucked among
many larger ones following the voices. I came upon two
guys, very young, maybe no more than 20, but possibly as
young as 17. They had a pick up truck near them full of
equipment. I noticed shovels, pitchforks, large pick axes,
and some machines I had no words to match. I knelt behind
some bushes listening to them. The taller one seemed to be
in charge. The short rotund one was digging, while the
taller was reading a map or something barking out
information.

"Jamie, I'm telling you this is the spot."
"That's what you said last night, man. I'm getting
tired of failing."
"Well, there's no guarantee. I'm, we're,
undertaking something beyond huge here. You know
anybody who's ever physically severed a state from its
country."
"I know Mo, but Christ, I just can't wait for this
fucking place to go. We'll be heroes."
I shook my head to try and wake up from the dream
or the hallucination I was thrust into by that homemade
madness. "That's the last time I do drugs made by the
brother of a dealer in Reno whom I just met." I told himself

110

giggling a bit. I watched Jamie digging and Mo took a pick axe and started hacking a ditch in a line seemingly in accordance with the paper he kept checking. The curiosity was getting the best of me and danger didn't seem evident with Jamie and Mo.

"So what exactly are you two doing here? Is there another gold rush going on?"

They stopped their work and Mo spoke, "I don't think it matters to you unless you're going to California."

"Well, that's exactly where I'm heading."

"What for?"

"The same reason anybody really goes anywhere I guess."

"Well, there are lots of reasons to go somewhere."

"Essentially though."

"See, that's a going to California answer."

Jamie said, "Yes, that's a typically Californian answer. Just why we're going to make that godforsaken place an island."

"Huh?" I said.

"Jamie, you know, you got a big fucking mouth!"

"What's the difference if he knows. No one's gonna believe him. First of all, his eyes look like he's been having way too much fun and second of all, the story's too insane. Then there's no proof we were ever here."

"We gotta wipe our footprints."

"Yeah, I got the check list, don't worry. It's on there."

"Just the same, don't tell anyone else, Jamie. This is big shit we're doing."

"Entertain me, guys. What do you got planned here?" I asked.

"Just what Jamie said."

"You're going to make California an island?"

"Yes."

"What is this a James Bond movie? Just what drug have you been religiously taking?"

"Do you see this line here where I'm digging. This is the directly above the San Andreas fault line. You now anything about geology?"

"Fault lines, templates, platonics." I said remembering a freshman course.

"You know the words. The meanings is what we're after. Typical going to California cat. All superficial knowledge. Dilettantes head west. Don't really know anything, you just know to go. We're standing on the most delicate fault line in the world. After last year's earthquake, you know the World Series one, which is all anyone remembers. Stupid baseball game was more important than the results of the natural disaster. The SA fault line opened even more and the template that we're on almost split. It was in all the papers. The right blast and California more or less goes to sea."

"You guys are really gone."

"Just like California will be." Jamie said.

Mo pointed to the truck and Stoker looked inside. There seemed to be enough dynamite to blow up the entire globe.

"Enough to send this fault line vibrating to the point of breaking. All we're doing is speeding up the process. It's geologically inevitable." Mo said.

"Kind of like Marxism. Inevitable historical forces and we're like Lenin speeding up reality." Jamie said.

What is it about Marxists? I seem to find them everywhere and they're all deranged.

"Can I ask why you're blowing up the state of California?" I was unable to keep a straight face.

"Go 'head and laugh cowboy. Just watch the news though and we'll see who's laughing.

"Ok." I said, wiping the smiling off my face. *"Tell me why."*

"We hate California."

"Really." I said sarcastically.

"You asked," Mo said. *"It'd take all night, but suffice to say Hollywood is the biggest scam of the century. A whole industry of assholes getting rich and making everyone passive in the process. Hollywood has sapped our integrity and energy. Every idea is no longer an idea, but something to put on screen. We want reality back. And the North. They're worse than Southern posers. Those hippie fools postulating utopia and writing bad poetry. At least,*

112

Hollywood is honestly full of shit. It's time to take our lives back from this lost state that is running all our lives into nothingness."

Jamie said, "It has the 7th largest economy in the world. This state has more money than most countries. Now, is that fair?"

"Where do you guys live?"

"Look when it's all said and done if you say a word to the FBI, we'll hunt you down. There are others scattered along the fault line doing exactly what we're doing. You'll be followed, so keep you mouth shut."

"Look, this isn't really happening and if it was and I told someone, I'd be put into an asylum, so not to worry."

"We suggest you go home. Where is that?"

"Boston."

"Why would you ever leave? Real people, Boston, a real life, not this illusory phony prophecy of California."

"You guys are as unreal as it comes." I turned around heading to my car.

"Bon Voyage. Don't get island fever." Jamie said and Mo and he laughed heartily as they resumed their digging. "Remember you'll be watched."

I got in the car and headed west passed a sign that said Truckee 64 miles. I pulled over at the first food area and got a newspaper and a large coffee and wondered if any of the last 3000 miles across the U.S. had actually happened. It was better not knowing.

I arrived in San Francisco with no skills, a damaged heart, wore youth on my sleave like a military decoration, and thought my subconsciousness could be disinterred through writing.

I figured I'd fit right into this city.

I got a cheap little room on Broderick Street across from the Kaiser Hospital. I didn't have much cash left after paying the rent. Luckily, it was a transient week-to-week place called The Gotham. I liked the name. Everyone wants to be Batman.

It was one room and a bathroom. It was furnished with a lumpy twin bed, an old rocking chair, a countertop with some drawers, a rusty sink, and a hot plate with a few pots. There was a fire escape that had a view of Kaiser. It became my porch. I smoked and read away the boredom there while ambulance sirens flashed and whirred below.

After a few days of walking the city, I started to think about a job. Having no skills and no diploma, I thought I would get a clerk job. Work in a bookstore, a movie theatre, whatever, but I didn't want to make six bucks an hour. I wanted to make some money. I had no romance with self-imposed poverty. I liked the name The Gotham, but the place was squalid and bleak. I didn't want to be The Joker. It would be depressing in weeks. Right now it was just plain sad.

I was no true bohemian. I was just a visitor. A tourist.

I planned my pose during these days. Scanning the want ads, I saw some bartending positions. That's what I could do. I realized I had had a lot of experience. An alcoholic father finally presented an asset. I always bartended for my old man. He was a big martini drinker. Dry Stoli on the rocks with two olives. He let me experiment sometimes. I would make them up, shaken, stirred, dirty, perfect. He taught me all of them. We even occasional ventured into Manhattans and Rob Roys, but the old man didn't like to do brown alcohols. "They were for real drinkers," he'd say. Our biggest connections were sports and booze. Better than no connection, I guess. I bartended family gatherings. The women cooked. I made the drinks. My father had made a little bar in the basement. I was an expert at opening wine by ten. Martinis by twelve. Blended drinks in the summers.

I'd invent the name of a bar in Boston. Tell the interviewer it had closed down.

I had more revelations. They seem to come all at once. Epiphanies seem to spawn each other like all the Bible begetting folk in Genesis. Epiphanies are incestuous. I decided after a few months in San Francisco and making a few dollars, I'd teach English overseas just like Lyra and I planned. I'd roll on undeterred, making peace with our tragedy and fulfilling the promise of it without her. I didn't need her. I didn't truly need anyone. I also considered a fishing venture in Alaska prior to trekking the world in case I was really hard up for money. I'd heard it was hard work, but good money in a quick stint. I had gone 3,000 miles west. Why not go all the way west until I got home. Keep going west. It was a good idea, Lyra. See the world, create, and settle peacefully into existence. She could have Clarkson for all I care. She could have Maple and Denise and the whole sorry bohemian lot. Maybe I was doing everything to spite her. My epiphanies were paved in bitterness, perhaps, but it was a healthy anger, a justified anger. She'd done me wrong and I deserved the flow of vitriol. I'd occasionally lapse into angry cockerel rants. They were curtailed by trying to visualize the vague angel at the bus stop who saved me. Other times, the hurt was boundless.

I would tend two bars in San Francisco. The first one lasted one night. The second was a little longer. Both ended rather climactically. Everything seems to lead to some form of orgasm when you're on the run.

The first one was in the tepidly seedy part of North Beach. I walked past City Lights bookstore, took a right by Machine Gun Al's Roaring Twenties All Nude Review, passed by some $1 peep show places, which I had already sampled during my walk the city first days, and finally some Thai massage parlors, which I couldn't afford quite yet.

I actually got the job on the phone. I had called from the Gotham lobby pay phone. They had an emergency and needed someone that night. They didn't even ask where I had worked. The woman asked if I'd had experience. Yes. She asked if I minded working with a partly gay staff and clientele. No. She said to be there at 5:30. I said OK.

It was on the second floor. The pink carpet was strewn with soft purple feathers. The place was empty. There was a small service bar with no stools for customers. It was in a lobby type room with big, 40's style vinyl wall couches that went around the entire room. In the center was a circular couch surrounding a fountain with a statue of cupid being the source of the water flow. Pure cheese and kitsch. To the right was a large dining room with big wooden tables and a stage. Feathers were scattered everywhere. There were voices coming from upstairs. I followed the voices to a smoky, windowless office with two paper covered desks. I knocked on the open door.

"Yeah."

"Hi, I'm the bartender. I was—"

"Oh, yeah, Kim called you?"

"Yes."

"She tell you the deal."

"Not really."

"What's your name?"

"Stoker."

"Good name. You from L.A.?"

"No, Boston."

"You're a long way from home, but we all are, right kid?"

"Sure." He was smoking and his voice matched his addiction. An overflowing ashtray sat on a pile of papers and folders. He looked over forty, had bad teeth, and thinning brown and gray hair. His nose may have been big at one time, but it looked like a boxer's nose. Hit so often that it was smashed back into his face. Cheaper than a nose job.

"So, Stoker, what are you waiting for? Show starts at 8:30. Suits show up at 7:30. Big Martini and Manhattan crowd. Scotches and Old Fashions will come your way. You know how to make 'em Boston boy?"

"Sure."

"Best Chowder I ever had."

"It's good."

"Chowdah I mean," he said, laughing like he was choking on salt water.

I just stood half smiling.

"Set up your bar, kid. They're going to love you here. Ice is in the freezer at the bar, booze is locked up, keys are hanging on the door where you are. Good looking kid like you will make some good tips. You'll do all right. Make sure the wait staff tips you out 10%."

"Ok."

"You'll have no problems, no, no, easy as pie, kid."

I started to leave.

"Hey, Boston boy." He said not looking at me.

116

I turned around.

"You came west for a reason right?"

"Sure."

"Everyone has a reason. Reasons don't matter. You'll do fine. They're gonna love ya."

An hour later I had set up the bar. I lined up the white and brown alcohols for easy identification, got enough olives, cherries, and onions ready and tried to remember all the Martini variations. I had no idea what an Old Fashioned was. During the set up, a half dozen or so young men came in and smiled at me before going up the backstairs where Billy was.

Soon those same men were elegant women dressed to the nines hanging around the bar. Several drag queens and me. I was as wet as an ocean behind the ears, but I tried to appear blasé by the whole queer scene.

"So, sweetheart, where's Jose tonight?"

"Who's Jose?" I asked.

"The regular bartender," another one replied.

"Well, I like the fill in," another said.

"Where you from handsome?"

"Boston."

"Lot a queens in Beantown. Ought to call it Queentown. They just aren't as out as we are yet."

I shrugged.

"I met my dream man in P-Town. What a weekend!"

"That's a long time for you sister."

"Shut your snotty ass mouth."

"Are you straight, dear?"

"Yeah."

"Don't worry honey, we don't bite, unless you'd like us to."

"How long you been in the city?"

"Oh, about a week."

"What a welcome. Right to the heart of our fair city. A transvestite club."

I laughed as did they.

"Well, well, I bet you've tended bar in those Irish, manly bars."

"Just one, back East."

"Look at that nose. It's so nice, big, but straight, full of soul, character, ooh, sweetie, if I had you for a night, I'd welcome you to my fair city."

"Leave 'em alone. Christ, Dale, you ingratiate yourself when no one's opened the door. You just barge right in, fake breasts first."

"Oh, I'm just having fun with him, you don't mind, do you cutie."

I rolled my eyes.

"What's your name?"

"Stoker."

"Oooh, that hits the spot, stoke me, Stoker." said Dale.

"There you go again. Listen, Stoker, Dale gives you a hard time, you tell me and I'll take care of her."

"I'd like a hard time from Stoker."

"Where'd you get a surfer name like that in Boston?"

"My old man named me after a character in an old film about a boxer who wouldn't take a dive."

"Integrity, huh. You won't find any of that here," she said, and they all laughed.

"My name's Melanie. Dale likes to rattle new bartenders, straight or not. Don't worry, I can tell you're straight as a cucumber. I know a sister right off the bat. One look in the eyes and sexuality is identified. Can't hide the core, dear."

"Bullshit, Mel. I've been hiding my core my whole life," Dale said.

"Dale, you don't have a core."

Dale looked at me. "We're all gay, sweetheart. I'll get you to come out of the closet like a bull in Pamplona."

The drag waitresses started doing their job, getting drinks for the very white, business-type crowd who were milling around the lobby. They were flirting with the men, who seemed to enjoy every moment of it. When 8:30 came, the lights went dim and Billy from upstairs got on stage in a tuxedo and played emcee for the singers. First there was Dionne Warwick, then Diana Ross, Judy Garland, and finally Barbra Streisand. Dale came by to keep me company during the songs. She was black, had giant eyes, a male jawbone, and an Adam's apple like a walnut. She was all man with tits and makeup.

"So, you never said why you came here?"

"I needed a job."

"No, to San Francisco."

"No, reason, really. No good reason, that is. Girlfriend trouble basically. Needed some geographic space. San Francisco's the last stop."

"You heteros are all fucked up. All caught up in forever crap. You're all doomed."

"Not all of us," I said. "We made it about two months into forever."

"That's a good run."

I laughed and tried to occupy myself with cutting fruit even though it was all cut.

"Sugar, I love that profile. It makes me all loosey, goosey and juicy all over. Fix me a whisky sour and I'll leave you alone."

We laughed and the night went fairly smoothly. I was on edge most of the night, but got a kick out of waiters/waitresses' sense of humor and the unabashed banter. I felt as if they had an edge on heterosexuals, as if they had one-upped us evolutionarily by stripping down and out of a social straight jacket. Saying sayonara to controlling family and friends and shedding the past like a molting lobster. Heterosexuals were too often zippered up in the mold.

At the end of the night, I told Melanie about my newly conceived gay philosophy. Melanie was pretty level headed and I didn't think she'd take it as a come on. Dale probably would have ripped my clothes off.

"Sweetheart, I wish it was that simple. We're just as fucked up. No one's got a clue. That's why we're here."

"Here?" I said looking at the club.

"No. San Francisco, dear."

At the end of the night, the waitress staff left. The performers were still in the dressing room changing back to another identity. I had about $50 in tips. Not too much, but

I only got tips from the staff. No direct customers. Dale tipped me out $20 and offered more than money.

I went upstairs to talk to Billy.

He spun around on his swivel, vinyl chair. He looked like a minor league Larry Flynt.

"Oh, kid, hey how are you? How's Dale? I heard she had the hots for you."

I didn't like him. Not at all.

"Billy, do you need me to work again?" I asked.

"Can you handle it?"

"I think my question answers that."

"Easy, Boston boy. You're a bit tense."

"Well?"

"Kid, it was a one shot deal. Jose will be back. You're too straight for this place. Thanks for the night. You picked up a few bucks, new experiences. That's what you're here for, right? Experiences, San Francisco style."

"You got me figured out. You're quite astute," I said.

"Kid, you're a dime a dozen. I've been in this crazy city for twenty-five years. There's one of you entering every five minutes and one leaving shortly after."

"I'll be leaving as soon as you give me my pay. I was told I would get $7/hr."

"Yeah, yeah. How many hours did you work?"

I looked at my watch. I added an hour to the total for putting up with his shit. "Ahh, it's 9 hours."

Billy fumbled around with some papers. Found a little piece of yellow scrap paper. He wrote something down. He put the paper off to the side. I saw it fall off the desk. He didn't notice.

"We'll mail it out to you, kid."

"I'd prefer to have it now."

"We don't print checks on demand."

"Petty cash. It's only $63."

"Kid, don't tell me how to do my accounting."

"You don't even have my address."

"Leave it on the bar."

I thought about telling him to go fuck himself, but I wanted the money. Or I was just a wimp.

I came up with a plan. "Fine. I'll leave my address on the bar on the way out."

"Good idea, kid. You'll be all set. You'll have your $53. Don't worry," he said without looking at me.

"$63."

"Whatever."

I headed downstairs. I could hear the drag performers upstairs. They were chatting and laughing.

I went behind the bar. No one was around. I decided to take my paycheck right now. I grabbed bottles of Crown Royal, Johnny Walker Black, Stoli, Courvoisier. That's close to $100, I thought. It'd help me get through some lonely Gotham nights. I put the bottles in a box as quietly as possible, throwing in some paraphernalia like a wine opener, martini mixer, and a cutting knife and board.

I headed for the exit, purple feathers bouncing in the air with every step. I heard steps behind me. Before I could turn around, I was yanked backward by a handful of hair. I was flat on my back and the box was taken out of my hands as I was falling. Above me were the scowling faces of Judy Garland, Diana Ross, and Barbra Streisand. Behind me was Dionne Warwick holding my arms down with her/his knees on my wrists.

"Don't fuck with Billy, straight boy, or we'll fuck with you," one of them said.

Then I saw Streisand pull her clenched fist back and crashed it down on my face across my right eye. I tried to break free, but Judy Garland had a handful of my balls and was squeezing them like a lemon. I felt as if I'd been hit with a brick. I could feel my eye simultaneously closing and blowing up like a balloon, but that pain was nothing compared to the agony in my groin. Sweat was pouring out of my forehead. I could feel streams down my temples and over my nose, dripping into my mouth. My vision was gone and all I could see was a kaleidoscope of black and white surreal stars and fleeting flecks of diamonds behind my eyelids.

"You ever come in here again, we won't be so nice."

I heard Billy's voice. "There's an experience for ya kid." He said amidst a cackling, tobacco laugh.

They got off of me, taking the bottles and laughing their way back upstairs.

I lay there feeling the pain recede ever so slowly in my loins and the pain increase in my soon-to-be shining black eye.

It took about a week for my eye to return to near normalcy. I spent a lot of my time in my Gotham room. I wondered if loneliness could get any lonelier than this. I was running from the world, but I wanted to run back. I couldn't quite explain the feelings. Lyra was the obvious, quick explanation. I knew more was simmering underneath. I hated the subconscious, the invisible and devious puppeteer. The true Big Brother dictating all. I continued my spontaneous expressions daily as if I were in dialogue with the interior. As if I were a miner. As if I could sever the strings of the marionette. I had little hope, but plodded on, stumbling into the depths. Or, at least, thinking I was in the depths. Maybe, the void was the last place I should be entering. Maybe, my internal trespasses were causing breakdown momentum.

I smoked a lot, bought some cheap wine to get through the evenings, and walked a lot, mostly in Golden Gate Park. I liked the serenity of the Japanese Tea Garden. I wrote some long letters to Lyra. They were pining, 'let's get it back' letters. At the end of that miserable week, I threw out the letters to Lyra. I put the spontaneous scribblings into a folder that was getting fatter.

One day on the way back from the park, I saw a Help Wanted sign posted at a pub called The 1907. Another strange bartending scenario was headed my way. This time it is was on the heterosexual side of strangeness.

A middle-aged woman was behind the bar. It was quiet. A few people were at tables eating breakfast. I could hear the griddle sizzling. I saw the cook whisking eggs furiously in a large tin bowl.

I sat at the bar and had a cup of black coffee. I inquired about the job. The woman's name was Eileen. She told me they needed a bartender immediately. She was the manager and had just fired a bartender this morning. I told her about my experience. I left out my only job with the gender benders. I preferred not to discuss getting my ass kicked by Barbra Streisand and Diana Ross.

I got the job on the spot. In fact, I was behind the bar ten minutes after walking into the place. People seemed to trust me instantly.

Eileen sat at the bar with some paperwork and a calculator. She had been bartending and doing the paperwork at the same time. She told me my timing was great and then she explained the drama that I was walking into.

"We are in the midst of an overhaul. The 1907 has been a local tavern forever, well since 1907, of course. There is a loyal group of regulars who come in nightly and we're lucky if they pay for one drink on their way to getting sauced."

She pointed behind me.

"You see that."

"Sears," I said.

"It's going to be a mall pretty soon. They're gutting the building and putting in a Target and a whole bunch of stores. Construction workers will be in here everyday for breakfast and lunch and, at night, for drinks. After they've finished, consumers will be at our beck and call, but we need to give the place a new look. The new look starts with bartenders who actually collect money for the drinks they serve."

She laughed.

"A novel idea, huh?"

"Revolutionary," I said.

"Is that too much to ask Stoker?"

"No. Seems reasonable to me."

"So, I've caught everyone in the act and fired them. They can't sue because I've had spotters in to nail them. Needless to say, I'm not too popular around here. They say I'm sucking the soul out of the place. Well, I say, we can have a soul and make money at the same time. Besides, it's a bar, not a church. I get my soul on Sundays."

While she was talking, the waitress put up some drink orders. Mostly regular and Irish coffees.

"You ready?"

"Sure."

123

I made the drinks while Eileen explained. Apparently, they didn't train anyone in San Francisco. You just go in and work. It fits. Laid back California. The uptight Northeast would send you to a 40-hour seminar to be a video store clerk.

"There's only one left. Oscar LaGrange. The owners want him out desperately. There's a catch. He's also an owner."

The chef walked over and delivered a plate of eggs, bacon, toast, and potatoes to Eileen. He was bald by choice. Eileen thanked him and he scowled at her as she looked away from him. He winked at me.

"Riley Port. Pleasure to meet you." He said shaking my hand.

"Stoker Caudwell."

"Welcome ab-b-b-b-b-b-b-oard," Riley said, face contorting wildly during the stutter.

"Thanks."

Riley left and Eileen continued.

"So, LaGrange owns a third. The other two-thirds are owned by a couple. They want him out, but it's hard to fire him. He's the damn owner. LaGrange ran the place for years. Too many years. But basically all he does is drink the profits and give away enough so the place is in the red. The owners hired me to revamp and modernize. Give it a facelift. The last surgery to this old dog is getting rid of LaGrange. So I put in all new rules. No comps. Before you gave out a few free drinks to loyal customers. No more. Every bartender has been nailed, but LaGrange. He's bound to screw up. When he does, he's fired. He'll still be an owner, but he won't be allowed in his own bar. We've had a lawyer check into it all. Then, the other owners will offer him a nice buyout package and we'll be done with his sorry, sodden ass. Stoker, Oscar LaGrange is the biggest drunk you'll ever see."

I nodded through the whole thing. I was really only concerned with my schedule and pay. I'd follow her rules, but I was here to make some money and then see the world. The little soap opera had nothing to do with me. I had my own.

124

"Ok, Eileen. I think I've got the big picture. Now, how about me? When do I work and how much is the pay and all that."

"Yes, yes. How stupid of me. Yeah, let me get the schedule."

My first night shift was a Sunday. It was a slow night. LaGrange walked in about an hour into my shift. He put two packs of Camels on the bar. He sat down at a stool and looked at me. He didn't say anything, but I knew it was him. He had a salt and pepper mustache, dark, puffy circles under his eyes, and he was well on his way to the great drinker's nose. The gin blossoms were on the verge of full bloom spring. He'd been living a life of April showers.

"Scotch and water, twist," he said.

I got him his drink.

"Is this Dewars?"

"No." I said.

"I drink Dewars."

"You didn't ask for it."

"Do you know who I am?"

"Yes."

"Eileen didn't tell you what I drink?"

"No."

"Do you know who I am?"

"Yes."

"I ain't like everyone else. I own this bar."

"I know."

"Do you think I should be paying for my drinks?"

"It's not my decision. I'm just doing my job."

"Would you pay for the drinks if you were me?"

"I couldn't tell you. I've been told to charge everyone. Even the owners."

"Davis and Helen are in here once a month. Big fucking deal. I'm here everyday. I work here. I put my soul into this place and now this hot shot from a chain bar wants me to pay for drinks. It's like charging me in my own home. Just ain't right. Just ain't the way we've been doing things here for the last twenty-five years. Who the hell does she think she is?"

125

I didn't say anything. I think I had a little smile creeping out as a result of his over the top tirade. I knew one thing right away though. I didn't like Oscar LaGrange.

"Stop smirking kid. Ahhh, what the hell do you know? You're a little wet behind the ears. I'll pay you. When you know the ropes, we'll talk? Work out an understanding. For now, here's your fucking $4. Next time use JB."

LaGrange put a $20 bill on the bar. I gave him his change. He was quiet for a while. The bar was dead except for him. There were a few people at the tables.

"You see those guys over there? You see the table of ladies. Let me teach you something about the bar business. What we do here is you pour me a pitcher and a round of Irish coffees and I'll bring it over to them compliments of you and me. Compliments of The 1907. That's how I've been doing business for years. I've been running this place since 1968. Did you know that?"

"No."

"This place is like family for me. People come in to see me. You seen my tokes. I make $100 a shift during the day. You know how many barkeeps do that in this city? I'll tell you. Less than a handful. I love people, kid. I like to see a smile on their face. That's what bartending is all about."

He coughed loud and deep from the depths of his blackened lungs.

He cleared his throat. He took a big gulp from his scotch and water.

"You buy someone a drink and they smile. I've been here twenty-five years and that's what keeps me going. A smile. The creation of a smile on a customer's face. When I put my head down at night and think about the day that just went by, I want to smile. That's the last thing I want to do every night is smile. Isn't that the meaning of life? Isn't that what it's all about? A smile as your head hits the pillow."

Oscar was slurring this sentimental monologue. From what I was told, he started drinking around eleven a.m. everyday. It was now 9 p.m..

"Oscar, I can't comp any drinks."

126

"No hard feelings. Fuck it. She wants to play hardball and so do you. Well, I say fuck her and fuck you. Bring a pitcher to the players and Irish coffees to the ladies. Pour yourself a shot and bring me a shot of Schnapps. That's what kind of guy I am."

I ignored the 'fuck you.' I started making the Irish Coffees.

"I'm paying for these drinks so bring me my shot first. Don't make me fucking wait. I ordered them and I own this fucking place. Christ!"

I stopped and got a frozen shot glass and poured Peppermint Schnapps into it and brought it to Oscar.

"You forgot yourself."

"I'm all set."

"You're not gonna let me drink alone, are you?"

"I don't drink when I work."

"Jesus Christ, you're a hard on. You ain't got a clue how to tend bar. Your tip jar's gonna collect nothing but air."

"I'll take my chances."

I hated him.

I brought the drinks to everyone and they all toasted, thanking Oscar profusely. He stumbled over to their table. I heard him telling stories about his days playing minor league baseball in Buffalo. Oscar moved his way down the table to the ladies. They bought him a shot. In a half hour everyone left. They were laughing as they left. They were laughing at LaGrange. Mocking his drunken Casanova efforts.

As they left, Duncan James came in after his shift down the street at Trader Vic's. I had already met most of the regulars when I was filling out paperwork. Duncan bought Oscar another shot.

"So they're trying to run me out, Duncan."

"Who?"

"Eileen and her little protégé."

"What?" Duncan said incredulously.

"Yeah, they want me out. Ain't that right?" he asked me.

"I haven't got a clue."

Duncan pressed for details, but Oscar was all over the place with language. Scattered thoughts were being voiced. His head was bobbing slowly in a circular motion and his eyes were all but closed, but the alcohol had a voice.

"Trying to get me, but they tried before...I'll be back. They haven't learned. I know what going on. I made $120 today. Who can make that in a day? I was telling Mark, AIDS, you know AIDS is fucking San Francisco up the ass. Why don't they just get the ten best scientists. Best in the world, lock 'em in a lab, pay 'em whatever they want and they'll come up with a cure. Eileen is fucking me. My sister's fucking gay. What a mess she made of her life. My old man. Breaks his heart. Should have been our bar. Instead, I got to deal with this corporate bitch, Eileen. Yeah. The job. Family. The 1907 is my home. I want to be buried here. Buried in the bar. The 1907 is my eternity. I've given everything I've got to this place, and, they, and..."

Duncan and I watched Oscar's scattered soliloquy fade as his head slumped to the bar, knocking over his scotch and water. His head fell on to his packs of cigarettes, cushioning the fall. The scotch spread into a puddle around his mouth, which was pressed against the wooden bar. He was out, but his eyes were half open. Then, his tongue crept out of his mouth. It started licking the puddle of scotch. That lasted a few moments and then he was out cold. The pressure of the cigarettes and bar pressing on his jaw formed an odd smile on his face as he lay there, a tired, old, beaten dog of a man.

Sunday nights were always slow. I picked up more shifts quickly. I was working four nights a week, one day shift, and one early morning shift. I started saving some money. I also started doing research on English teaching jobs and the Alaska fishing scene. I figured that in a month or two, I'd have enough to leave San Francisco. I was getting to know the regulars more and more during this time. They were the core of The 1907. The hard core.

There was Sean McGrath, who was working the morning shifts on Saturday and Sunday. He was an out-of-work welder. He'd always claim to be hard pressed about finding work during the recession, but he picked up odd jobs here and there, often with local pubs that needed minor work done. In turn, it would erase the healthy bar tab he ran up.

The cook, Reilly Port, was also a regular. His extreme stutter originated during his days at Colorado State. He said it was part stutter, part Bell's Palsy. Reilly left a $40,000 a year job as executive chef at a swank hotel downtown to take The 1907 kitchen manager job at half that salary. Reilly explained the pay cut as "m-m-m-money c-c-c-can't buy f-f-f-friends." Reilly had also been in the service during the 80's to escape what he called his gun toting, psychotic ex.

Reilly's best friend, Duncan James, was sitting in the corner. He'd worked at The 1907 for eight years, but quit the day after his wife died. His wife was on her way to the hospital to pick up their newborn boy, who had stayed a week later because he was a preemie. Duncan asked Oscar for the afternoon off to go get his son, but Oscar said no. As a result, his wife went and was killed in a car accident by an afternoon drunk. Duncan quit the next day in a rampage at LaGrange. He went to work down the street at Trader Vic's and was now the manager of the restaurant. About two years later, he reentered The 1907 on Reilly's suggestion and quickly became a devout regular again, without one word to or from LaGrange about what had happened.

Next to LaGrange was his most recent groupie, Carter Eddy. Eileen told me LaGrange usually had a young male friend with him. The friend would change every several months. Carter had quit Pacific University after two years. About three months ago he quit selling water filtration systems. Like countless others, he went from regular to bartender to regular.

LaGrange, Sean, Duncan, Reilly, and Carter were exorcising their rage at Eileen and plotting their own coup d'etat.

"We've got to stop this. They're killing the heart and soul of my bar." LaGrange said.

"Davis and Helen are making a huge mistake," Sean said agreeing with LaGrange. I'd like to give Eileen a chance, but she wants trouble right away. She's trying to roll all our heads. I told her, Rollins had promised me after a month I'd go from $6.50/hr to $7. She told me Rollins doesn't work here anymore. 'New boss, new rules' she said. She's testing us. I think she wants us all out and wants her own staff. I'm gonna stay just to spite her. I got offered a full time job back at my old job, but I said no, just to make her sweat it out."

"Jesus, Sean, you've been trying to find a job for years and now you ain't taking it to screw Eileen over 50 cents an hour?" Duncan said.

"I've got principles, Duncan."

"Too many. Principles get you into trouble," Duncan said laughing alone. He looked over at me. "It's like I said Stoker, if I could bottle common sense and sell it for $10, I'd be a rich man and help this God-forsaken race of humans, too."

"I don't need you to tell me what common sense is. This is beyond common sense. What I need is for my fellow bartenders to back me up. Rollins promised all of us that 50 cents an hour. We've all got to ask for it. What do you say Stoker and Carter?"

"It's not that important to me," Carter said.

"Ahh, Fluffy, nothing's important to you," LaGrange said.

"That's not true, Oscar. I'm a new bartender getting experience. I'm gonna stay with this thing, so I'm not gonna let 50 cents screw me. And cut the Fluffy stuff out, huh. I'm tired of it."

"I'm just busting you."

"It's getting old."

"Ok, Fluff, take it easy."

"And you Stoker?" Sean asked.

I pretended to be watching the Giants game on the TV above their heads. "Huh?"

"You gonna get your raise? You gonna ask for it?"

"No."

"Why the hell not?"

"I got hired by Eileen, not Rollins. I don't even know the guy. Besides, Carter's right. It's 50 cents."

"You can't see the forest for the trees."

"Whatever." I didn't know what he was talking about. However, I was used to the arena of drunken logic for most of my life. The bottle was my third parent. Maybe, that's why I was here.

130

"Stoker, you're a typical Red Sox fan. It's just like what happened to Dwight Evans."

"Sean don't start this." He loved to break my balls about Dwight Evans.

Reilly jumped in, "St-St-Stoker, Sean's right about Evans, the Sox d-d-d-dissed him."

"No, they didn't, man. It was time to move on for him and the Sox."

"He's got kids with major health problems. He'd been with them for fifteen years and two World Series and they said 'fuck you.'" Sean said.

"They got Phil Plantier ready to go in right field. Evans's production dropped off lately and it was time. You're too sentimental."

"I agree with Stoker," Carter said. "They want to win and Plantier's a can't miss rookie."

"You would be a fucking Sox fan, Carter."

"Sean, what are you getting so hot about?" Duncan said. "It's freakin' baseball."

"Duncan, can't I express some passion about something? Christ, the Red Sox are pathetic. Seventy-two years they've been waiting and I'll tell you why. They don't take care of their players. They drop 'em like bad habits. Babe Ruth, Reggie Smith, Fred Lynn, Burleson, Fisk, the list goes on. Dump them for money. They want Plantier for short money, not to win. The Yanks take care of theirs."

Sean grew up in his father's pub in the Bronx.

"Our pub is turning into the Red Sox. Losers. We've got to get this bullshit corporate kiss ass Eileen out of here," LaGrange said.

The morning shift was strange, but peaceful. The regulars didn't begin to feed their addiction until near lunch. Morning sobriety reassured them that they weren't drunks. It was 6:30 a.m. The TV was off. I had put Al Green on the jukebox. Reilly was slicing mushrooms and onions in preparation for the day's soup. He was also chanting his morning soliloquy. It was virtually the same 'I've ruined my life' mantra every time.

"That's right, ole Riley Port, you just done gone off and quit Colorado State to end up cutting onions in a dime a

131

dozen pub. Yes sir, g-g-g-g-g-ood move there kiddo, you were a wise young m-m-m-m-m-an. Right now, I could be down in some chic Embarc-c-c-c-c-adero office being a lawyer handling divorces and servicing beautiful women in court and out. Oh yeah, g-g-g-g-g-great sex and g-g-g-g-g-g-reat money. Instead, I ain't g-g-g-g-g-getting' shit either way c-c-c-c-c-c- cuttin' mushrooms at sunrise. I ain't drinkin' today Stoker, you hear me?"

"Good idea, Riley," I said pouring myself a cup of coffee. "How 'bout some coffee to take care of you while you're on the wagon," I said, playing Riley's game.

"I'm not fuck-k-k-k-k-in' around. I'm off the booze. I'm going back to school. I'm gonna be a lawyer. It ain't t-t-t-t-t-too late."

"Carpe Diem, Riles. Quit the booze first and then get your degree."

"Like I told you, booze is tough for me. I got that Native American blood in me and we're genetically alcoholic thanks to the fuckin' Europeans who came here and introduced liquid evil to peaceful, proper p-p-p-p-p-pot smokin, land-connected folk. We've been disconnected every since. I'm a born alcoholic and my soul comes from folk who don't believe in possessions and materialism. T-t-t-t-t-tough to live in the world with that genetic make-up."

Reilly had a great grandfather who was one-eighth Arapaho, according to some family tree company that he paid. This made Riley one sixty-fourth Native American.

"You can do it, Reilly. You can overcome that Arapaho blood." He usually didn't listen to me.

"Yeah, law school's the tick-k-k-k-et. Ain't too many stuttering lawyers out there, though. I'll show 'em"

"How 'bout that coffee?"

"Hell yeah, I can't quit and do everything at once."

I brought Reilly a cup of black coffee. He was moving on to green peppers.

"Hey, be a buddy and put a little Bailey's in there, Stoker," Reilly said as I put the coffee down near a mountain of sliced mushrooms.

I looked at Reilly, shaking my head and grinning.

"I'm just kiddin', ole Stoker buddy. You're too serious sometimes, brother. You need to let go of that B-B-

B-B-B-Boston edge of yours. Take off the straitjacket and relax with me, my man."

"It's in my blood, like your alcoholic Arapaho past."

"You're right. Genes are strong. Can't get rid of 'em. You g-g-g-g-g-otta k-k-k-k-k-keep 'em in check."

I sat at the bar after I refilled some coffees to the three or four people eating breakfast. Reilly was now into his Bermuda mantra. "Yeah, the ex-wife was hunting m-m-m-m-me down with a shot gun. Damn crazy woman took a few shots at me. I was hiding behind some big Oak tree. She blasted square into the center of the tree. The d-d-d-d-d-damn bullet went all the way through. It was peeking its pointy edge outside the back of the tree. Right between my eyes. She reloaded and I ran as fast as my Arapaho legs c-c-c-c-c-c-ould take me."

Geronimo.

I bet every male regular in every pub has been wronged by his woman. Every time it was the woman's fault. Every time. It has nothing do with them. The guilty are never guilty. The alcohol keeps the truth at bay, diluted in the veins. Quenches the subconscious thirst. Let's them get from sunset to sunrise. Softens the sting of ole angel midnight. If only my woman hadn't wronged me. It's the drunk's Tao of existence. There are exceptions to every rule and philosophy, however. Duncan James was the exception at The 1907.

My role at The 1907 was as the unofficial scab on management's side because I refused to give anyone free drinks. I was following Eileen's rules. I loathed the nihilist slow suicide of the drunks. A white flag life. My contempt was also surely my own cowardly revenge at my old man. Redirected at The 1907 regulars, but revenge nonetheless. The less free drinks I gave, the less time I spent hearing the stories of their life over and over and over again. They'd often tire of me and my policy and head down the street to The Fireside Pub.

The crew was at their stools, Reilly, Duncan, Oscar, Sean, and Carter. Another long time peripheral regular, Albert Jones, occupied his favorite corner stool. He would stoically read his newspapers every night and drink two

Jamaican coffees. He rarely conversed with anyone. LaGrange was irked by this. It didn't fit his people first, smile before sleep credo of bullshit. However, Albert rarely recognized LaGrange's existence. Albert had history on his side. He was the most respected man at The 1907.

One night in the late 70's LaGrange was putting on his sloppy drunk of a Don Juan moves on a beautiful blonde waitress. She politely accepted a post-shift drink from her boss. While LaGrange was hitting on her, it came up that she had a boyfriend and that this boyfriend was black. Oscar responded instinctually. The river of scotch flowing through his gloomy veins had worn away any social filter. "Honey, why on earth would you want a nigger touching your beautiful ivory skin?"

The following day when Oscar was behind the bar for his afternoon shift, Albert Jones came into The 1907 for the first time.

"Are you the manager?" he asked LaGrange.

"Yes sir, Oscar LaGrange, what can I do for you?" he said politely.

"I'd prefer we speak in private?"

"Do I know you?"

"No."

"Would you like a drink?"

"No."

"I'm a little confused."

"I would agree. I prefer you come away from behind the bar and I tell you this in private at a table. It's quite important."

LaGrange poured himself his Dewars and water with a twist and grabbed his Camels and walked around the bar. LaGrange must have been walking on eggshells pondering his fate with this man he'd never met. Albert Jones was six-foot-five inches tall. He had powerful, steely eyes that could make you feel half your size when he glared at you.

Albert walked towards LaGrange and grabbed him by the shirt. LaGrange was defenseless. His hands were occupied by his drink and cigarettes. Fear occupied his heart. His drink crashed to the floor. Cigarettes tumbled into the scattered glass and ice. Albert let fly a crushing right hand into Oscar's left temple and Oscar spun like a top

134

backward and crashed to the floor. Oscar was out cold and was taken to the hospital, where they discovered his ocular bone below his left eye was shattered. He stayed away from his bar for four weeks, while Albert became a regular. Oscar came back, tail between his legs, apologized and never uttered a racist word in public again. When Albert would bring in one of his many girlfriends, all of whom were white, Oscar would always give them drinks on the house.

And a smile.

So these men sat and drank and talked and drank and talked and drank and talked and drank, while Albert read his paper. Reilly was bemoaning his latest femme fatale and Duncan was trying to cheer him up.

"Let it go, brother. It's over. You've done too much. She was good woman, but your self-respect is at stake here."

Reilly sat with his head between his hands looking down at the bar in silence.

"You know, Meredith asked me to tell you to stop the flowers, the letters, messages. It's starting to freak her out, Reils, you've got to move on."

"I c-c-c-c-c-an't believe it. I love her and d-d-d-d-d-d-d-did nothing but show her that," he said with his face contorting as he stumbled longer than usual over some letters.

"Reils, ole pal, you've been moping around for a month. Come on, snap out of it. Get back on your horse, cowboy."

"Ain't no horse left," Reilly said.

Sean jumped in. "I've seen enough man. Goddamn it, cut the fuckin' shit. You only went out with the girl for a few damn weeks and you're acting as though you were married for a decade. Reilly, you're acting like a goddamn idiot. I give you no sympathy 'cause you eat it up like Red Sox fans eating up first place in June." Sean winked at me.

Duncan said, "Ease up Sean. It doesn't matter how long the relationship was."

"Sure it does! Easing up ain't doing him any good. Look at Rollins. His first wife was a coke addict and his second he found secretly stripping down at North Beach one

135

night at one of those $1 peep show joints. Now he's married again and we all know what a great woman he has now. You pick up the pieces, get up and go on. Christ, when Joline left me, I didn't bring everyone else down with me. I moved on."

"Huh?" Reilly muttered.

"I said I didn't do the nosedive you're doing when I lost my honey. You're being ridiculous. It's like some teen movie. Freakin' covering her car with roses."

Reilly lifted his head and his face was red. He got off his stool and took his pint of Bud outside to the few plastic tables on the weedy patio and sat down alone with his back to us.

"Why don't you lighten up a bit on him?" Carter said.

"Oh, Fluffy, man he'll eat that shit up. He's been eating it up for weeks now. He needs new medicine."

"Maybe Sean's right," LaGrange said.

"Seems to me, Sean, you were pretty bad when Joline left you. You were pretty down, too, like you ought to be," Carter said.

"I didn't do the shit he's doing."

"We're all different. He's doing it his way, and you do it yours. Besides, you weren't treating your lady the way Reilly treated his."

"Fluffy, what the hell are trying to say?"

"You told me yourself you could have done better. Treated her better."

"This ain't about me. Ain't your business, Fluffy!"

"Some nights it is."

"Says who?" Sean was starting to fume.

"Easy boys. We're family here," LaGrange said.

"Says you. You go on and on about it some nights," Carter said. He was holding his ground better than usual.

"You don't know shit about it, Fluffy. You're talking out of your ass. The point is Reils doesn't have to drag everyone else down. I gave him two weeks before I started withdrawing sympathy. Christ, two weeks to mourn a four-week relationship."

"When was the last time you had a full time job?" Duncan said, getting Carter's back.

"What's your fuckin' point, Duncan?" Sean barked.

"All I'm saying is you haven't worked full-time since you and Joline broke up. It takes time. Just giv'em some slack. I mean, I agree he needs some tough love, but you don't have to bash him over the face."

"I'm not working full-time because I can't get work. Believe me, if I could, I'd be out there, but you check out my union. We're getting no offers. They're hiring non-union for half the pay and I'm not working for $15 bucks an hour and crossing union lines."

LaGrange jumped in. "Listen, why don't you stop your bickering and have a goddamn drink. Stoker give us all a round of that German black gold and send one out for ole Reils." LaGrange said, using the foundation of his entire life as an olive branch.

Reilly came inside just then. "I'll have it in here, you fuckers and I'm buying. Ole Stoker here needs his money 'cause he's a pro doing his job and ain't nothing wrong with that. I've been a dick and I'm goddamn glad Sean let me have it. When you're a dick, you n-n-n-n-n-need someone to say, hey, you're being a fuck-k-k-kin d-d-d-d-d-d-d-dick. But I'm back and getting back on that old horse, goddamn it."

"Reills ole pal, you're alright." Sean said.

"Sean, you were right. You can say I told you so," Duncan said.

"No need for that. Stoker, get Duncan a beer on me and tell me one thing."

"What's that?"

"How many championships have the Sox won since I don't know, Amelia Earhart got lost in the Pacific?"

"Damn Yankee fan. I come to San Francisco and I get stuck working all day with a damn Yankee fan," I said, somewhat smiling.

"Red Sox luck, Stoker! All part of the sweet curse." And Sean let out a big laugh from deep in his belly. Snapping Reilly out of his funk had Sean glowing. He was feeling proud and had forgotten about Duncan's work comment and Carter's jabs at his failure as a boyfriend. Hours later the pride was diluted as LaGrange's olive branch reached its true delusion.

Sean had been up and down the stairs a few times with Duncan and Reilly trying to pump up alcohol's slow down with "snow honey" as Reilly called it. LaGrange had slid out of his seat and stumbled across the street to his 3rd floor apartment that had been his home for twenty-two years. Albert Jones had had his two Jamaican coffees and left with his girlfriend, newspaper and his only words of the night, "Night, gentleman."

It was one a.m. and I was sitting at the bar with the remnants of the platoon. There were no other customers. The waitress had gone home.

"You want some?" Sean asked me.

"Yeah."

"Here's your tip," Sean said, shaking my hand and putting a little pack in my palm. "You guys go down and I'll watch the bar."

We did a couple lines each and headed back up. The bar was still empty. I got behind the bar and started to clean up. I refilled everyone's beers on the house.

"Now I know how to loosen you up." Sean said.

"Temporarily." I said.

We all toasted.

"When our glasses hit, Reilly let out a mammoth sneeze, that made Sean jump in his seat spilling some of his beer.

"Jesus Christ, Reilly!"

"What?"

Reilly let out another sneeze, even louder than the first. Duncan was laughing.

"Fucking Reilly, I hate that."

"What?"

"Your goddamn sneeze."

"How can you hate a sneeze?" Reilly asked sincerely.

"Cause it don't have to be so sonic. Why you gotta amp it up?"

"I wasn't amping it up."

"Bullshit! You could have lowered the damn volume a bit."

"Sean, brother, what the fuck are you t-t-t-t-t-t-t-alking about?"

"What the hell kind of question is that?"

"It's a question meaning, now you're being the d-d-d-d-d-d-d-dick."

"Reilly, I'm just telling you a sneeze doesn't have to be an earthquake."

"Sean, that's my damn sneeze. I like it that way. Christ! You can't c-c-c-c-c-c-ontrol everything."

"Boys, calm down," Duncan said.

"His sneezes drive me crazy. It's not about control. It's manners. They've been bothering me since he moved in with me. Sneeze like a human or get the fuck out of the apartment."

"Sean, we're all having good time. I let out a bodily f-f-f-f-f-f-f-f-unction and you lose it."

"You're losing your damn room if you sneeze like that again."

"Really?" Reilly said.

"I, myself, have always liked the sneeze. It's rather cleansing. Therapeutic," I said.

"Go back to fucking Boston!" Sean said without any hint of humor.

Reilly got up. He grabbed a pepper shaker off a table and poured a pile into his hand and began sniffing. After a few moments, he began an exaggerated sneeze prelude and then unleashed a titanic, volcanic sneeze.

Sean got up and looked at Reilly. "You prick! You're lucky I don't knock your sorry ass out right now." Sean shook his head, got up and walked out.

Duncan, Reilly and myself spent the next few hours finishing Sean's tip and several pints. The Sneeze was the topic of our conversation and would be for most of the next week.

The insane, meaningful meaninglessness of the sneeze and every other conversation at The 1907 was wearing me down. I was close to making a decision on teaching English or catching fish. Either one would transcend being an alcohol dealer.

One evening near the end of my 1907 tour of duty two semi-regulars were engaged in the same conversation they had always had. I had witnessed the words flying above and around, but never truly took them in. It was like a duel with automatic weapons. Two men stood ten paces apart and the hundreds of bullets sprayed from the gun's dark hole, but no one ever got hit, just like in the cartoons or bad action movies.

Heimi, a short, bald, mid forties man, was saying, "Reagan screwed me, us, everyone, but the top five percent. Can you believe a guy helps a mere five percent of the country and gets elected because ninety-five percent of the country gets duped. What a life!" Heimi let loose a stunted giggle disguised as laughter.

Wilbur Jacque was a tour guide driving the fake trolleys and showing the city to tourists all day. He lived with his mother and trumpeted the causes of Choayam Trungpa Rinpoche's form of Buddhism. He carried copies of Wallace Steven's *Necessary Angel* in his bag. He gave them away to all those who would take it, only asking for a "snifter of Courvoisier in return, if possible, thank you very much." He was Wimpy, gone spiritual and moderate drinker.

Wilbur responded. "It's not Reagan that blinded us. We're all walking around with cataracts. We need to pry off the layers that are dimming our vision. Once we see, we wouldn't even need politics. That's just a ruse fulfilling our blindness. Politics are cataracts. Politics are a temporary evil."

"Bush is still reaming us, too. I got screwed in the '82 recession and again right this moment as everyone's downsizing and a forty-something Jewish man's the first to go. I got two houses and real estate's dead. I can't sell 'em and the rent doesn't ever cover the mortgage. I don't know why we can't see through them. Trickle down my ass. The only thing trickling down is the damn runs I've got from shattered nerves. The rich people are laughing so hard at how we bought the package lock, stock, and barrel. Trickle down. Yeah, when I finish pissing, that's my trickle down. He-he-he-he."

"We aren't seeing through ourselves. Trungpa didn't get drunk, he got intoxicated. Once we understand the difference between drunk and intoxicated, we'll begin to see.

We won't be near sighted anymore. We'll be deep sighted."
Wilbur nodded, agreeing with himself.

"If I sell my two houses, I'll lose $50,000. While I
rent, I lose $1,000 a month. Thanks Bonzo. Jesus Christ.
Bonzo went to Washington. What a country!"

"When we're intoxicated, we climb. We see. We
envision. When we're drunk, we flail, sink, and regress. We
need the intoxication of Rinpoche. Politics is simply our
lack of intoxication. Politics are for the drunks."

"The Soviets are dead and we still spend thirty
something percent on the military. How do you explain
that? We could pump that money into the economy and
create jobs and I could unload my damn houses and get the
albatrosses off my tired, achy back."

"Stevens said, 'The truth seems to be that we live in
concepts of the imagination before the reason has established
them. Reason is simply the methodizer of the imagination.'
That's my mantra that I say every morning when I wake and
every night before sleep. 'Reason is simply the methodizer
of the imagination.' Over and over and over and then the
necessary angel gives me peace and I live wholly without
concepts of mortgages, recessions, houses, etc."

"You live with your mother." Heimi scoffed.

"Irrelevant." Wilbur said.

"I don't know about this Rimposh guy, but…"

"Rinpoche."

"Whatever. I heard Jerry Brown's running for
president and he wants a flat tax. Everybody pays thirteen
percent and you rip up the rules and loopholes that let the
rich pay shit now. Goddamn poor and middle class hold the
country on our backs like Atlas, while the rich sit on lounges
chairs counting money from our labor and sweat. We're like
19th century Chinamen building railroads. What a life!"

"I came back from Boulder without a dime in my
pocket, but rich in the words of Rinpoche. Have you read
that book, Heimi?"

"Huh, what book?"

"*The Necessary Angel*."

"An angel's not necessary for me, unless it's willing
to buy my property."

"Reason is the methodizer of the imagination."

"You know Wilbur, I never know what the hell you're talking about."

During my first days of The 1907, I was intrigued by the California madness. I was curious about the edge of America circus. I was taking the clowns too seriously. Lyra must still have been flowing within my blood. I was like Reilly on the inside, but going Bogey on the out. I was wound all tight. Sean was right. Maybe, it was being around all the booze. Maybe it wasn't Lyra. Maybe, it was something deeper, older, gravitating in the shadows.

Paternal shadows burrowed deep within.

I often took cigarette breaks outside to escape the endless chatter. From The 1907's vantage point high on Van Ness Street you could see the tip of the Golden Gate and the hills of Marin just beyond it. I could see the billowing roll of the fog quickly draping the black night in dark, sensual mystery. I'd wished the fog would tumble right into the bar and whisk the drunken talking heads away. The vapors would be the real potion to send their beaten souls back to life. The rolling heavens would exhume all their spirits that have been dulled and drowned in alcohol's unforgiving freefall. Pull the original spirit out and leave the decayed, defeated body behind. My illusory moment would end when I'd gaze into the bar and see all the faces in the mirror; Albert, Duncan, Sean, LaGrange, Reilly, Carter, Heimi, Wilbur. I looked at all of them. Each set of eyes in the mirror. Each head with its mouth moving or eyes watching TV. It was an all-in-one reflected panorama that was a great and sad film of hollowed existence. Youth had slipped through their fingertips and there was no preparation for the loneliness that lay ahead. Nothing left to do, but mourn yourself on a stool, night after funereal night.

It was after midnight. Just a few regulars and LaGrange hanging on later than usual. He'd been out boating with some friends and looked tanned and healthy. The fresh air and sun did him some good, temporarily cleansing away his barroom complexion. Albert Jones had gone home. His seat was taken up by an occasional regular,

Jean Filbert, who was from France and rubbed Sean McGrath the wrong way.

"Maginot line? Jean, explain that one to me." McGrath asked beginning his attack.

"Sean, explain Vietnam."

"Two different things. We learned our lesson. That was growing pains. The Maginot line was sheer stupidity. Let's built this huge, intricate wall with transportation systems built in and spend years on it, just so Hitler could walk around it. How could the French think that Hitler wouldn't go through Belgium like the Germans had done in WWI? Seriously, all kidding aside, I think it was the dumbest move in military history."

"Stoker, can I have a Pernod, please? Growing pains, my derriere." Jean said.

"You guys did the same damn thing in Vietnam. Don't throw stones in glass houses, Frenchman."

"We did it before you and warned you. It wasn't growing pains. It was runaway American ego."

I poured Jean a Pernod. He was going to need it.

"The Germans did it to you in WWI and you let them do the same thing. Déjà vu shall we say," Sean said with mocking laughter. "You built a wall and they walked around it. What a joke!"

"Why do you care?" Jean asked Sean.

"Historical curiosity. I'm a student of history," Sean said, washing down the words with a half a pint of Bud.

"Sean, why do you always nail people on one thing and never let it go? The Maginot line, the Red Sox with Stoker," Carter said.

"Jesus, Fluffy, I'm just busting people's balls, making conversation. It's that touchy feely shit that you expect and that's why we call you Fluffy."

Jean drank his Pernod quickly and left.

"Au revior." Sean said.

"You see, you drove him out of here," Carter said.

"I never liked him. I saw him steal someone's money off the bar."

"Whose?"

"That's not important. He's a fucker. French or whatever, he's a fucker. I don't trust him. I grew up in my

143

dad's bar and the one thing you don't do is take someone's money. You can insult him, say whatever you want to a point, but touch a guy's money and you've crossed the line. We all leave our money out, go the bathroom, use the phone, and come back trusting each other. Money's there when you get back, but not with Jean. He's a Euro-trash thief. Period."

LaGrange interrupted. "Listen, speaking of thieves, I've got to tell you something that's been on my mind for a long time. Out in the sun today on the water with my friends and a few beers, it all came together. I know how to nail Eileen and get her ass fired and make up for all the drinks we've been robbed of. No offense, Stoker."

"None taken, Oscar."

"You're not the problem. You're just a pain in the ass. It's that tyrant of a woman who's the problem. I want her out and I know how."

"Let's hear it, Oscar," McGrath said, finishing off another pint of Bud.

"Let's rob the place," LaGrange said.

"What place?"

"This one."

"The 1907. It's your place, Oscar!" Carter said. "You gonna rip yourself off? Brilliant plan!"

"It ain't my place, Fluff! They're taking it away from me. They're ripping me off. I can't have a drink in my own goddamn establishment."

"So, have you thought it out? How do you want to do it?" Sean said calmly.

"Us. I want us to do it. You, Reilly, Duncan, Fluffy and Stoker, even you. I know you're a by the book tight ass and all, but—"

"I'm not by the book. I'm just doing my job."

"What's the fucking difference, kid?"

"Cause if I were by the book, my life would not be here listening to your lives. I'd be elsewhere."

"This place ain't a prison," Sean said. "You're free to go, Boston boy."

I half smiled and nodded at Sean. I considered running with the prison metaphor, but I steered away.

"Yeah, I'm going. I'm—"

"I know. I know. You're getting out of here anyway. Thailand, right?" LaGrange said.

"Taiwan, maybe. Maybe Alaska first."

"Whatever. I've seen you come and go in my city over and over again since I came here in the 60's. San Francisco eats your kind up. Every time. What did you come here for anyway? I bet you can't answer that."

"What the hell do my plans have to with this?"

"As expected. I oughta write a book about trespassers looking so hard for that something they can't define. Can't find something you can't define, Stoker."

"Whatever, Oscar. You got it all figured out."

"He makes sense," Sean said.

"What you're really looking for is right here. Right among us. Brotherhood. Camaraderie. Selected family, not the one you're forced into. One you choose."

Carter said, "Can I see option B?"

"Yeah, the door is right there, Fluff." Sean said.

"I'm joking. Christ."

LaGrange continued. A day of sunshine had Oscar firmly diluted in his own alcoholic pathos.

"The point is we're together by choice. Family's got its place, but this we can control. We stick together while Eileen's trying to rip us apart. She wants my ass on the street. Well, we pull off a robbery and we get her ass in trouble and, as gravy, we get those drinks we should be getting now."

Sean said, "Again, how?"

"It's as easy as pie. Listen. Wait, Stoker, are you in? I was just bustin' your balls. Don't take it personal. The rest of you? I'm not telling the plan without knowing you're in."

Sean said, "I think I speak for everybody by saying we're not in until we hear the damn plan."

"Fine. After closing Sunday night, because that'll include the whole weekend drop, we take the cash, which will probably be about two grand. We take it and make a run to Tahoe and let it ride in blackjack. We get a little run and try to get to ten large and split. If we drop to a grand, we stop. We divide the money and I'll set up a comp list for us, so all our drinks are on the house for hopefully $10,000

worth. We'll stick it in Eileen's face ordering free drinks.
Let her bring in the spotters because it'll all go on account.
Davis and Helen won't know what hit them. They'll give up
trying to outmaneuver ole wily Oscar LaGrange. Reilly,
you're the player because you got luck on your side. You're
a new man just getting over that woman. When I got over
my divorce, I hit it big in Vegas. We lose the first hand and
we're done. We get on a roll and we're set. If we lose, we
head back and break the lock and leave the safe open. The
bartender's safe because we'll be witnesses saying you made
the drop. We got ex-bartenders all over town who have keys
to this place and know the combo: 19-0-7. What kind of
combo is that? Christ, those two are idiots. I've been telling
them to change the combo for years. And if we win, we
return the money and keep the profit. No one knows the
difference. I'll say I inherited some dough and set up the
tab for all of us."

Nobody said anything for a few moments.

Then Duncan said, "Well, I'm out. I got a job to
protect and two kids overseas to feed. Best of luck, though."
He left me a $5 tip and left.

I was surprisingly impressed by LaGrange's plan
and wanted the extra two grand for my Far East days. I said,
"I'm in, but I don't want a tab. I just want the cash. I'm
leaving right after."

Reilly said, "They might suspect you if you split
right away."

"No. They'll never suspect you because you're by
the book, Boston boy. It's gonna be an old bartender they'll
suspect. Oscar's right," Sean said. "I'm in. They didn't
give me my raise and this is what they get back."

"Me too. It's a good plan and just-t-t-t-t-t-t-t-t-tified
larceny." Reilly's face twisted and contorted and tilted in
the effort to get out 'justified'.

Everyone looked at Carter.

"Solidarity to the family," Carter said, smiling.

"Yeah, cosa nostra." I said.

"How 'bouts some drinks Stoker, on the house?"
Oscar said.

"What the hell," I said.

"Well, look at that," Sean said.

146

"Yeah, ole Stok-k-k-k-ker is l-l-l-l-l-l-l"

"LOOSENING UP for fuck's sake!" Sean said.

"Thank you." Reilly said, laughing with everyone else.

I refilled everyone's beer, LaGrange's scotch and water, and offered a round of shots.

Sean said. "Make up some kamikaze's in honor of our mission."

Carter, LaGrange, and Reilly plotted the details and I went downstairs to count out my draw. Sean joined me, pocket filled with ammunition, of course.

"You want a little?" Sean said, offering a small, neatly folded piece of paper.

"Not tonight. I want to stay clean while I plan my move out of San Francisco."

Sean went to another room and pulled a mirror off the wall. It had a picture of the Golden Gate Bridge on it. Sean opened up the paper and proceeded to cut the coke from its little clumps into a fine, smooth powder. I enjoyed how meticulously and diligently Sean went through the cutting process. He liked his lines to be clean, smooth and exactly equal in size. His apartment and life, for that matter, were a dark, cluttered mess, but his lines were crisp, clean, and organized.

Sean took a brand new $20 bill from the drawer that I had just finished counting out, rolled it up, and gave it to me.

"No, thanks."

"You sure?"

"Yeah, I'm sure."

Sean did the lines quickly and efficiently. His nasal passages and sinuses were singed of any blockages or biological obstacles. The cilia must have been burned deep through their tiny follicles. The white poison had eliminated everything in its path, like a mighty river eroding its own banks.

"So, what do you think of the plan?" Sean asked, downing his beer. He usually drank his pints of Bud into two large gulps.

"I think it'll work. I'm a little worried about being a suspect, but there'll be no proof. Worst they can do is fire us and I'm leaving anyway, but you guys—"

"I don't need this job. Hell, I just did it as a favor to Rollins. Who the hell wants to work Saturday and Sunday from 6 a.m. to noon? They're thankless shifts."

"Why do you do them?"

"I just said, Rollins."

"But he doesn't even work here anymore."

"You don't get it, Stoker. Things aren't as simple. Ain't so black and white as you see them."

"Should be."

Sean shook his head. He stuck the bill up his right nostril, pressed his left nostril with his free hand, and took another blast. He had another pint of Bud waiting for him. He had brought two full ones down. He dipped the index and middle finger of his right hand into the beer and stuck them into his nose. He inhaled deeply and loudly, shaking and moving his fingers in his nostrils.

"I don't know if I'd trust LaGrange though, with that tab," I said. "He drinks more than all of you and he's liable to piss through your portion of the tab, drinking and giving it away to every decent looking woman he sees."

"First of all, it's his idea and his money he's fronting the theft with."

"It's not really his money. He only owns a third."

"I don't want to squabble over damn percentages. It tears you apart when you get into that shit. I don't ask for a five spot for every line people do with me."

"No, no, you're right."

"It all works out—you catch me some drinks, we hang together, companionship ain't got a currency. Drop that East Coast accounting mentality. Things, us, are so much bigger, man. Much, much bigger, Stoker. You people from Boston," he said laughing and slapping my back.

"Yeah, yeah, I know."

"You know I'm only breaking your balls when I go off about the Sox."

"You're just jealous. You wish you could root for a team that never wins. There's something noble, heroic in that."

"You're right, in a way. Noble, heroic, masochistic. Yeah, you're right. Just like this stuff. A strange, perverse nobility," he pointed to the mirror.

There was some silence.

Sean ended it quickly. "So what the hell's in Taiwan, anyway?"

"Well, it's far away, for one thing."

"And for a second thing?"

"I'm just going to run while I'm young. I guess I hope it gives me some future peace. Got to get rid of some energy before it gets rid of me."

"I hear you, off and running for awhile. No time to stop. Don't let the energy get you. I like that. I know that, but don't know if it's as easy as you say. Something tells me at the end of all the movement, you'll be right back at the beginning."

"Maybe so. I had this ex-girlfriend and we kind of got brainwashed by some avant-garde professor who went on about Kerouac, strange underground art movements, weird bohemian New Yorkers, mad post-WWI characters in a revolutionary cabaret and on and on. I followed her lead and after she left me for another guy right in front of my eyes."

"The vexing femme-fatale."

"It's not her fault. I don't know. I'm tired of blaming her. I'm living my life."

"Somehow, it just doesn't get easier, Stoker. No matter how much you unleash in the twenties. I don't know. It's worth a shot. Get it out in the twenties, so it won't be like the parents."

"Truth." I said.

"Maybe I oughta get out of here, too. Maybe, I didn't get enough out. I saw some ads for courier work in Australia. I got to go to a place with English. I can't deal with not knowing what the hell is going on."

"I think I want that. I mean, I more or less don't know what the hell is going on knowing the language around me, so what's the difference."

Sean laughed. "Nobody fuckin' does anyway. We're all just pretending and going along. Riding the conveyor belt. I don't know. Get some career going though pal. Don't end up behind the bar forever. It's misery. It's not a life."

"Like a LaGrange."

"Yeah, but he doesn't know any better. It's his world, booze and all. We all got our own worlds. That's his. So be it, but get something going, like teaching or something. There's real nobility. Help some kids, make a few bucks, and get summers to unwind and loosen up some of that energy that will never go away."

Sean bowed to the mirror and snapped up two more, one for each side.

"I might just do that. I'm gonna teach in Taiwan. Teach English. It's a start."

"Definitely. Stick with it after. You can fall off the train for only so long before they just don't let you back aboard. Then they throw the 'It's a start' patronizing phrase at you. I want to know what's the end, screw the start."

"I know."

"I don't think you do."

"Maybe not," I said.

Sean took out some more rocks and began cutting and shaping. He put a healthy dusting on his index finger and coated his gums. He pointed to the mirror for me to do the same.

"No, thanks."

"You really don't know. No, you don't. Twenty-four years old doesn't know shit. You're like a top spinning around with no clue as to who pulled the string. I know who pulled the string now, but I can't get her back and I'm still spinning like a fool. Ahhh, but my twenty-four was different than the 80's bullshit. It's all changed. The way they look at you now. Oh, don't get me wrong. You can still screw up at twenty-four and pull it off, get away with it. They'll let you even at twenty-six or twenty-seven, but back then, messin' up was an art form. It was hip when that word meant something. It was heroic, real, human. Jesus. There was more than one damn road and inventing, falling off the detours, was envied. It was life. Now, even youth has bought the ticket and even the ones who snub the system, don't do it right. I'm not talking about some Mohawk-haired, ear, nose, face-ringed punk idiot. They're disturbed to the core, cornered by some bad instincts built in young. I can't understand their pain. It's the regulars I'm talking about like us, looking elsewhere, somewhere, I'm talking about. It's so lamentable and I'm not even talking about my Joline who I lost three years ago."

Sean's words were racing out of his mouth and his nose was running.

"Jesus, I worked too much she said. And now. I can't work a full shift outside the bar. I get calls from the union for new construction sites, but no, I just can't do it. Don't tell no one 'cause I keep saying the recession's the reason, but Christ I can't do it. The energy's gone. Now, an eight-hour day is like an eternity. Ahh, the hell with it, I'll get back on the train. It just takes time. Healing whatever damn wound is open."

"There's always time," I said.

"Yeah, time. Damn clock is ticking so loud it echoes in my skull. To hell with the past. More importantly," he began, "I had that waitress a month back, Sandra. Remember her?"

"Sure. Short, blonde, cute."

"Right in the tub. Three times. Christ. I shocked myself. Thirty-seven and still messed up, but I gave it a good ride. Triple-header, but that's not even it, though, it's the way they do it now. Can't stand it. It ain't worth it. Not sex, I mean, that doesn't change. I'm talking about youth."

"Your generation was different."

"Hell yeah. We messed up together. You guys do it alone…but you, you're not really screwed up. You're ok. You got a good head on your shoulders, not giving away free drinks when the pressure was on. I respected that. You're just screwin' up a bit early on. A little ride. Fishing in Alaska then Taiwan and then you'll head back and teach and get married and the ride will pay dividends. In my twenty-four we stayed together for a while and look where it got us. We all got married unhappily or burnt or brainwashed by the pursuit of money. It just took longer to splinter. Maybe your way is better. The single plotted line without any hold ups like friends. You guys, though, I don't know. You took our failure and let it die. Never took the torch. The fuckin' 80's. An embarrassment to youth. What a farm we're pillaging. You following me? Ahhh, to hell with San Francisco. It's one big mirage hidden under the fog. Hell, some of 'em still owe me money and I'm spackling and painting the damn 1907 for side money. I'm the goddamn weekend morning bartender for $6.50/hr serving all night speed freaks at seven a.m. and they owe me. Can you believe that?"

"You oughta get it back."

"What?"

"The money they owe you."

"Fuck the money. What good does it do? They owe me more than that and it can't be paid back. It will never be paid back." Sean was talking really fast. His brow was furrowed and he was shaking his head steadily to reinforce the negative words.

We were silent for a bit. Sean wet his index finger and ran it across half the mirror, picking up residue and then he rubbed his gums and teeth.

When we got upstairs everyone was quietly and attentively watching TV. Other than the movement of drinks moving from bar to mouth, there was total stillness. I looked up and saw a female lion hunting a turtle. Oscar loved shows on nature and animals. The lioness was growing frustrated with the turtle, who had quickly retracted all his appendages and lastly put his head inside his shell. She pawed at the empty holes and even tried to force her head inside the hole that housed his head. She quickly pulled out shrieking as the turtle had bit her fiercely on the nose. There were drops of blood coming from her nose and mouth. The lioness changed strategies in her rage and began gnawing at the turtle's shell. The turtle put his head out occasionally to peer at what was happening, but quickly went back inside when the lioness made a move towards its head. LaGrange and Duncan were cheering for the turtle. "Get the bastard," one of them yelled. After many tries, the lioness was able to sink her teeth into the shell at its peek point. Reilly said, "She'll never get through. The little guy's s-s-s-s-s-afe inside." Eventually, one of the lioness's great incisor teeth broke through the shell. Big pieces of the shell were ripped off; while the turtle's head madly and wildly circled the outside world trying to bite the enemy, but the lioness

152

smartly had gone to the rear. When the turtle tried to extend his feet to move, she clawed at them drawing blood. The final scenes were of the lioness and now a lion eating the turtle's totally exposed soft body on a plate of his bottom shell, while his upper shell lay scattered around him in broken pieces.

"I thought the shell was impenetrable," LaGrange said.

"Damn lions." Carter said.

"Tomorrow night," LaGrange said. "And he looked at everyone for confirmation."

"So, what do we need?" Sean asked.

"A car and the money," LaGrange said.

"We can use my car," Sean said.

"It's a regular night. We all come up and then leave before last call. Stoker, you make the drop like normal and get a free witness by giving away a drink or two after hours. Maybe Jean, the bastard Frenchmen, or Heimi. They'd never turn down a comp. Let them see you make the drop in the safe. Of course, the bags will be empty. Take the cash and leave the credit card receipts. Get the last minute witnesses out of there and walk down to Sean's and we'll be waiting for you. Oh yeah, most importantly, leave the safe open and mess the place up a little like a robbery happened. Leave a bottle of Jack and half-filled pints of beer on the bar. Leave the lock on the door, but open. Then if we lose, we're covered. If we win, Sean puts the money back when he opens the next morning."

The theft had suddenly turned LaGrange lucid.

"What if we really do get robbed? We're leaving the place unlocked," Carter said.

"All the better. It's our back up. Ain't nothing to steal but booze anyway," Sean said.

"We can't get bogged down in what ifs," LaGrange said. "It's time."

We all agreed.

Everything went smoothly. Heimi and Wilbur were there doing their conversational dance. They saw me make the drop. The safe was behind a mirror that had a team picture of the San Francisco Giants on it. All the regulars knew about it. I had $2,100 in cash. I ran down to Sean's. He and Reilly were coked up. LaGrange had just woken up and was groggy and still drunk from the previous night. Carter was a bit bleary eyed from his allotment of beer. We got to Tahoe at 4:30 in the morning. Everyone was getting sleepy and cranky. McGrath was out of lightning and the boozers had no toxic nectar to sooth their skulls and stilted souls. Reilly suggested coffee for all when we arrived at the bar in a swank hotel with casino lights blinking and slots thumping and jingling in the predawn. "Remember the plan" is all everyone said. Thousand dollar hands and ride the roll-up to ten K and then split. Reilly kept rubbing his hands while we all drank the coffee and started coming alive.

"Warm hands will bring good luck," Reilly repeated several times.

So, we headed out and Reilly selected an empty table with just him and the dealer. He had picked out the cutest female dealer and sat down in the center seat. McGrath gave the lady our two grand and asked for two chips.

"Changing two thousand," she chimed to the pit boss, who came over with a curious look.

"Trying to up my inheritance a little," LaGrange said.

"Good luck," the dealer said, giving the two chips to Reilly.

"L-L-L-L-L-L-L-uck always helps, young lady. Think p-p-p-p-p-p-p-ostively as you deal out some winners for us."

Reilly got twelve on the first hand and the dealer had a seven showing. Everyone was saying hit, but he ignored the advice and waved his hand to stay. She opened and had an Eight and then drew a King and busted.

"Never b-b-b-b-b-b-ust. Gotta give yourself a chance to win and the d-d-d-d-d-d-d-ealer a chance to lose."

McGrath said, "It's Reill's game. Everyone shut up and let him go." Everyone nodded.

LaGrange said, "Oh, that awakening from the

154

femme fatale has lit him up. He's got horseshoes wrapped in four leaf clovers up his stuttering ass."

"Jesus, Oscar, shut up. You'll kill the run," Carter said.

"It's just words."

"Fluff's right. Let it go on its own," McGrath said.

Reilly got a pair of Eights on the next hand and the dealer had a Five showing. He split them and drew a Queen and a King. The dealer drew a Two on fifteen.

"We're up three grand." Carter said quietly.

Reilly put two chips in his pocket and put one up as his bet.

"Up your bet, Reills. You're on a roll," LaGrange said.

"Quiet p-p-p-p-p-lease," Reilly said calmly.

He stayed on a fourteen with the dealer showing a Two. She opened a face card. It was a Jack.

"Jack be nimble, Jack be quick," Reilly said.

"Holy shit," McGrath yelled.

"Never bust, keep the trust," Reilly said smoothly.

"Double your bet," LaGrange said.

Reilly put up one chip. He had an eleven with the dealer showing a face card. Reilly put up another grand to double and got the face card beating twenty.

"God almighty," LaGrange said. "We're up six grand. We're almost home, baby."

Reilly put up six chips. "Time for the k-k-k-k-k-ill," he said.

"Put it away, Reills. One more time, baby!" Sean shouted.

Reilly was dealt a fifteen. He stayed with the dealer's Ace looking right at him.

She opened a three.

"Christ, Reilly, what the fuck! We're going to blow it," LaGrange said.

"Oh shit." Carter covered his face but peered through his splayed fingers.

"Relax boys," McGrath said.

"Soft fourteen," The dealer announced calmly.

I was shaking my head. Carter's hands were now intertwined tensely. Reilly kept nodding his head confidently.

She drew another card. The few seconds seemed hours.

"Jesus Christ!"

"Oh my God!"

"Reilly! You mother fucker!" LaGrange screamed.

Six hearts stared at all of us.

Faces fell into hands and Reilly seemed catatonic. Nobody said anything for a while.

"All bets in?"

"Sir?"

"N-n-n-n-n-n-n-not this one."

"Never b-b-b-b-b-ust, keep the trust," McGrath said. "Fuck the trust," McGrath walked away.

"Lady Luck l-l-l-l-l-left me boys. I'm sorry. Really sorry," Reilly said.

Carter patted Reilly on the shoulder. "You had a good run, Reills. We got greedy."

"Lady luck. G-g-g-g-g-g-goddamn lady luck!"

"Fuckin' stuttering asshole," LaGrange said.

Reilly stood up and got in LaGrange's face. I was hoping he'd pop him, but a lot of words and banter would precede it. I didn't stick around. Lady Luck had left Reilly and I had left San Francisco. The regulars would disintegrate. They would find other bars to take shelter. LaGrange, though, would stay at The 1907. I imagined him being buried beneath the hardwood floor with a bottle of scotch and two packs of cigarettes in his coffin. A smile etched on his cold face by the mortician. It was all over. I walked out of the casino and as I was heading out I saw McGrath at the bar. He lifted his pint of beer and nodded at me. I nodded back. I knew the words he didn't say.

I hopped on the next bus north. I never bothered to find out what actually happened to The 1907. It didn't matter. It was life mired in daily tragedy and I didn't have time for it anymore. I wanted tragedies to be in my wake. I kept thinking of all the regulars sitting on their bar stools as the bus pulled out of Tahoe. I liked all of them, even LaGrange, in my departure. I wished they were put in an

156

isolation chamber and forced to drink water for a month. They could cleanse all the evils littering within. A new, purified start for them. A clean and sober second chance. I thought of Lyra and how much I still loved her. I thought of the transvestites. I thought of Dale hitting on me. I thought of the beautiful whore in New Mexico and sex with her seemed as though it never happened. It was somebody else's memory trespassing in my mind. I thought of Maple and his distended, red face as he invoked his father. I thought of my family. My father. I hadn't consciously thought about him in a long time. I thought about how much I missed him. I would return home and tell him everything. Everything. Start new with him.

In the end, none of it and all of it really mattered. Everyone and everything would find their destiny in the eternity of words.

The words would come. Meanwhile, it was time to see the world.

jay kard
The Living Novel

It was time. I knew it.

I wiped the mirror free of steam from my shower and lathered my face. I still used a bar of soap and an old wooded-handled brush to create shaving cream. None of that aerosol produced cream. I took my old west style, silver blade and sharpened it on a one of those barbershop leather straps. My barber right here in Mill Valley, California gave it to me. Then, with nice long strokes I took the graying whiskers off my face. I liked the sound of the steel knife slicing off my stubble. I always tried to finish in the least amount of strokes possible. I strove for shaving efficiency. When I finished, I pulled the rubber drain stop and let the water run out. I analyzed my severed whiskers lying on the white porcelain. I have always stared at my molted face in the sink. Facial precipitation. Thirty-five years ago I grew it to see if I was a man. The more whiskers, the bigger the balls. Testosterone daydreams. Now, I still do it out of habit, out of peaceful delusion. When I finished, I cupped my hands together and splashed the hottest water I could stand on my face. Then, I put the stop back in the hole and filled the sink with boiling hot water that I had already prepared from the kitchen. I took the big cast iron kettle by the wooden handle and poured the bubbling water into the sink. I put a big towel over my head and leaned over the steaming water. The vapors blasted through my skin and pores. I stayed extra long in the facial sauna this morning. After the water became tepid, I dried my red face, splashed cheap aftershave on my hands and patted my entire face with the stinging alcohol.

I took a deep breath.

It was time.

I really knew it. True knowledge, free of the hazy maze of self-doubt. Zen knowledge. Bone and blood flow

knowledge. Corporeal knowledge, not cerebral chess
maneuvering that outwits yourself.

I looked at my skin. It looked good for my age. I
smiled and checked my crow's feet. They seemed the same
as yesterday and the day before, but not like a few years ago.
Maybe they're growing about an eighth of a centimeter
every year. They're like the rings inside a tree that tell you a
tree's age. I respect my crow's feet. I inspected my nose,
wondering if it was too big as I had wondered since the 7th
grade. I never truly knew. Some days I thought it was
striking, 50's leading man quality. Other days I felt like
Gogol in *Diary of a Madman* and wanted to lop it in half.

My gray hair still had its silver sheen to it. I was
happy about my hair. I hadn't lost any and women liked the
color. I didn't want to change my hair. Zen contentment.

I took another deep breath.

Life had been going along well for me, but things
had recently changed. Like the Bob Dylan song from the
movie, *The Wonderboys*. "Things have changed." I was
nearly Dylan's age. I loved Dylan and I loved Dylan
Thomas, too. *Do Not Go Gentle into that Good Night* is my
favorite poem. I loved Michael Douglass's character in *The
Wonderboys*. I have a lot in common with him. I smoke
pot, but not as much as the character. I'm an adulterer, but
not covertly like him. I'm out in the open. My wife knows
it and even strangely endorses it. It's a long story. He had a
manuscript that never ended. Two thousand seven hundred
or so pages if I remember correctly. I have a manuscript,
too, but I don't want mine to end. There is no end and I like
that. Made me feel eternal. I hate all endings. Nothing
should end. We must defend infinity. If death is the end, I
want my book to end when I do, but hopefully I'll still be
writing it with divine ink in the cozy, white lap of eternity.
Infinite infinity.

I've been putting the living words of my life onto
the page for over thirty years. I now have twenty-four
novels, 7,250 pages, and 2,350,000 words. It's really one
novel in twenty-four books. My own ego-driven legend.
Like Kerouac's Dulouz legend. Same as kids building a fort
and imagining war. The creation of one's own legend is
human honesty. My enormous novel is my life and I could

160

care less if anyone ever reads it. Honestly. My poet friend at the local bookstore balks at my use of the word novel. He says a novel is not something taken down like dictation as I do. Mine are oral novels transcribed from audiotape to page. I transcribe my reality. Almost verbatim. I record events and conversations and they become novels. None of this third person, omniscient narrator façade. The citizens of the twenty-first century will see that form as archaic. Turning one's own life into art will be embraced as the only true way to engage reality. Poet friend says a novel involves creativity, manipulation of events, merging fact and fantasy, people real and unreal. I say every moment of every day is manipulation, fact and fantasy, real and unreal. He claims I have an illness, Hypergraphia, whereby I'm addicted to writing, an alcoholic of the written word. I am compulsively obsessed with writing in order to shape and escape reality as an alcoholic does with booze. I tell him he's had too much therapy. He thinks I live in some "crazy, cocoon universe". He claims I've "eclipsed everyday vision into a concocted, cockeyed written existence." His aspersions at my life's *raison d'etre* are fine with me because his universe involves verbal fallacy. He writes to please everyone else except himself. Misguided reality. He's written mostly poetry and I really like his poems, but he's also tried a novel, a screenplay, and a play trying to get recognition. He's a lost, feckless artist. He should stick to poetry. He said he wants to write another novel. Take another crack at it. I tell him his problem is the "it" he seeks. Poet friend says I'll be his protagonist because I'm virtual fiction already. Of course I'm fiction, just like him. Life is fiction. It's quicksand. Black tar in the desert heat. Constant motion. Change. Reality lasts a second. How could it be otherwise with the earth rotating completely around in twenty-four hours, chasing the sun, the moon orbiting us, all of us pursuing the star Vega. If this weren't enough, our galaxy housing all this mercurial madness is in motion at thousands of miles per second as it expands. Sometimes, I think every action we undertake is to try and just slow it all down.

I've also got a protégé like Douglass's character in the film I mentioned. Tobey Maguire played the role. I've got a 23-year-old kid from the East. He believes I'm a true bohemian. That's what he calls me. He says only a true bohemian "has no concept of the American Dream. Only a true Bohemian let's the Joneses run wild without a hint of jealousy or insecurity." I told him to read Joseph Mitchell's *Joe Gould's Secret* if he wants to know who I am. Of course, that's on the assumption that I know who I am. I do know what I've become. I know what I've done. I'm obsessed with that. I'm at home with that realization. We must be the sum of memories. I am all my writings, but I do not pretend to know who I am. That is a tremendous human assumption no one could purely answer.

I've had other protégés. They will come and go. They come west looking and searching like all exiled, eastern kinsmen of meaning's mystery. His end of America reconnaissance will come undone, unraveled, scattered in a love interest that fails its original, seductive offering. Adam and Eve retells itself over and over again. But I laud protégé's efforts. One of my favorite quotes is by Andre Gide.

"Believe those who are seeking the truth; doubt those who find it."

All my writings that I've purged to the page seek the truth. Not one has found it and not one ever will. Gleeful missteps. Holistic revelry. Poet friend will never even enter the arena of truth until he leaves the arena that entered him. That makes me laugh. Peacefully. I'm hard on poet friend, but he has one point I give credibility to. He believes my "writing illness" is a result of being an orphan and not procreating. I have no known lineage before or after and therefore my existential dread is more acute than the average human. My world begins and ends with me. I have no before or after. Every word I write is the parents and children I've never had.

Maybe.

Maybe not. It's all gray and I embrace it.

I put my weary bones on the couch in my writing room. Fifty-three-year-old bones according the Asian method of counting, which only makes sense. You have to count conception to birthing. They might be the most important months of life. Full of absorbed energy and the creation of the deeps seas of the subconscious must begin

162

and spread in those first months. That's what I presume humbly.

My wife is upstairs watching soap operas as these scattered thoughts flow in my mind. I am tired. Really tired. It should be the happiest of exhaustions because it's from excessive and extensive intercourse. I have been fucking so much, so deeply lately that my body is giving out. I've been fucking like my ne'er-do-well poet friend should be. I've been fucking like my protégé will with some California woman before it all turns inside out and upside down for reasons neither can truly answer. He'll get hooked offstage and off-guard by the mighty dream of connection. Of course, the source of my fatigue is a woman. Man's only truth. From Eve to Helen to Cleopatra to Juliet to Joan of Arc to Garbo to Marilyn to the inevitable next. What else is there in life? We are powered by the potent combination of our cocks and our hearts. We spend our life trying to keep either side of the seesaw from grounding. It's difficult terrain, but I've been lucky.

I've had many women over the last decade of my marriage. Since my dear wife had a stroke, she has permitted the affairs. Daisy lost her sex drive after the stroke. She told me during dinner one day about ten years ago that I could see other women. "Jay, my sex drive died, not yours. I don't want to lose you because of this change or have you live a deceitful life. Here are the rules..." She made me promise never to leave her and never to fall in love. She said to keep them simple, carnal and short term. Very few people believe me, but it's true. I was only moderately surprised. Daisy had always had the bohemian blood. She was always disturbed by conventional marriage and fallacious nature. The stroke hadn't changed that.

Poet and protégé are always shocked to hear of my open marriage. Sometimes, I am too. But I've kept my promise never to leave and never to fall in love. The affairs are not constant, just one or two a year. It hasn't been hard to resist falling in love or finding an occasional lover. Bourgeois women find me fascinating. I'd like to think it's my shiny, silver hair, sometimes leading man nose, gentle voice, but it's not. They look at me as a circus act. A harmless, side-show freak in their middle class circus. They got money and bills and kids and dull husbands couch-bound at night and televisions and brunches and graduations and dinner parties and video rentals and two week vacations and car pools and mystery novels and soccer games and the nightly news and weather and lawn mowers and pool cleaners and cleaning ladies and new stereos and soft rock music and and and and and...

The Joneses.

Then they meet me. A dog-shit cleaning, middle-aged man who's written twenty-four unknown novels and refuses to stop his own game of charades.

This current woman though is different. She's outside the circus, or above it I should say. She's tender, sweet and dangerous. She is brilliant and beautiful. She is cataclysmic. Seismic. A gorgeous, sensual, intelligent, innately spiritual woman. Not some western poseur. Not some bored housewife. A magical woman. Her parents must have sensed must have sensed her preternatural essence during pregnancy Her Japanese name translates to Rainbow. Rainbow could be a Geisha girl and let me do things to her that I had never done to any of my many previous lovers. New positions, contraptions, voices, role plays, costumes, places all causing orgasms that rattled my middle-aged bones. Magik's pussy drove me mad. I never enjoyed engaging a woman orally until Magik. I'd always done it just to excite the woman. Jump into her with my mouth for selfish reasons. Warm up. Get the juices flowing. Licking her with me in mind. Couldn't wait to finish, so I could enter and get those few, precious seconds of pure ego joy. But with Magik, I truly enjoyed letting my tongue glide along her velvet Japanese portal. I loved her pleasure. I even came once licking her into ecstasy. I get going just thinking about it.

Rainbow could also be a tough, hard-as-nails, Jewish mother of a woman and set me straight when I would let doubt undercut me or allow the demons to bear their long claws within. Stuck. Whining. Playing Winey Cronhaeur as we called these moments. She'd take charge and give the carpe diem routine that every partner needs from each other. Next thing you know, we'd be intertwined in bed, Magik's

164

long, black, silk hair cascading all over me, her voice all gentle sensuality.

Rainbow was all woman in all its magnetic, seductive, riddling sphinx enigma. Rainbow was a question to every answer.

I loved her more than any other paramour. But Rainbow was dangerous. Rainbow was a threat to my cozy, cocoon world. Rainbow was the one affair that threatened my marriage. She could snap the springs of my perfect, constructed universe.

That is why I had to leave. She had a hold me that I hadn't had since I met my wife. Everyone else was carnal fun. Good, meaningless sex and talk and fun and fuel to another day. We each benefited from it. It added excitement to their life and they had no problem detaching from me. They could never really be with someone like me. I was safe for them and it would sustain their house of cards marriage. I could never really be with them either. I loved my wife. But this pattern was broken with Rainbow. Rainbow truly wanted me. Rainbow put my heart and soul back into sex. Rainbow turned sex into making love. That simple.

And I was scared to death.

It was time to leave.

I bought a brand new map of the United States. I'd always loved maps, but this map was different. It was an ordinary wall map in appearance. About six feet in length and three feet high. It had good size and I needed the size. I wanted every little town shown on this map. It was different because it had a purpose besides dreamy viewing and wondering and geographical knowledge. This map would determine where my wife, Daisy, and I would live next. This map would determine destiny. I had to leave Rainbow and that scared the piss out of me. But I rationalized staying would be scarier. My sexual and soulful connection to Rainbow would pull me away from Daisy. I couldn't leave Daisy. She and the recording of my life in words are my anchor, my connection to this mad, spinning Ferris Wheel world. I had to go. Daisy would go with me. She wouldn't even question it. We'd pack up and start anew. Magik's power over me was enormous. I had no chance. She was too much and I couldn't tell her about it. I just had to go.

I was shaky and sweaty lying on the couch trying to convince myself this was the way to go. It would be a good surrealist decision to throw the move to the fate of a dart. Aragon and Breton would be proud. I was tired though. I wanted to stop thinking of Magik. Stop replaying our deep, soulful conversations. Stop picturing our bodies naked and entwined. Stop conjuring the palpable energy I felt in her presence. I consciously tried to change the direction of my thoughts to my next novel. I wanted my next novel to filter my life into the key episodes. An encompassing, Christo-like canvas of the world, rather than the usual specific, tightly framed life novels I did. I wanted to spontaneously remember the large events onto audiotape and distill them in a linear retelling of what got me here. A nice, clear scaffolding of my reality. My memories. Me. I let my mind drift into the past. I was sleepy in body, but alive in mind.

Adopted family life was in New Jersey and my destiny was most shaped by crazy Aunt Hellie. She was a little Jewish pariah of my adopted family. We were all Catholic and my mother's brother's first wife had had a nervous breakdown and ended up in a sanitarium. My uncle remarried Hellie, who was crazier than his first wife in many ways. My devout Catholic grandmother couldn't stand to have a Jew in the family, and this combined with Hellie's confrontational, brash manners, made her the effigy of our little clan.

Hellie wanted to save the world and was a verbal communist. Whenever we had parties, she critiqued everyone and everything as bourgeois and phony. She and my uncle traveled everywhere and only wanted to talk about their trips or the politics of egalitarianism. Aunt Hellie was about 4 foot 11 and her skin was ravaged by the sun and bad genes. If wrinkles measured wisdom, Hellie was a genius. She was about ninety pounds, but she had the Napoleonic complex down. We called her Aunt Hellion.

Aunt Hellion impacted my life. Because everyone in my family was virtually the same middle-class mold hatched into life with conversations on jobs, money, sports, all the this and that of no consequence, Hellie was different. She squawked like a septuagenarian Macaw about the mistreatment of blacks, the bullshit middle-class morality, read the Beats, elevated the Soviet Union, and whined with Whitmanesque fervor that the President and the Cabinet should be poets and philosophers. "Leave the legislature to white bread, homogenized gentiles. The amalgam of the two polar opposite would create a real society, not this mockery we endure." However, all the political and social superficial, rabble rousing gripes drifted to the background of one sentence she uttered many times at every gathering.

We'd be having a cookout or Christmas dinner or something and halfway through she'd come to me and stick her little, shriveled, baked apple face into my ear and say, 'Jay, every conversation is the same, every time I'm here. Don't you hear it, Déjà vu all over again. It's sick how these people can say the same thing in 1945, 1950, and 1955. Nothing changes, except for maybe the products and brands. Oh, what a life.'

Now, I'd just listen and nod because ole Hellie was more or less correct, but what she didn't see was that *she* said the same thing over and over again. The people around her were saying the same thing over and over again and she was doing the same thing as those she whined about. I never told her this and the hypocrisy annoyed me, but years later I missed Aunt Hellion. Because I was an orphan, I think she felt connected to me. She was more a less an orphan in our family. She married into it and my grandmother crucified her for killing "our Jesus". I think every family should have an Aunt Hellion. She helped disrupt the monotony with her own version of monotony.

I was sitting in a bar on the Lower East side of Manhattan. I'd just finished high school and was pondering college or whatever. It was 1958. I was with my high school girlfriend drinking ten cent glasses of house jug wine. It was spring and all was well. Then my world split open and in the chasm a path appeared.

There was a guy reading a book at the bar drinking five cent mugs of Narragansett beer and he drank them ferociously under his protruding, heavy brow. The brow of the artist, pained and serious, and wallowing in the gravity of everything and refusing to make that transition into the necessary. Instead of pawning his youth for comfort, he was the kind who'd pine the moment because the moment wasn't what it should have been.

I asked him, "What are you reading?"

"Does it really matter to you?"

"Not particularly."

"*Joe Gould's Secret*," he said dismissively.

"Never heard of him."

"I bet there's probably about five billion or so names you've never heard of," he said derisively.

"Yeah, but there's not five billion titles with names in them."

"Perhaps there are."

"Perhaps," I said, willing to play this game of verbal brinksmanship.

"How do you know he's even real? How do you know it's not fiction?"

"I don't. Either way I've never heard of him, real or unreal."

"Does it matter?"

"That I've heard of him?"

"No, if he's real or unreal."

"Maybe for him."

"Does it?"

"What's the book about?"

He slid the book my way and took a final swig of his beer and got up to leave.

"Have you finished it?" I asked.

"No."

"Well finish it. I can read it another time. Since you're such pleasant company, we can meet again."

"It's a stupid book. The guy's a fraud. Besides, I hate words. They get in the way. There is no more flagrant lie than words. Without words, we'd have no lies. With words, we have no truth. Gould should have written that down in his oral history. Put that in your pipe and smoke it. You take it. No painter has any use for *Joe Gould's Secret*."

He left.

My girlfriend, Surya Romanavich, a Russian Jew I'd met at the New York Public Library one afternoon, said, "You know, those abstract painters think they have a monopoly on anger and nihilism, as if the world had only done them wrong."

Turned out this Joe Gould guy was real in the molecular sense. He had graduated Harvard and then dropped everything to settle on a Bohemian existence and came up with the idea to pen an oral history by writing down conversations he'd heard on the street, in the subway, at artist parties, anything at all. He had claimed to have written 10,000 pages and had them stored away in various Bowery motels, flophouses, and second-hand bookstores and other locales where he'd befriended someone. He'd taken up a collection called the Joe Gould Fund and wealthy types involved directly or indirectly contributed to the fund. He was homeless most of his life until a benefactor put him on a stipend to finish the oral history.

Turned out Gould was a fraud, just as the heavy-browed, cheap beer drinking artist had said. He'd written the same couple of chapters over and over again. One was about his father's death and another about an Indian tribe in North Dakota, with whom he'd lived for six months. In sum, the guy was an eccentric clown. He'd sometimes go into a whirling dervish and squawk like a seagull. Gould claimed to have been fluent in Seagullese. He would do this at parties after too much to drink. However, his fraud and failure became my calling.

I was eighteen and I knew exactly what I wanted to do and it had nothing to do with money. I have never wavered a moment, since the day I met the angry artist. I'm now fifty-two years old and have been doing just what Joe Gould didn't do. I've been transcribing my oral history. Every time I finish a section, I take the tapes and transcribe them. Then I cover them and bind them at a local printing press and my reward is the book that rests on my shelf. No money, just the Defense of Infinity. Money is irrelevant and fame a myth. A sad, pathetic pursuit taking one to the very core of nothingness. This life, my life, has showered me with peace. The books are my currency. They solved my youthful struggle with voids and eternities. I lost my fear of Hemingway's *Clean, Well Lighted* nada at a young age by knowing a pure posterity was in my beautifully lonely hands. When I discovered that my wife and I couldn't have kids due to my sterility, the books became my kids. I knew I would never die and peace has been in my grasp ever since. I lost it only once. I slipped into an abyss, but deep down I always knew I'd climb out.

Before I began my oral history, I decided I needed to study. I didn't need an education, which was just the pursuit of a paper for ulterior motives. No, I wanted knowledge. Honest knowledge.

I went to Columbia University and in the fall of 1958 I took my first course, Western Civ. I simply went to the class and got the syllabus and attended all the lectures, while reading all the books in the New York Public Library.

Nobody ever said anything to me as far as my lack of matriculation. I was considered a bit odd because I wasn't in the Freshman Dorms, but rather living in an apartment near Times Square. However, I'd made some friends on campus and went to some parties, had a couple beatnik girlfriends, but most of the time I read and studied. The enrollment was a lie, but the education all true.

Because I knew what I wanted, I didn't have to waste time searching classes for inspiration nor did I have to fill those requirements like Math, Economics, Science. I was on a four year plan. The first two years would be Western History, Religion, Philosophy, Literature and Art. The third year would be the same, except I would study the East. Eastern ideas weren't as trendy then, so the courses were limited and books were a bit sparse. One year would suffice. My fourth year would be overseas living abroad, learning a language and culture. I'd always romanticized Rome. I started studying Italian from the beginning as preparation. In my fourth year I'd master Italian and stowaway in some classes over there. I'd also begin my oral history on my first morning in Roma. I thought my oral history should begin overseas. You've got to leave home to understand home. My Oral History, in the fourth year of my self-designed education, would be my thesis, my dissertation. Except, my thesis would be eternal.

Nobody asked any questions in the large lecture classes for obvious reasons. When I started taking smaller seminar courses, I always made sure I spoke a lot and exhibited my interest, which was pure anyway. When the professor mentioned I wasn't on any list, I just told him that I was auditing the course in addition to my regular load and couldn't get approval for bureaucratic reasons. I said it would be my honor to just sit in and be a part of the class. The result was always the same. I imagine math and science types would have gotten a little more anal, but the humanities types usually liked my bureaucratic reference and must have felt they were snubbing the system for the benefit of the individual. They also liked the attention. Those in the arts or humanities seemed too in touch with their lonely cores and attention always seduced them.

I had a bunch of jobs at that time. I worked in a cigar store; painted houses in Long Island; worked for the city cleaning Central Park; and walked dogs for rich, upper class types. Usually I'd work a couple months and then quit when I had a few months rent paid in advance. Then I'd have more time to plunge into my autodidactic universe. The fact that people pay $100,000 today for an education to me is insane. It's all right there in the Public Library. Sure the professors helped, but more or less they weren't teaching. They were fulfilling their required presence more than anything. They just framed what I needed to do.

When I finished my three years and felt the peace of knowledge, the energy to explode the oral history out of me was, like the times, atomic. I painted as many houses as I could in Long Island. Whenever I painted one, someone on the block would ask me to do theirs. Bohemians whine about the keeping up with the Joneses mentality of material types, but that's what got me comfortably to Italy. I drew my line on eccentricity, unlike Joe Gould, on homelessness. I didn't want much, but I wanted a room, a kitchen, and a bathroom.

A couple months after Kennedy was sworn into office, I got a passport for $2 and I bought a one-way ticket to Rome for $68. I still can't fathom inflation. Economics

171

will forever be mystifying to me and I think I like it that way. I saved $1,000, a little goldmine to me, and I was off. When I arrived at Leonardo Da Vinci airport, I got on a bus to the center of Rome. One of the first things I saw was a movie theatre with the sign saying, Alberto Sordi in *Un Americano a Roma*. I knew the fates were talking. The next day I began my oral history.

"I just dropped it all." Walter Graves told me for the thirtieth time or so. We lived in neighboring rooms in a boarding house near Villa Borghese in the center of Rome. "Dropped it all, Jay. Jesus, Jay, I'm swelling up in guilt. I can't sleep at night. I just listen to all the Vespas whipping by and Fiat horns honking, thinking I'm completely insane for having done what I've done. I really believe I'm physically swelling from my anxiety, from my guilt."

"That's not guilt, ole pal of one month, that's pasta."

"I left my wife the day before the wedding. I humiliated her. I can just imagine her face, the tears. I can't get over it."

"Maybe it's the sauce, cream sauces. Maybe you're eating too much Northern cuisine. Order more tomato sauces, *sugo*, as the Italiani say."

"Stop joking around. This is serious."

"Then go home."

"That's not the answer."

"Then stay."

"If that's the answer, it's not a very good one."

"This answer takes time, perhaps. *Devi Provare*, Walter."

"Don't speak Italian to me, Jay. I haven't learned ten words since I came here. I'm so nervous. What does that mean?"

"You have to try."

"It's not easy."

"Did someone say it was?"

"Maybe she'll take me back, but it's not right. You know, Jay, sometimes, on those rare occasions, when I'm not drowning in guilt, I am euphoric, ecstatic with my escape, but after thirty or forty seconds, I'm guilty over my euphoria. How dare I feel good after what I did, I tell myself."

"Good Walter, in ninety or so years, all those thirty second blocs will give you one great day."

"You know Jay, you're younger than I am, but you're one sarcastic know-it-all bastard. Smug, too. You don't get it. When I left Chicago and that life, I saw the sky. For the first time in years, what seemed years, what seemed forever, I noticed the sky without the prompt of a plane or thunder. Just looked up and saw all that blue. Miles and miles of blue. Infinite blue. I realized I'd been walking unconsciously for ten years with my eyes down. All weighed down from my meaningless job, meaningless town, and soon-to-be meaningless marriage."

"What exactly do you mean?"

"You're always breaking my balls. *Rumpo le mie palle.*"

"*Rumpi le mie palle.*"

"Huh?"

"You said you break your own balls."

"Did I?"

"Yeah, but it's appropriate. You do break your own balls all the time."

"Shit, yeah, *Rumpi* is you. I'll never learn Italian."

"Walter, your bleakness is starting to get to me."

"Help me out."

"Why don't you try drugs?" I suggested.

"Thanks."

"Spontaneously flying to Rome the day before your wedding and dropping everything isn't your scene, but you did it. Hell, you should be proud of yourself, basking in the glee of escape. You realized you couldn't marry this woman before it was too late and you had kids and mortgages, grass, grills, garage doors, hedges, interest rates, linoleum…"

"Ok, Ok, I get the damn point. You're right."

"Smoke a little tea with me, Walter."

"One step at a time, Jay."

"You're right, Walter."

"Maybe I should write her a letter telling her my fears and that it was best to do it early, nip it in the bud,

173

rather than down the road, like you said, with kids and a mortgage and all that married for ten years stuff."

"Good idea. She'll never understand, but it might clear you up a bit. Then start learning the language, get a job, meet one of the many Mediterranean beauties, and really see the sky. Leap right into all that blue, Walter ole pal."

"Yes, I just want to see the sky everyday. Is that asking too much from life?"

"No, Walter, that's reasonable."

"It's not too greedy, right?"

"Not at all. I can't think of a better, more down to earth desire out of life than seeing the sky everyday. Yes, down to earth. Pun intended, Walter."

I landed a job at Villa Borghese, a public park in the center of Rome. It's surrounded by the mechanized insanity of thousands of tiny cars and motor scooters. Millions of spinning wheels zipping across lumpy, ancient Roman roads. Mixed in with this were the sounds of humans laughing and fighting, verbal jousts from balconies above and cafés below. Everyone, young and old, complaining about everything. One would walk through this strangely rhythmic score in the theatre that is Rome and suddenly land in the sanctuary of Villa Borghese. Noise was everywhere, but I found a quarantine walled in by great trees and softened underfoot by miles of grass. It was as tranquil as a place could be in the middle of mighty and comic Rome.

My job? I cleaned up. Not only didn't I mind, but I loved my job. I have never understood the American concept of success. In fact, maybe it was Aunt Hellie's perverse influence or my being an orphan, but making as little money as possible while surviving decently has always been my manipulation of success. I mean, thirty years later I was cleaning up dog shit for a living in California. A few months before Rome I was cleaning Central Park. At that time I daydreamed of cleaning parks in all the great cities, from New York to Paris to Beijing to Moscow. I wondered if anybody had literally cleaned the world as I might. I think I could sleep peacefully through the night well into my sixties with a million words stolen from unsuspecting voices and having cleaned a chunk of mother earth.

I got paid under the table or *Banco Nero* as the Italians say, which was the only way I could be paid, being illegal. Clearly, my boss was skimming from the budget. He must have paid me half the Italian wage and kept the other half for himself. I didn't care because my wage covered my minimal expenses and my job was simple. In fact, of all the various cleaning jobs I've had, this one was the best. I roamed Villa Borghese all day in my green uniform with one white stripe across the thigh and forearm. I worked four hours in the morning and four hours in the late afternoon. I had a three-hour siesta in between. I was virtually unsupervised. My boss was always in his office working with the books and figures (skimming is hard work). I was free to do what I wanted as long as the litter was under control and garbage cans were emptied every night. My boss didn't work much beyond making his end of the black market function efficiently. However, he did do a quick check of the grounds every night at eight o'clock. If the garbage cans were empty and there were no egregious piles of picnic waste, he was satisfied.

To relieve my guilt and help clean the world beyond the anemic aegis of my boss, I usually worked the first and last hour of my split shift. The rest of the time, I found a nice place under a tree and read the remaining books on the syllabi from my new Italian professors. Professors who never got my name. Class sizes were in the hundreds and getting to know students was irrelevant. They were merely there to dispense knowledge to the ignorant. I was getting nearly fluent as a result of living and working in Rome, the rigorous self-study I'd done in New York City, going to class and from reading my history, literature and philosophy, all in Italian.

Once a week I'd also clean a small zoo on the grounds. Cleaning the zoo was my favorite part. The animals were a mess. Shit was everywhere. No one cared about the animals. Zookeepers did the bare minimum. Italians were teetering towards communism. After two World Wars on their soil, much of their humane spirit had been bled numb. Making sure the baboons had a clean cage surely wasn't a priority, I presumed, after their own cages had been devastated and their lives destroyed or ineffably damaged. However, I was the innocent American to whom war was simply discussed or read about in the newspapers. Besides, the animals were also a great relief from Walter's namby-pamby orations.

I was the happiest man I could imagine while being without a woman. I'd lived in two great cities. I planned on living in every city. Every. My Wolfean blood curdled at the thought of permanence. I imagined myself in Barcelona, Oslo, Lagos, Lima, Calcutta, Tangiers...I'd be writing my oral history with chapters from everywhere before eventually settling in the States from where the majority of my eternal work would spring. While in Rome and the future cities I would inhabit, I was particularly on the lookout for Americans. When in cafes, at work, wandering Rome's crooked and crowded streets, I had my mini-tape player tucked in my coat pocket waiting for a conversation. Sometimes, I caught those Americans who could speak Italian and I would translate as well as transcribe. I caught the tourists, ex-pats writing the exiled great American novel, artists discussing the next movement to invade the spiritually naked and hungry, business people scheming for the next great product or import, lovers quarreling and loving, students loosening the seams, and, of course, Walter and me. Rome was simply stop one among many cities where I would prelude American oral history with Americans abroad.

At least, that was the plan until a chance meeting during my siesta in a café on Via Veneto. From that point on every city I imagined resided in the eyes of one woman.

"Jay, she's got kids," Walter said after I told him what little I knew of her.
"Walter, I don't care. What's the difference?"
"Jay, she's married."
"Still irrelevant."
"How can a husband and kids be irrelevant?"
"Because she's the one."
"For her husband and kids."
"She can't be the one for her husband and kids otherwise we wouldn't feel this way. One moment of eye

contact and I knew it and so did she. Besides, she's already separated from her husband. I'm prepared to be with her kids. This is not conscious. This isn't something you consider. You do it because all your insides are directing you. I don't have a choice. It's not like voting for a president. I'm being carried by our primordial attraction, not by a rational choice of the way she looks or her personality or her background. She's just the one I'm going to spend the rest of my life with."

"What about your nomadic soul searching ancient cities. What about all that stuff about writing the rhymes and reasons of existence from the voices of the existing, as you put it."

"Joe Gould intended to write the oral history of Manhattan. I'm going to write the oral history of Northern California. According to Daisy, it's another planet and that's appealing. She's my gold rush in 1961."

"Jay you're really gone over her."

"We talked for hours and it felt like seconds. Yeah, I'm gone."

"Jay, I don't want you to go. I'll be gone without you."

"First of all, I'm not leaving yet."

"When?"

"I don't know."

"Let me come with you."

"Walter, you're scaring me. We'll be friends for life, but not Siamese twins."

"Maybe I should go back to my fiancé."

"That's a mistake Walter. We've talked about it."

"I'm gonna miss you."

"Me too, Walter. I'll miss you."

Walter went out onto the balcony that the five second-floor rooms shared and smoked a cigarette.

I felt sorry for him.

Daisy and I spent two weeks traveling Florence, Tuscany, and Sienna. It was beyond romantic. The stars were realigned. We were like kids building pristine little Lego worlds in the pure, pre-video game days of childhood. She told me she felt as if she were living in a mirage. That everything would just melt before her eyes one day because happiness wasn't as possible as this. I told her when you meet the one, it is. In Montepulciano overlooking Tuscany with a bottle of wine and paper cups sitting on an isolated precipice, I asked her to marry me. She said yes on the condition that I wait about six months. She had to complete her divorce and give her kids some time to adjust. When the time was right, she'd send me a letter saying to come to Mill Valley, California.

Poor Walter surrendered to the inevitable. He returned to his family and would ask for his fiancé's forgiveness. He told me, "Jay you have an advantage. You're an orphan. Your emotions are free, but a family twists them into knots. I can't live like this. I have no business here. Running away to Italy. A bohemian fool thinking I could start a new life. The old life never lets you."

"Walter, you have to let the new life come to you. Your one is out there and she's not your wife. Otherwise, you wouldn't be here."

"I shouldn't have come here in the first place. Jay, I don't have a one. I've fallen in love a hundred times with beautiful Italian women here. I don't have a one. I have a thousand."

"You're talking about lust, Walter. I see a hundred women a day that I want naked and screaming my name in my bed, too. Screw sex. I'm talking about spiritual union. If the universe is orchestrating our lives and some elements go together harmoniously and others cause negative reactions, what the hell is the difference with people? You and your wife don't go together. It's no one's fault. It just doesn't work. I can't explain what I'm feeling with Daisy, but I know you're not feeling it with your wife or these Mediterranean beauties you want to undress. Give it time and the elements will join correctly."

"Jay, you'll fit in California. I'm lost here, spiritually dead. At least back home, I'm not lost."

"But you're spiritually dead, which is why you're here. You have to try to be alive. It won't happen by changing landscapes."

"I'm happy for you, Jay, but I'm not you."

We had several more of these conversations, but Walter finally left a few months before Daisy's final letter would arrive. I wouldn't see Walter again for fifteen years and when I saw him he had finally shed his old life.

When Daisy went back, I worked on my oral history. It had already started before. I kept my mini-tape recorder in my pocket like an undercover cop covertly gathering evidence. Every night I'd go back to my room and transcribe almost everything I had heard. In fantastical fits of onomatopoeia, I'd even try to put a language to the sounds of Rome as Joe Gould did to seagulls and Kerouac would do to the sounds of the sea at Big Sur. All my transcribing helped soften the ache of loneliness that filled every pore of my young skin while Daisy and I were separated. We wrote each other everyday. I'd sit in Villa Borghese reading her letters and painting her image in my mind and then writing her back the moment I finished her words.
This went on for months.

While recording my oral history Book One – Rome, I finished my university experience. The university of myself. I had finished attending classes in Rome at their great and ancient school, La Sapienza, The Wisdom. The classes were always packed and nobody asked anything. A Professor stood in front of a chalkboard at a podium dispensing knowledge, while four hundred Italians crammed into two hundred seats. The Italians were smoking furiously, sitting in the aisles, standing, and taping this bored *professore* lecturing. This was the one place I didn't have to hide my mini-recorder. I actually taped many passages and put it in the book. Word for word lectures from La Sapienze, 1961, from classes on Literature, Art and Political Science. By the end of these classes, I was fairly fluent in Italian and reading with ease. About three months into my exile from Daisy, I decided I was done with my degree. The remaining three months I would finish my thesis, book one of my oral history. At my university, I was my advisor, my Dean, my President, and if I needed to change a requirement or a direction, it was quite simple. All I had to do was ask myself. Ending a bit early didn't bother me. I had done what I had set out to do. It was around the time of this decision in my last class that I met the major character of Book One, an Italian anarchist named Dario Uguale.

Dario and I would find cafes near La Sapienza and we'd sit and talk and do speed, which made our conversations eternal. I often ran out of tape during our talks. I would only put what I'd recorded in my oral history. If it wasn't recorded, it didn't really happen. I was the curator of my reality and my reality was what made it from voice to tape to page. This particular reality of Dario Uguale mostly condemned America and bemoaned Italy. As I said, Italy was teetering towards communism after the disaster of WWII and its tenuous togetherness as a nation, but Dario hated communism as much as American democracy. He most recently had fallen for the anarchism of Emma Goldman and Thoreau, but was now "transcending them as well."

When he wasn't criticizing "make believe" America, he was buying nasal inhalers from the *farmacia* and breaking them apart to inhale the base, which was filled with benzedrine. Benzedrine was a pharmaceutical amphetamine that kept you up for hours and hours.

"Ohh, Americano, I tell you America is the end of the world, but *grazie Dio* for these sinus *decongestione*. This benzedrine is my *Dio* now."

"Hopefully, the government won't catch on," I said.

"*Il governo non e' stupido, Americano.* They've got a stake in the profits. They probably know kids in the states are sniffing their brains into orbit, but that's what they want, oblivion. Send those mad beats into internal oblivion."

"Oblivion isn't such a bad place."

"I've been to worse places. Try Latina."

"Where's Latina?"

"South of Rome, about an hour. Mussolini built it. There's even a building built like an M. Damn Italians still haven't destroyed it. You know amico, a lot of people still think Mussolini wasn't bad."

"I always liked the goose step myself."

"I'd have taken Il Duce over Hitler, and Stalin, of course." Dario said. "Yeah, Il Duce wins in that triumvirate. You see, that's why the States look so good. Look at the damn competition. *Madonna Santa*, Roosevelt is the second coming compared to those madmen."

"Dario, I really could care less about government. I can't think of something I'm more detached to than *il governo*."

"Si, me too, Americano. That's why I flirted with the anarchists for a spell. I loathe government."

"You loathe, but I don't feel anything."

"True, *Americano*, we're different there."

"I guess if I cared, I'd vote anarchist."

"Now that's a contradiction."

"What?"

"Vote anarchist."

"So what made you drop anarchy? Last time we spoke, Emma Goldman was your new *Dio*."

"No more *dios,* Americano. We atheists must stop searching for replacements. I got tired of Goldman's arrogance. Damn anarchy to her started sounding like another political party. Now Thoreau, I still respect. A more lonely anarchy. Anarchy of the soul without others. There's a great American, *Americano*. His passage on the pyramids is epiphanic. Everybody goes, how do you say, bananas for the pyramids. People travel thousands of miles to visit the pyramids and Thoreau thought it was insanity. All these fawning people to witness the results of human slavery. His exact words were genius. "So many men could be degraded enough to spend their lives constructing a tomb for some ambitious booby, whom it would have been wiser and manlier to have drowned in the Nile, and then given his body to the dogs." Now, that Americano, is genius. Booby! I love that word. There's no true translation for it, other than *seno*, which is just breast, not booby.

"If you follow that credo, you ought to loathe all of Rome."

"And loathe Rome I do. The constructions and sites of Rome are built on human misery. Piazza Del Popolo was an execution ground; Il Coliseo, a symbol of debauchery and

181

the nadir of the human spectacle. It's my brethren, the *popolo* itself that I love. The conversations in the cafés and on the road. Two teenager girls holding hands on their way to school. Two boys kicking a soccer ball in a polluted field. That is the true Rome. To hell with Ayn Rand and all that humanity has built because all that humanity built was built on inhumanity."

"And now where?" I asked, curious to hear Dario's follow up to Communism and Anarchism.

"Now, *amico mio*, I've got my new panacea."

"God, your English is so good."

"Summers with the queen, real English, as the British high-brow boobies say."

"You learned well. So, tell me, Italiano, what's the next philosophy."

"This is beyond philosophy. Philosophy is a dead end. Politics is a slow death and art is a tease. This, my friend, is a state of being, which is the state everyone is searching for—socialist, communist, abstract expressionist, Christian Democrat, capitalist—whatever your pious, fraudalent road, this is the state of flowing peace all the dysphoric searchers haplessly envision and never see."

Dario was a handsome, dark skinned Italian of Sicilian descent. He had vibrant, mahogany eyes that radiated energy above tired, dark circles, which were the result of excessive reading, caffeine and Benzedrine. Sleep was an irregular rarity. His powerful, piercing eyes bespoke desire and life, set in the appropriately contradictory frame of fatigue. His words and eyes produced an irresistible and mad charisma.

He always engaged my mind and filled my first running tape with the great Italian bohemian madness. Long dead, Joe Gould was probably shuffling in his box or his spirit was doing cartwheels in the clouds.

"Immediate Nostalgia. The feeling of nostalgia within the moment of its origin."

"Nostalgia without the wait," I said.

"*Essato*, Americano."

"How?"

"You remember, Gianfranco Guerrini?"

"Sure, the Neurology student."

182

"Yes. We've been working together. Nostalgia strikes at the most unpredictable of times and the melancholy of nostalgia has been drowning me in frustration. I mean here are these moments, times, that in memory become what they truly could have been, beatific moments of life. Yet, we can only experience them from afar, with the distance of time gone by. Take, for example, this very moment now. We're talking. We're enjoying our kindred company, but two years from now, alone wherever we may be, only then, will we realize the essence of now. That is tragic. Tragic magic. *Tragico magico.*"

"It's better than not experiencing the essence of now, at all," I said.

"Si, Americano, the glass is half full. That's America, *Americano*. That's the spirit of your country. You may be an anti-materialist oddity of your world, but there's still some American in you, *Americano*."

"It's true."

"*Si, certo*, it's true, but what would be more true would be to capture two years from now and experience it today."

"But how?"

"That's where Guerrini comes in. He's taking neurological readings of my brain waves when nostalgia strikes and researching the sensations. He's hoping to find a stimulant, a pill, that can create the same neuron output thereby giving us nostalgia without the pain of separation and time elapsed. Without the loss of the event."

"It would be a miracle."

"What better place for a miracle than glorious Roma."

"And in the meantime?"

"No idea, *Americano*. I think I'll be in a café talking the rest of my life, creating nostalgia. What else is better than that?"

"Not much else."

"If I take a position in life, say a teacher, or whatever, some acceptable role, I therefore declare I accept this life and I don't accept life as it is. It's an atrocity. It's absurd. So, I'll stay in cafés and complain the rest of my life. *Americano*, I'm Italian, true and true. I loathe any group, but my blood is my blood and in my blood I've got a millennia of complaints. We, Italians, love to say what's wrong. That's what I like to do. You, *Americano*, are an optimist. Italians are natural pessimists. We've been there too many times to think it will work out. Americans are babes in the woods, but they'll get there in a century or two."

The benzedrine really fueled Dario's anti-philosophies. We often started light, but invariably, he drifted into the depths of existence and the ideas of new orders, new ways out of the absurdity. He was my introduction and I couldn't have wished for a better prelude. My books would be about life and living existence and I couldn't think of someone who cherished and lusted for life more than someone like Dario Uguale. Someone who condemned existence and loathed so much of life because he pined for so much more. Dario Uguale also awakened me to the realization that my oral history was a vain effort of capturing the nostalgia of the moment.

Book One, Rome, was finished near the end of 1961, days before Daisy wrote me saying she was ready. I was on a plane the next day.

When I arrived in San Francisco, Daisy was waiting for me. I had all my possessions in two bags. One small valise had my tape recorder, Book One of my homage to Joe Gould, a few pictures, a camera, and few scattered shaving/hygiene supplies. The other bag had my wardrobe, which consisted of t-shirts and jeans. Other than my oral history growing exponentially through the years, I never wanted my possessions to grow beyond one suitcase. This, of course, would be youthful fantasy. I must have at least two suitcases to my name.

Daisy and I kissed madly at the gate. I tasted her sensual lips and caressed her long, strawberry blond hair. We got to her house and didn't have the patience to make it to the bedroom. Fortunately, Daisy's two dogs were not jealous and they just watched us rolling around and greeted me after.

For a week, we more or less continued rolling around in the various rooms of Daisy's house. In between, we slept and talked and drank wine. Daisy's kids were with her now ex-husband and Daisy had stocked the house with food and wine. She had planned our hibernation and I very willingly agreed. This was our honeymoon. She wore the ring I gave her, but we would never marry. We saw no point in that. We were already married. She was already my wife. I married Daisy the first moment I saw her.

After our honeymoon, I decided to make a change in my life's plan. I had already given up on cleaning/seeing the great cities of the world. Daisy and I both decided that some money would help get us going. We had her kids to raise and a mortgage to pay and Daisy's divorce settlement wasn't much beyond the house. Given my new responsibilities, I tried to get a job for money and, in fact, I got one, but I couldn't keep it. I answered an ad for a sales position in a coffee company. In the interview I said I had a business degree from La Sapienza. They wanted to promote Italian-style coffee in America.

"We need someone who has lived in Italy and can help us market our product. Americans have no time anymore because of work. So a smaller coffee, like an Italian Espresso, would take off. We want to market the time factor to men and then market the elegance and class of Italy to housewives who long for a better, more interesting life. For that matter, both sexes long for a better life and Italian coffee will give them a taste of the better life, European style." This is what the interviewer said to me.

I took the job and quit after a month. Daisy agreed that the madness of marketing coffee as my existence would lead us down a sad road. She said a new dishwasher and a car wasn't worth it. I was making $2,000 a month, but wanted to kill myself sitting in an office all day having these ridiculous meetings and talking about coffee all day. I missed Villa Borghese. I missed the park, cleaning up the world. Daisy said quit, and we'd find ways to get by with more meaningful, but lower-paying jobs.

A month later I was in Golden Gate Park picking up trash, which to me was more meaningful than wearing a suit and marketing 'the better life, European style'. Dario Uguale would have been proud. I did that all through the 60's and had so much to transcribe from eavesdropping on the people of Golden Gate Park. My oral history was growing. Life with Daisy was wonderful. We lived frugally, but happily for many years. Our extended family eventually included a not-yet renowned Sam Billingston, who had married Daisy's daughter. Their marriage didn't last, but Sam and I became true friends and spent many days on the road sharing memories. One of my oral history books came from our driving conversations. One of Sam's books also came from this. He told me he was crediting me in the book. I never read it. I didn't have to read it. I didn't want to read published, fictionalized reality. Sam and I had lived it and I had the truth down, not some filtered, molded version made palatable and tempting for the public and critics. This was always an issue in our friendship and the conflict and tension led to some of the best conversations in the oral history.

Sam and Elise divorced and we were given their house as gratitude for the help we had given the young, doomed couple. Elise moved to Hollywood and has struggled through a career of minor parts. Sam has struggled through a career of major parts. Whatever the outside trappings, the spirit shall struggle.

And so we had a beautiful, little home with no mortgage to pay. We sold Daisy's house and had some money invested. I continued cleaning up the park and Daisy worked part-time in an antique store, where she began her own kind of oral history, which was a collection of nostalgic, old stuffed animals. Around the time my oral history grew to be 4,000 pages, tragedy struck. This was 1976.

Suddenly, by some cruel act of eternity, Daisy became a shadow of the person she'd been. She had a stroke and the amount of blood that had been cut off to her brain damaged her mind in the way a lobotomy would. She wasn't a vegetable, but she would just tune out the world for hours and hours. She would have moments of lucidity and we could communicate like before, but those happened only occasionally. Her only real link to her previous life was her continued fascination with stuffed animals and she'd spend hours with her growing collection. However, now it had devolved into whispering to them and holding them as a child would. Apparently, her brain had gone backward to a place of her youth.

Adding to the tragedy, this place of her youth didn't include sex.

During one of her moments of lucidity, she told me, "Jay, listen to me. I want to tell you something important."

"Go ahead, sweetie."

"You're free to be with other women."

"Huh?"

"We can't, but that doesn't mean you can't."

"Daisy—"

"No, Jay, it's not fair for you. It's not healthy. You still have desire. I remember your desire, but I just can't fulfill it. There's no drive in me, but you are free to be active, but just to appease your urges from time to time. I will keep you this way. Just don't abuse the privilege and never, ever fall in love with them. Promise me."

"I promise," I mouthed, slack-jawed and eyes wide.

Lucidity left and Daisy went back to her dolls.

I was as shocked as I was relieved. Perhaps my temporary loyalty during the early years of the stroke was good karma. I was honored by Daisy's decision. I promised myself at that moment to honor Daisy's transcendent recognition and selflessness. She had eliminated her ego from her heart. I promised myself never to leave her.

To be closer to home in Mill Valley, I took a job at a kennel nearby the house. I would take care of dogs, which for the most part meant cleaning out the shit from the cages. Of course, I loved the job. I loved dogs and being outside and the pay gave us more money than the park had. Mostly though, we were now living off Daisy's disability check. We didn't have money for fine wines or vacations, but Daisy had her stuffed animals and I forged forward with my oral history, which would soon include my new open marriage world.

The rhythm of my new, openly adulterous life was broken by two major events. The first was a dark depression that rendered me suicidal for a period. The second was falling in love with Magik.

The depression hit hard. It was shortly after the high of my open marriage and several affairs. Perhaps, despite all the bohemian talk of a natural state of sexuality that was not encumbered by monogamy, my infidelity had rendered me dark. Or perhaps it was in my family. My last name was an anagram for Dark. All my life I hadn't really considered the significance of my surname. Perhaps, my name had been Dark and some ancestor played with the letters to break the curse. Being an orphan, my name never seemed important. It was just an insignificant tag, label, like one on a shirt. However, maybe it was smashingly logical where my name came from.

The depressions slid bleak and formless, consuming my days. At work, I'd just sit and cry, like a kid. Sometimes, I would be with some dogs, who tried hard to cheer me up by wagging their tail or nudging their snout into my face. Failing this, they would join me in my depression and lie down, droopy-eyed and sad. They would just put their heads down on the ground and stare up at me. They'd give up and join my sadness, forever loyal to all our emotions. Their eyes made my pain worse. Dogs' eyes are more emotional than people's. They feel as much or more than we do.

The darkness was invisible, which made it all the more numbingly frustrating. There were no images of my past, missteps I'd made, faces of those I hadn't loved or loved too much. There weren't moments of indecision that led to loss. There weren't moments of exaggerated effort that sent me tumbling foolishly ahead when stability was needed. Something lurked inside, a faceless, crippling monster, omnipotent and omnivorous.

At the time, the oral history was catching up to the present. I'd described Dario Uguale, Italy and Walter, California, and Sam and I, my affairs. I'd filled several binders. I had 5,000 typed pages of the voices and conversations around me, the graffiti on the walls, the voices on the subway. I was cultivating Joe Gould's seed and seeing it through to fruition.

When the darkness set in, I stopped. I was in a tunnel and the clichéd light at the end couldn't be seen. I quit work and spent weeks in bed, sometimes sleeping sixteen hours a day. Sometimes, the darkness welled up and the tears came down like a long expected rain after days of dark clouds. Words are impotent at trying to describe the sadness that rendered me physically and mentally atrophied. Sadness has its own unknown language.

Daisy got a shrink to come in and talk to me and he wrote that it was for Daisy, so the state picked up the bill. Some days I was too deflated to talk, which was hard to believe considering my runaway mouth. Through our conversations, I came to a conclusion. Since he was of the Freudian school, where the shrink rarely gave an answer, but just paved the road with questions that would lead you to your own answers, I discovered I was terrified of the present; of my newfound freedom handed to me by Daisy. It was several years and lovers later, but the therapist led me to believe guilt had enveloped me. It had pushed me off the cliff and into the sudden, paroxysmal depression. It hadn't hit me because I was still living in the past with the events being penned in my Oral Histories. But now my words had caught up to me. The present came to exist in both life and escape, and I was terrified of my freedom.

What I had to do was accept my freedom as legitimate and pure. This was step one. My realization of the fear cast some sun at the inexorable nights of my recent days. I got out of the house and started living again, going to the café and reading the paper and listening to those around me and recording them. So many of the conversations around had to do with money, possessions, mortgages. The late 70's had become a very different time. Daisy and I were living on what now seemed pennies. In therapy, I discovered further guilt over our free house and lack of earned money. I was guilty over Daisy's government checks. I was guilty for many things. Naturally, the Freudian led me to childhood and into the underlying guilt and rejection of being an orphan.

Painful realizations seemed to bring me further down after the brief respite of peace. I stopped therapy and made a great leap forward from my darkness by a strange and sudden urge that overwhelmed me quite by accident.

Shoplifting.

It started small and comically, just like it would end. I'd stuff a can of tuna in my coat. The next time I'd put some cases of soda in the bottom of my carriage and the cashier wouldn't notice and I just wheeled it out, free of charge. We were living on Daisy's monthly disability check of $425 and my pittance from the kennel, so the thieving was euphorically practical. Whenever I was stealing, the darkness was gone. In fact, I was happy to the point of giddiness. It was my thieving utopia. Shortly thereafter, the darkness would begin its steady creep back to the surface like a Six Flags roller coaster grinding and churning its way up the first slope before unleashing its relentless fury around hairpin turns and corkscrew loops. Fearing the descent after the peak, I'd start planning bigger thefts. They were all aimed at the Safeway over on Calistoga Road. Suddenly, our house was filled with food. I also never paid for a newspaper or magazine from Hall's. Those were easy pickings, but the Safeway started getting difficult. I got caught twice with my rucksack filled with steaks and dog food. The manager banned me from the store for six months and the darkness was exhumed. I tried stealing from other stores, but it didn't work. I only wanted to steal from that store and I couldn't satisfy my urge elsewhere.

I went back to Dr. Loom, and of course, I came to all sorts of quotidian conclusions about childhood needs and orphan syndrome and guilt over my liaisons beyond Daisy, but the talking cure was inept. Besides, Dr. Loom never ventured an analysis. The burden was on me. Everything was an interrogative from him. I grew tired of the process. I needed to steal and steal from Safeway. I needed larceny. I had no interest in the why of my intoxicating, inane urge. I just wanted to follow its lead. An addict needs his fix and I couldn't wait six roller coaster months.

So, I bought a disguise.

I actually went to a costume shop and got a professional set up. I grew a mustache, but bought a mouthpiece that changed the shape of my jaw. I bought a wig of real human hair. Once a week I'd go to Safeway and Daisy thought I was playing dress up. As if it were Halloween or some game and she started doing the same, which was very depressing. So, I stopped letting her see me

190

in disguise and began secretly leaving the house and returning out of disguise.

It all came to an end when I got caught with two prime pieces of steak. The blood had leaked out of my coat and onto my pants.

"Hey, mister, you ok?" the rent-a-cop said.

"I'm fine, thanks, you?" I said casually, while checking out with a couple of cheap items.

"There's blood on your pants."

"Huh, oh, well, I had a cut there and it must have opened up. It's no big deal."

"There's a lot of blood and it's not in a good area, mister."

"I'm fine. Just a little embarrassing and all. You know, the location. I just need to get home and clean it up. Change the dressing."

"You sound familiar."

"Huh?"

Then the rent-a-cop had his little epiphany, which kind of made me feel good, thinking this is a story he's going to tell for years. The day he caught a thief after years of boredom and flunking out of the Police Academy or something. He pulled off the wig and screamed, "Kard!"

I just smiled sheepishly and he handcuffed me and called the real police.

Safeway decided to press charges and I got thirty days in the Marin County jail. The judge appointed a state therapist to come and visit me. She wasn't a Freudian and didn't hesitate to render judgments and conclusions after a few visits where I did most of the talking.

"Jay, I think a key point is why you were so obsessed at robbing only Safeway and no one else," Dr. Bensin said.

"Sounds important."

"You want my state appointed analysis?"

"Sure."

"Ok, here's my take. You've lived this very bohemian, pariah lifestyle that hasn't really bothered you on the surface the way it would most people. After years and years of just getting by monetarily and staying devoted to

191

your craft of transcribing your world, you had repressed so much angst. The angst of not "keeping up with the Joneses" as you often say, and your complete non-recognition of the alleged American dream was actually recognized within and surfaced in these deep depressions you started having. What else could Safeway represent? The name itself is like a sledgehammer metaphor for middle class. You'd go there and see all the ease and comfort of people buying cartloads of groceries, while you and Daisy barely got by. This angst was excavated when your recordings caught up to the present. You must have felt the settled part of your life in a fairly wealthy town. While you really didn't belong, aside from the characters working at Hall's that you've described; the ex-cabbie poet friend, youth protégés on the run from the East. However, they weren't in the Larkspur community. They were transients. You were here to stay. Years of cleaning parks and dog cages made you bitter, but you've kept it in check with the recollection of the past. When you arrived at the present, it unraveled the buried bitterness. Jay, no man is an island, despite your brilliant efforts."

"It sounds eloquent, yet sophomoric. But you probably have a point."

"Jay, I'm just scratching the surface here. We haven't even begun to get into the guilt of your affairs or the tragic stroke that has turned your beloved wife into a shadow of her former self."

We did get into them and the only result was I started getting more depressed. All this talk about hidden pain coming to the fore made it worse. Hell, I'd rather have it hidden. Besides, the damn shrink seemed to be culling out neatly placed sorrows tucked away comfortably in the soul. They had their place of repose. Who says all repression is bad. It's damn human. It's life to have repressions. Mine were packed away in sturdy, organized boxes that didn't need to be opened. Dr. Bensin was disturbing everything. Hidden truths need to hide.

I stopped confiding so much and cut down my visits. She knew me too damn well. I didn't think that was so healthy and my depression was getting worse. While I was in jail, I read an article about the long-term affects of amphetamine use. This, coupled with the reality of my darkness still stunting my days, sent me elsewhere. Once I was out, I went to see Daisy's state funded neurologist and he filled me in.

"Residual Amphetamine Depression," the Neurologist said. He had an office on 7th Avenue overlooking Clement Street, which was a busy mix of Asians, mostly Chinese I believed, but the restaurants catered to Vietnamese, Thai, and Koreans as well. Just outside his window across the street I could see a video store with Chinese characters. In English it said, "The Best in Asian Nymph Video."

"Residual what?" I asked.

"Residual Amphetamine Depression. There's a theory that heavy speed use can slowly damage the brain tissue along the synapses. Concomitantly, the chemical activity bounding through the synapses gets altered. However, the whole process takes time and the result can be horrific periods of sadness. Actually, sadness may be too soft a word. Deadness might be better. Just as you described your recent months. So, this black hole is opened up and you fall into its void. So goes the theory."

"Do you believe it?" I asked.

"I don't discredit it."

"If it's true, what do I do?"

"Well, we can try medication. I'm not a big believer in therapy. That is, the conversational type. I believe most of our problems are biochemical. I'll have to do some neurological tests to determine potential deficiencies or excesses in your chemical activity. Of course, this whole thing was caused by your excesses long ago. San Francisco types always mystify me, so to speak. They think they can indulge and have no effect thereafter. Your depressions could be a punishment for your past."

"Bad karma. What goes around comes around," I said, thinking of Dario and wondering what his mental state turned out to be as he indulged more often than I did. I didn't even know if he stopped like me.

"Usually," the doctor said.

The doctor prescribed me some pills. I went to a pharmacy next to the Asian porn video store and got a bottle of the purple and red gel-coated capsules. I walked outside on Clement Street and looked around, watching everyone. I turned on the recorder in my pocket. I was trying to embrace the present. I'd hoped it would soften the "deadness", bury it, even. Bury the deadness. I listened to a conversation in Chinese between two fifty-somethings. I wished I'd understood what those two men were discussing. It was probably nothing, but I felt as though it would have been like uncovering the mystery of existence, had I understood it. I needed a new language. An unknown language. Non-linguistic even. Like Gould speaking Seagullese. I decided to transcibe the sounds of this Chinese conversation into English. I was feeling a little better. I listened to the high-pitched lilt of their language. Threw in letter patterns to match their multi-tonal, piercing sounds. Unlike Japanese, the Chinese were loud. Screamers, in fact. Mao must have hollered like a banshee in order to speak to a crowd because the Chinese couldn't shut up. It's as if they had to go over their 5,000 year history everyday.

A couple or so nights later I was home in my transcription room. Daisy was upstairs with the dogs and fixing her dolls, which occupied most of her time. I was romanticizing the Clement Street Chinese I'd heard days before. Bleakness whispered, but I felt some control over its primal grip. I was throwing myself into the truth of my transcription, formulating phonetic words from a foreign language. I was realizing I loved truth. I occasionally dallied with the notion of editing and fictionalizing my tapes, but I hated lies, fabrications, fictional fictions. I approached every novel I've ever read as truth. And they are truth. Truthful imaginations. Manipulations of events. Yet, I wanted no part of that manipulation. The golden chalice of everyone's undiscovered palace is at the end of the road of real events. Somehow, this path would be reached by the appreciation of the events around me. My path was interrupted by the phone.
    "Hello."
    "Jay?"

"Yes."

"It's Walter."

"Walter! Hi! My God, how are you?"

"Good, and you?"

"Not bad. I miss you. I've tried getting in touch with you, but never could. It's been a while, where are you?"

"California. Marin County."

"Jesus. You're close. We've got a lot of catching up to do." I turned on my recorder, excited about a variation in my present. I held the recorder by the receiver's mouthpiece.

"Yes, but I can't."

"Can't what?"

"Catch up."

"Why not."

"Just can't. I'd like to introduce you to someone named Gurdjieff."

"Why?"

"I think he can help you."

"Help me with what?"

"Everything," Walter said. He was speaking in an apathetic monotone.

"That just about covers it. Is this God, Walter?" I said, laughing a bit.

"Not really."

"Who is he?"

"Meet me at Muir Woods Park tomorrow night at 7:00."

"So, we can catch up?"

"No."

"Walter, what the hell is going on? You sound strange, very different from Rome."

"I am different. Rome was a long time ago, Jay. See you tomorrow."

I arrived at the park a few minutes before 7:00 p.m. the following night wondering just who this Gurdjieff guy was going to be. What was his particular spiritual schtick? I was thinking he might be some Eurasian mystical guru, displaced from the Sixties and Seventies. That debris still

195

floated far and wide. We were in Muir Woods and it was a peaceful evening. I saw the soft red earth with omnipotent sequoias rising up while the sun sank below the tree tops. There was a tent with benches beneath it and podium in the center. About fifty people were walking around drinking from paper cups. Some were staring upwards at the Sequoia ceiling and others were milling about. One was lying in push-up position with his ear to the earth. Then I saw Walter.

"Walter! Old friend, how are you?"

He didn't respond. His eyes gestured something indecipherable to me.

"Hey, you can at least say hello."

He nodded no. Not angrily, just no. Precisely then, I noticed the other people weren't talking. No one. My words were the only ones in the air amidst the sounds of birds, leaves, the wind, footsteps, running water, plates and other kitchen sounds. I immediately sensed that my initial vibe might be right on. Californian cults for those who simply couldn't move on, but I told myself to be open-minded and I turned on my recorder. It didn't appear that I'd be getting many words from this muted collection of lost souls. I told myself to stay non-judgmental. Stay open to the opportunity of possibility for a new direction of the oral history. I decided to be quiet and observe the gathering. Walter looked at me and nodded in affirmation, sensing my analyses. I truly wanted to talk to Walter and get his tale on tape as a way to connect the past to my present. For some reason, I was also recognizing the dissipation of my deadness in a way unlike anytime in recent memory, aside from the adrenal rush of petty thievery. Yet this wasn't a rush. This was peaceful dissipation.

I spent about a half hour walking around looking at the others, wondering about their lives. At that point, my cult suspicions were realized as a man in a white, monk-like robe stood by the podium and spoke.

"Can one come into contact with the whole situation rather than force oneself into completion?"

Silence.

"You won't be here again. Every moment you die and are reborn. How deep and essential can you make each rebirth is the approach to the mystery you shamelessly ponder."

Silence.

"Many of you have written that you want to grasp the truth behind words, beseeching me to speak directly, beyond abstract aphorisms, as one of you wrote."

Silence.

"The question is truth and you mock the question by expecting an answer. When we don't know or understand something new, we frame it in words. We surround and therefore stampede the answer under all these weighted words, which aren't even ours, but were given to us by others, always others. It's a cultural labyrinth and the way out of the maze is not by asking or answering, but by allowing."

Silence.

"In our conclusion and the order we believe we've found through verbal language, which is never from within, we think we've happened on a solution. Every new place is lost in the reformation of an old place. We fear. We desperately need to be right instead of real and if we attempted to stay in the new place, we may get touched. A vision may come, but it can never be given."

Silence.

"The comedy of errors that is God has sidetracked us tragically into millenia of empty tears. It's all been so wrongly manifested by our rush. Our haste. Our questions. Every voiceless feeling is the message. Again language has disrupted the processes by which we attain God. It exists within the silent dialectic of messages evolving into questions and again into message and higher question. This is spirituality. Our religion. Our God is the highest distortion of humanity. Money is the highest defamation of everyday reason. Our feeble attempt at organizing through church is again the innate need to frame the mystery, when the mystery should just be allowed to spread within a wild peace that it deserves. Our relentless sprint has taken a black, Jewish spiritual nomad who might be considered a quack today and made him a white, blue eyed CEO of the corporation that is religion today. We can't go to God. It, not he, comes to us."

Silence.

"In Persia, a monument reads, 'Repair the past, prepare the future'. We don't know how to pray. Pray to a friend. Think of him. Think of your relationship to him. Inwardly change toward him in the way you feel, not think, you should act with him. Elevate yourself to him in a different way. A higher way. Eventually, he will unconsciously treat you differently and you will have repaired the past for him and prepared the future for yourself. This is prayer. Never do it with your family. Never pray to them. Leave them out of spiritual ascendance. Their weight will hold you down. Our prayers too often center on them. They shouldn't be in the process. Without involving them, you may one day come to them."

Silence.

"We must release the hierarchy. Allow it to melt. Truth is on a plane and requires forward steps, not upward leaps. The sky hasn't the answer. We walk and run and take steps everyday, but have we ever taken one true forward step to true ego-less spirituality?"

Silence.

I couldn't find Walter after. He'd disappeared. I took it that he wanted me to take in the words alone and undisturbed by our reunion. There was silence and people ate. I saw a brochure at a table, which explained that this was:

"A reinterpretation of Gurdjieff though the lens of the ancient stoics, who believed that repression was a glorious, healing path, if the repression was sufficiently understood. This wordless, voiceless ascendancy, mixed with Gurdjieff's religious doctrines of Eastern meditation and calmness, would combat the angst, anxiety, materialism, and ennui of 20th century existence. There is no guru, no leader. We are all leaders and each week at a meeting one member speaks about his/her enlightenments gained during his/her quietude and reading Gurdjieff and P.D. Ouspensky. All money is through donation and strictly limited to maintain an outdoor place to meet and eat. We will never build anything beyond silence and chiseled words spoken by only one each week, the temporary leader. Permanance is another false frame. We offer a book by Gurdjieff for free,

which must be read in order to come to a second meeting.
Thank you. "

I wasn't sure what to think. I really wanted to talk to
Walter and get some words to frame this whole strange
thing, just as I wasn't supposed to. I wanted to have a beer,
find out all his news, and wax nostalgic about bygone
Roman days. I wanted to hear about the return to his family,
which I'd assumed had happened, failed and led him to this
ethereal path. Everything just said was against everything I
have done in my life. I was obsessed with words and trying
to frame my life though the voices around me. Using words
to give meaning. Now, I've just heard that more words take
one further away from God, from IT, from the intangible and
invisible.

As I was thinking, an epiphany uplifted me and
soothed me with the energy of awareness. Epiphanies are
too often slippery and elusive. Yet, this had force.
Momentum. My whole oral history was simply my form of
prayer, about which this man had just spoken. In my own
way I was praying to friends by giving their thoughts a
tangible place. It was prayer to my parents, whom I'd never
met. It was prayer to children I would never have.

It was prayer in my own mad form. My own
religion. Obsessive and neurotic, perhaps. But my prayer.

As these reckonings spread within, the deadness
dissolved into a redirected darkness that hovered nearby, but
far enough away to be controlled. One step ahead of
melancholy. For reasons I can't truly explain, having it
nearby rather than gone was more comforting. More real.
I needed its presence, but now it was under control rather
than controlling me. Present and real, not interred and
whispering. I wanted nothing more than to go home and get
to work seizing the present of my oral history. Make
dramatic changes. Worship my wife again. True love for
her would be to deny her offer. Be true to her when I was
told I didn't have to be. Re-channel all the sexual energy
into another path. Transcend the libido.

"Jay, wake up!"

Daisy was shaking my shoulder. I opened my eyes.
I wasn't sure if I had been daydreaming in a half-sleep or

truly dreaming. It all seemed real. I think I thought I was awake. If I had been dreaming, so be it. The dream state might be more real than the waking state. Truth seeps in after midnight.

I got off the couch and went to the bathroom to check my nose and crow's feet. I felt like I had been in some form of sleep for years, like Rip van Winkle. So many events piled upon events. We don't realize how famous we are in our own living movies.

I looked the same.

"Are you ready?" Daisy asked.

"I'm ready, honey."

"Ok. Who throws?"

"You, my dear."

Daisy stood about six feet from the map.

"It only counts if it lands east of the Rockies, like we agreed." I said.

"Agreed."

I gave Daisy a dart. She closed her eyes and threw it.

My eyes opened wide when it landed. I went over to the map and looked.

"You're not going to believe this, honey."

"Home?" she said.

"Damn close. Point Pleasant, New Jersey."

Daisy said, "Time to go home, Jay. Time to go home."

"Yeah, it's time," I said.

"Time to go to the other side of the rainbow, Jay," Daisy said with a long, lucid stare and a wry smile.

I nodded at Daisy.

"Actually, my dear, I'm done with rainbows altogether."

"Yes, Jay. It's time."

dixson naturian
Gone West

I packed up my Chevy Chevette with my art supplies, some clothes, a few books, and $2,000. As any youth on the run from the tired east would do, I went west. I went to San Francisco.

Of course.

I was blazing a trail where countless trails had been blazed. The soil was worn. San Francisco had been played to death by youth, but that didn't matter to me. It still had subterranean renaissance in its imagery. It seemed the only city worth a damn in America. End of America. The edge of the new world aging.

It wasn't really my idea. I wasn't original or daring enough. It was Xeno Waterfield's idea. Xeno was an eccentric, college friend of mine. Xeno had been in a few of my art classes, but he wasn't much of a painter. He liked all forms of art. Writing, film, photography, sculpture, paint, whatever. He'd throw his hat into any ring of creativity. He was also a big fan of found art. He would scour the streets the night before garbage pick-up and find things to use for artistic endeavors. His whole existence was about creations.

"Start with nothing and end with something," Xeno would say. "It's that bloody simple."

Xeno headed west with a plan. He wanted to start a literary journal that celebrated all forms of his religion.

Creativity.

He had a title, Imagine Incarnate, a desktop publishing program, and all the mad cerebral energy circulating under his fiery, red hair. He convinced me to join him out west to get the flighty journal off the ground.

But he had bigger ideas than the journal. Imagine Incarnate was just the starting point of his fantasy. At the University of Rochester he had been part of an art house. A bunch of student artists and writers lived together communally and sold their art through local auctions. Occasionally, a local businessman would make a sizable bid on a young artist's future success. All the money was shared. Xeno called it artistic socialism. "Socialism went astray with politics," Xeno would say.

Xeno hoped the journal would create a group of artists committed to a new order, a path beyond resumé and capital building.

"Beyond money lay something far more enchanting. A real Oz, my friends. Let's open the doors."

These artists would start up a new, mature art house. An Art House West.

I thought the whole thing was delusion. Bunk. Xenology. At least, the post-journal fantasy. I had no interest in living with a group of artists. I would prefer to live with a group of auto mechanics. It'd be more real. Xeno was cut from a different cloth. He was born in Berkeley and moved east as an infant, but Berkeley circa 1966 never left his blood. He was certified Bezerkley, but a part of me that I refused to fully realize was a kindred spirit to this aspect of Xeno.

I was willing to buy into the journal. Xeno wanted my sketches and paintings to illustrate the first issue. I figured I had nothing to lose. It'd give me a little taste of minute fame. Maybe I'd meet some strange, perverse women who dug my paintings. I had a whole regular life in front of me. Why not detour a bit? Jump into now. I'd go west, let youth holler for a while, and return home and become an art teacher in my hometown. I'd teach the kids who hated spelling tests, just like I did. Spelling was the bane of my educational experience. Yes, life would get simple down the road, but for now, I was drawn to complexity and a little disorder. I'd throw some caution into the wind before the ordered simplicity would begin. I'd look back from the rocking chair and say, "Yeah, I had my reckless days. Sowed my spiritual and sexual oats." I would deal with regretted action rather than non-action. I'd heed Greeley's "Go west, young man."

I'd say I was gone west. Really gone.

Why not?

I drove out to California alone, as did Xeno. We figured we'd use the loneliness for a muse and arrive in San Francisco with materials for a first issue ready for publication. I didn't paint or sketch a lick the whole trip until I hit the California coast. It was an uneventful, lonely drive. I stopped only for gas, food, or cheap motels. I didn't meet any women, nor take in any sites. I just drove, ate, smoked cigarettes to kill the boredom, and slept. It would have made a good, avant-garde minimalist film. True minimalism. Nothing happened.

Once I hit San Diego though, I felt ready. Nothingness crept up on my being. The energy of nada can be potent. On the way up to San Francisco via route 1, I stopped along the wild, rugged coast. I sat on the edge of cliffs overlooking the mighty Pacific and painted small abstracts. I didn't paint landscapes or any Ansel Adams or John Muir fit for the office waiting room scenes. But the landscape motivated the abstracts into new directions for me. I had done all my painting in the coffin-like basement of my parents' home, university art studios, or dorm rooms. I never thought of unleashing the subconscious with nature all around. I lost myself on the edge of the Pacific. I found moments of intense serenity. I found moments of feral energy that seized me and put me into a trance. An internal slingshot had been pulled back all along the 3,000 mile drive and once I hit the end of the road, the slingshot sprang forward with savage velocity. I was producing paintings and sketches prolifically along Route 1. I stopped two or three times a day and painted for hours. Most importantly, I liked what was coming out. I felt the painter that most influenced me, Arshile Gorky, would have been impressed. Yes, one of these would be my "Liver is the Cock's Comb."

The trip from San Diego to San Francisco took longer than the trip across the country. It took me a week to reach the Pacific. It took me three weeks to reach The Golden Gate Bridge. I stopped immediately after crossing the bridge. I parked at a vista point. Tourists were everywhere. Japanese were filming every nuance of vacations they weren't actually taking. I walked down to the base of the majestic entrance. I painted my final coastal abstract right there with shutters snapping shut and Asians laughing and giggling.

I found Xeno's apartment and entered with more than a dozen creations. He was ecstatic. Red headed, burly, mad cap excitement. He was bouncing up and down with giddy fury about my paintings and his words that were to become the first issue.

"Dixson, my crazy friend, we're going to make this happen!"

After the initial fervor mellowed, I had to get settled. Xeno and I were in different situations. He had already been in San Francisco for a few months. He had a job and a girlfriend and was starting a life there. He'd met Hannah at a café. He was taking an acting class next door to this café and went in after every class for a coffee. Before long, she was spending every night at Xeno's small studio in the Richmond district. There were three of us there. Three of us in a very small place. Tight and compact. A lot of energy. A little space.

Xeno would go off to work every morning. I'd look for work and search for an apartment half-heartedly for part of the day. I didn't want to be alone. The loneliness of the 3,000 mile drive lingered. I wanted connection. No more paintings were coming, but the energy lingered. The other part of the day Hannah and I would work on the journal. We'd do rough drafts, and jot down ideas. Get something ready for Xeno to see after work. Most of the time, though, we just talked about our lives. The excitement and the unease.

I knew I was in deep when I saw her reading Anaïs Nin. Definite trouble. She had just seen the film, *Henry and June*, and got turned on to Nin's diaries. She had been keeping diaries for years. She was now a pious diarist. Xeno wanted to publish sections of the diaries, but she wasn't sure. They were honest, raw, and revealing as any diary should be. Xeno thought a pseudonym would take care of that. Hannah didn't think so.

"The words enter the universe regardless of the name," she told me.

"Well, that's probably what you secretly want anyway."

"Maybe so, but I want it secretly."

She wrote honestly about the incest of her childhood. She wrote about her father's sins. She wrote the insidious dreams that invaded her at night. She thought words would help pacify the past that just wouldn't leave her alone. It was all too personal for her to expose. She never read anything to me. She sometimes started to talk about what she wrote that day or the day before, but she'd always stop herself. For the first few sentences it was as if she were talking about another person and then suddenly her eyes would widen, and she'd realize she was talking about herself.

She had the momentary escape until the escape caught itself.

However, she loved to read Nin aloud to me. It appeased her need vicariously. We spent long afternoons in the Golden Gate Park reading to each other and talking and leaving the journal for another day.

"We have an opposite Henry and June thing going here," she'd say.

"Yeah, two men instead of two women. And we're all straight."

"So we think," she'd say.

I nodded.

"Do you feel a connection among the three of us?" she'd ask.

"Yes, I do."

"The two of us?"

"Yes."

"In what way?"

"I don't know, just a connection," I'd say.

"Did you get lonely driving here?"

"Extremely."

"Are you lonely now?"

"Not so much."

"Me neither."

Our flirtatious conversations went further every time. She started wearing lower-cut shirts with me. Bra straps were more visible. Occasionally, bra straps didn't exist. Sex games were on.

I was getting very attracted to Hannah.

I slept in the living room of the studio. Xeno had turned a walk-in closet into his bedroom. It was a big walk-in that could fit a double mattress. He had a milk crate stuffed with books and lamp on top of it. He had pictures of Emily Dickinson and Jerry Brown thumb tacked on the wall. "I come to San Francisco, Dixson, and I go into the closet." He had howled when I arrived.

I'd listen to Xeno and Hannah fucking from their closet bedroom. I knew I needed to find my own place and a job fast. I was going to lose control. I wanted her. I was jealous. I could feel the chemical pull between Hannah and me. So, could she. We would talk about it.

Fools.

"Why should we be scared about the feeling?" she'd ask

"Because it could lead to betrayal," I'd say.

"But the feeling itself is beautiful."

"Yes, it is."

"Why should we run from love?"

"Is it love?" I asked

"A form of love. It's pure. It's honest. I don't want to be afraid of true connections."

"I don't either. I feel strongly about you, but I love Xeno, too. Just differently, of course."

"Is it that different?" She asked with a wry smile. She was a provocateur. It excited me.

"It's different," I said.

She nodded.

"We're walking a scary line, Hannah."

"I don't know if it can be controlled. I love him too, you know," she said.

"Maybe destiny is linked to this whole thing. Maybe I came west to find you."

"Yeah, true love. Destiny, my dear Dixson."

We both laughed and then smiled at each other.

There was silence.

I finally found an apartment and a job at a bookstore. The apartment was down the street from Xeno and Hannah, but the bookstore was in Marin County. Some distance from the city would be good. Some distance from Hannah was vital. I believed the timing would slow our dangerous momentum. "I am in charge of the art books at Tamalpais Book and Coffee. Head of the art section for $6 an hour. I was going places, taking the American dream by the horns and wrestling it to the ground," I told Xeno and Hannah. We were planning a little party for my last night at the Xeno's. Hannah and I bought some wine and food. Xeno was at work and we decided to have some wine in the afternoon.

Mistake.

The conversation led into our attraction, of course. The wine propelled it further. We didn't want to let the momentum slow. We put it on the table. Expressed it candidly with the help of a jug of cheap red wine.

"What if we make love just one time?" I offered.

I knew I was walking off the edge. I saw the plank. It was right before my eyes.

She thought for a while. Then said, "We just keep it a secret between us. A secret for our friendship. A moment to remember for our friendship. Just one time. A moment to remember the momentum."

"Maybe, if we do it once, we'll calm this energy between us," I said.

Splash.

"It is too magnetic," Hannah said.

"Xeno senses it. He says it's palpable."

"He knows?"

"We talk about it. He knows we have a connection. He's not surprised."

"Is he wary of more?"

"No. He trusts us. I don't want to hurt him. He knows I love him."

"I love him too. No hurt."

"It's all about love," she said laughing.

"Love," I said.

"Yes, love."

"Yes."

"Love isn't a bad thing, ever," she said.

"It's all good. Love has to be good. What else is there?"

We were smiling at each other, playing the game. Sipping wine constantly.

"I can't think of anything else, Dixson."

"Everything is done to get, keep, or recover from love."

"We just have labels to distract us from the real reality of what we're doing."

"Yes, real reality and unreal reality. Like work," I said.

"Dinking."

"Money."

"Homes."

"Drugs."

"And Sex."

"Yes, definitely sex."

"The greatest distraction of them all."

"I wouldn't mind a distraction," I told her.

"Which one?" she asked.

"The greatest. Why settle for less?"

"A lot of reasons."

"Let's not think of those."

"Now?" she asked smiling and lifting her right shoulder slightly, coquettishly.

"It's building between us. Can you feel it?"

"Stupid question," she said.

"It will be our secret."

"Yes. Our little love secret. It will die with us. Birth and death just for us."

I smiled. I wasn't sure what to do. I felt guilt and desire with desire winning fast.

"Distract me," she said smiling.

Desire.

I kissed her. We let everything go. We kissed passionately. I took her shirt off and touched her breasts softly and then aggressively. I ran my tongue across them. She took my pants off. She caressed and kissed me as my pants fell to the floor. She grabbed and squeezed my ass hard while her mouth went along my chest and then stomach. I pulled her cotton skirt down to her ankles. She stepped out of it and pushed me down onto my makeshift bed of couch pillows in the corner of Xeno's studio. A bed fit for a dog. Fitting for me. She got on top of me and put it in her mouth. She licked and sucked me and then wet her hand and massaged the middle of her breasts with her moistened fingers. She sat on my thighs, locking them together. She slowly bent down and lowered herself until her breasts draped over me. She slid up and down with her hardened nipples gliding across my loins while her breasts enveloped me. I almost came, but she pulled off just in time for me to control it. She kissed me on my lips.

Softly.

Deeply.

"One time," she whispered. "Only once."

I didn't know what she meant. I didn't care. I wasn't thinking. All the blood flow was heading south. It took all cerebral activity with it.

She slid back down me. She used the back of her soft fingers to caress me slowly before she got me moist again with her tongue. Then, she got on top and eased me inside her. We made love slowly and gently. We were savoring the "one time." I held her ass and pushed myself inside her as deeply as possible. She rocked back and forth on me. She leaned forward and pushed down hard on my shoulders as I pushed hard into her. I moved my hands along her back and then around front putting one finger on each nipple. Pressing. Circling. They hardened again and she came. Her body rippled with soft screams and quivering muscles. As soon as she finished, I brought her down to me, wrapped my arms around her, held her tightly, put my feet against the wall and we did it again hard and fast.

We lay side by side on our backs breathing heavily. Sweat dripped down my brow and temples. I still tasted her. Smelled her. Senses were hyperactive. We didn't say anything for a while. We just held hands. I was looking at one of Xeno's found art exhibits. There was an old, white wall tire attached to the wall. Xeno had written "Aloha" in large letters with chalk on the top of the tire, below the threads and above the white stripe. Inside of the tire there was an ancient, beaten up, wooden cuckoo clock. An arrow was sticking into the opening of the clock where the bird would have popped out. A Hawaiian lei hung from the tip of the arrow. My mind wandered to the ceiling, where a solar system poster stared down at us. I looked at the planets observing their distance from the sun. Mercury, Venus, Earth. We're third. Mars, Jupiter. The sun was huge in the picture. I remember a science teacher saying that the sun was four and a half billion years old and that it would last for another five billion years. It would then turn into the White Dwarf.

"Our secret, right? One time." Hannah said with her head now resting on my chest.

"Yes, my erotic bird."

She laughed. "Ok, my happiest man alive."

"That's me. The happiest man alive. No hopes, all happiness."

"No resources," she said, following along.

"No, no resources. Just memories of experiences. The truest of resources."

"And now we can get over the mystery, happy man."

"You think so?" I asked her.

"You don't?"

"It was good. Real good. Maybe too good for just one visit," I said.

"Yeah, but…it would get ugly. Let's not ruin it. I want to treasure this. When I feel down and lonely, this will be a blanket. We keep it up, secretly screw behind Xeno's back, we'll get caught. Then it's all dark. I'll lose you and him. Everyone will lose everyone."

"Too much loss."

"We'll just tuck it away. This way it won't lose to time. It makes it precious. It will be our warm blanket on cold, lonely nights."

"The sun is old," I said.

We celebrated that night with Xeno. We didn't want to betray our friend. We were on some perverse path and wanted to taste deceit and dissolution. We wanted to break the rules. Test the teacher's will and boundaries. We crossed the line, but it meant nothing. I still wanted her very badly again. Our perverse pact wasn't going to last long. One time. Just once. An antidote to loneliness in the future, but it didn't recede into the past. It was all present and potent. I didn't want a warm blanket. I wanted her body. I wanted her on top of me. Great notion Hannah, but not this time. I was lonely now. Horny. Ready. The Animal House Angel and Devil on each soldier. Id was kicking superego's ass.

"Don't screw over Xeno."

"Screw Hannah."

"Think about the ramifications, the friendship."

"Think about being inside her. Gliding in and out."

"Think about the deceit."

"Even better sex with that."

We drank wine. We chatted. Xeno held Hannah's hand firmly all night. He was conscious of our connection. He even verbalized it because Xeno believed all expression was the path to Blake's great temple. Expression was sanctity. Holiness.

"I know you guys dig each other," he said. "I told Hannah that a while ago. I knew if she dug me, she would dig you. In fact, you guys are connected more in some ways. Dixson, you had more torture in youth than me. The alcohol, divorce, all that strife and stress. I didn't have it. Suburban apathy, but not the intensity. Your paintbrush rages across the canvas. You're releasing internal furies. You're like the Nolte character in that Scorsese film."

"*New York Stories*," I said. "I liked *Oedipus Wrecks*."

"So did I," Hannah said. "I Love Woody Allen and that's my favorite title, *Oedipus Wrecks*. It's all one big Oedipus Wreck..."

"Yeah, but the Nolte character, that's Dixson's painting. All raw and manic mad art. Hannah's the same way in her raw journal. Real pain. Art is an open door to all. She's blind. Room for all of us, though. You know, it's a funny thing these triangles. I was never good at geometry." He laughed hard. We did, too, but it was a stilted laugh. "I don't know. Can't even say the word I'm thinking of. I want to say every word right now all at once, not just one. You know me."

Xeno laughed from the depths of his big belly.

211

"It's all a hootenanny. I love that word. That's the word I want. Yeah, you guys got pain fueling you. Me, I don't have that. I just observe the madness of the earth with a squirt gun like that carnival game. Just trying to aim the water straight in clown's mouth and ring the bell above and knock some damn sense into the packed suburban sardines and sheep grazing blindly across life. Missing the drum beat beating right in their ears. Yup. But that's all right. Right honey? You love me, right? Doesn't matter the source of my void. You love all of me, right?"

"Of course, Xen," Hannah said, hugging him and burying her head in the nape of his big teddy bear neck.

"It's on the table, right?" he asked.

"Yes, sweetie," she said. "All over the table."

"Full house, right, baby?" Xeno said.

"We're a winning hand, my dear."

"You wouldn't do anything to hurt me anyway, my kindred spirit, would you?" Xeno asked me.

"No." I said. I wanted to crawl onto the doggie bed and hide under the pillows. The libido was limp. Superego took charge.

Xeno picked up the big, cheap jug of red and filled our glasses. "To the triumvirate of creations." We toasted. Xeno got up and went to the bathroom. We looked at each other.

Fuck the superego.

We both leapt at each other, kissing passionately, angrily. We stopped at the turn of the doorknob.

Xeno returned.

"What do you say we call it night? I got to get up early, and Dixson you got to get your ass out of here tomorrow. Give my sweet lady and me our space back."

My apartment was in Mill Valley. It's a posh little town just after Sausolito. Two towns after the Golden Gate Bridge. I got the apartment out there because that's where the bookstore was. I figured I'd rather commute into the city to work on the journal and hang out with Xeno and Hannah than commute to work everyday. I could walk to work where I lived.

The apartment was anything but posh. However, it suited my soul. I had one decent sized room. A room that would be a small living room in a middle class home. I had a futon on the floor, art supplies scattered about, milk crates for my socks and underwear. My clothes were neatly piled on newspapers in the corner. John Kennedy Toole's *Confederacy of Dunces* lay next to my mattress. The closets weren't big like at Xeno's place, so they functioned as closets. There were two. The kitchen was big enough for a two-person kitchen table. The bathroom was tight. My knees scraped the wall when I shit. The whole place was Lilliputian for me. I could feel the hair on my head touch the ceiling. I'm six foot five.

I'm quite an oxymoron for an Armenian. My Middle Eastern brethren are usually short and squat. Armenians in Armenia excel in weightlifting and Greco-Roman wrestling. When I used to go to church, I was always the tallest. I'm also quite thin for my size. One hundred ninety pounds, soaking wet. A big, lanky Armenian. Oxymoron. My final physically black sheep quality is my lack of hair. I'm the least hairy Armenian ever. I only need to shave twice a week. I barely have any body hair. Armenians are normally as hirsute as prehistoric man. Some of my uncles have a full coat of fur on their back. It's repulsive. I'm glad I'm not like that, but I'd like to be somewhere in the middle. A decent 5 o'clock shadow, some chest hair. A little masculinity. A little balance. Balance was something clearly missing in my life at that point in many ways.

I sat at the kitchen table a few days after moving in and wrote a long letter to Hannah. I told her I truly loved her and maybe someday we could be together, but I valued Xeno's friendship so much, too. We got caught up in our little Henry and June thing, but it wasn't us. We weren't perverse enough. We just got consumed in an energy spiral and we twirled downward. My moving out will give us some space. Let's do what you said. Hold onto its beauty before it turns ugly. Who knows the future? A few days later, when we got together for a journal session, she told me she loved the letter. She agreed. It was done. We stopped the madness short. No one gets hurt.

I agreed, but I was hurting. Little internal soldiers were taking formation, surrounding the heart and adding reinforcements daily. The trenches were wide and deep. The numbers proliferated daily. They were far superior to me, outflanking my thoughts, while I couldn't get behind enemy lines. I missed her and wanted her and I was damn lonely out in Mill Valley thinking about Hannah and Xeno together and me across the Golden Gate.

Alone. Pathetic.

When you can't win the war, you learn to exist with it.

I bought a used black and white TV and put it on top of the fridge so I could watch Giants or A's games while I ate. Eating was the loneliest time. The TV was a good distraction. Not as good as Hannah, but not as dangerous.

So, I spent a lot of time in my apartment during the post-Henry and June days. Just as it had during all the cataclysmic times of my life, art became sanctuary. I spent most of the mornings on my porch working on the sketches I had done along Route 1. I was turning the sketches into paintings. I had painted the small canvases right in the moment. But I'd also done sketches of larger, Pollock-style canvases. I attached a canvas to the outside of my apartment and worked right on the porch. I wanted to keep the outside, natural vibe going. I never wanted paint inside again. My upstairs neighbors thought nothing of my artistic activity. I was in the San Francisco orbit. Here, everyone's aloft.

I loved painting with the fog rolling overhead across the Marin hills and into the mad city. I think the fog carried with it some mystical molecules of the San Francisco dream. The whole city's history was hunger and want. Gold. Art. Drugs. Cults. The city screamed to get out of the American strait jacket.

I felt the fog inspired me. I believed it flowed into each stroke. It rolled magically and ethereally overhead every morning. When I slid into true dreamy delusion, I likened the process to Van Gogh and the Arles sunshine.

When the fog really penetrated, I even perversely hoped an institution loomed in the dark horizon. A place to go. A place to reinstall boundaries and frame this avalanche of freedom. Fill in the crevices of invisibles chasms.

Sometimes, it was just too damn much. But that was wishful thinking. I just wasn't mad enough. The fissure was narrow enough to get through the night. It was a gentle madness. My paintings reflected it. They were wishfully mad. Posing. Hoping for agony, but expressing anyone's pain. Despite Xeno's analysis, I didn't see the rage on the canvas. Perhaps, I was just too immersed in it to see any of the truth I was trying to express.

The aesthetic Catch-22.

I figured I'd stay as long as it took me to finish the big abstracts. If Xeno and I got the journal going, I'd stay longer. If not, I'd head home. Move back in with my grandfather and start a normal life.

Balance. Reality.

No more fog.

I could feel the costume shrinking on me.

Meanwhile, I kept my distance from Xeno and Hannah. The longer I stayed away, the more my desperate need for Hannah faded. The soldiers retreated. It didn't have legs. It wasn't real. We were just another of the distractions we talked about. I kept convincing myself it wasn't love, just the alchemy of time, place, and need. The alchemy of loneliness and common demons. What was real was Xeno and me. We were true friends. Kindred spirits. When he asked me why I was such a stranger these days, I hid behind the art. I kept telling Xeno to get the nuts and bolts part of publication down while I finished my painting. I assured him I was onto something. He hooted and howled with joy over my artistic commitment. He was happy, while I was dealing with internal waves of disgust and self-hatred. I didn't like what Hannah and I did. I didn't like that the urge and energy still lingered. Sometimes, when that urge went beyond lingering and the alchemy found the right potion, I tried to convince myself that we were just in the throes of youth and experience. It wasn't a big deal. Sex is just sex and society has walled us into superficial boundaries preventing physical expression. Beyond Good and Evil. If Nietzche could proffer it, who was I not to dance with it? The sex Hannah and I flirted with was just our expression of the moment. It had nothing to do with Xeno. Hannah and I

215

had a pact. If no one knew, no one would get hurt. I worked
with all these ideas and California Aquarian sophistries from
time to time. Bought into them for a few fleeting here and
theres. Digested the fog. Let it invade the blood flow.

But most of the time I just felt like an asshole.

Mostly I felt the reality of it. California is one giant
landmass of concocted, cockeyed reality. The Lost Horizon
hotel.

During these lonely couple of weeks work helped.
I worked from 2 p.m. to 10 at night. After painting the
mornings away, I needed to fill my coffee drenched stomach
and relax uprooted spirits. I'd head for lunch at a nearby
Mexican restaurant. I'd start with a Margarita on the rocks
with extra salt on the rim. Then, I'd eat rice, refried beans,
carne asada, and wash it down with a Dos Equis almost
everyday. There was comfort in the creation of habit. I'd let
go of the rush of now and newness. I'd taken that too far.
Hurt myself. Almost hurt others. Maturity through
mistakes. I felt it coming.

After lunch, I'd go downtown. The bookstore was
in the center of Mill Valley. It was half bookstore and half
café. That was very fortunate. The bookstore alone would
have been dull and slow. Caged in by dead adventures. The
café added energy and young beautiful women. I spent some
of my time in the art section, organizing and researching new
books to give the section more breadth. This didn't take
long. Most of the time I just read about artists. I read entire
biographies on Picasso, Gorky, De Kooning, and Kahlo. As
for women, my self-loathing wanted me to be lonely. There
were many attractive women, but I made no attempts to flirt
with any of them. They responded similarly. I figured the
loneliness was my penance. Perhaps, I just feared more
rejection at this moment.

Just simple ego fears.

I worked and hid in the art section for the first half
of my shift. At six o'clock the manager and other clerks
went home. Maggie Gaines worked the rest of the shift with
me. We alternated between taking breaks and working the
counter until about nine. I'd go out back and eat free food

from the café and read the evening away. For the last hour we were at the counter together before closing up.

There was a large square behind the café. There were tables for people to drink coffee and have some light food. Beyond the tables, the patio extended into a social gathering spot for Mill Valley folk. Aging hippies kicked around talking and playing chess. Teenagers smoked and flirted with each other. Pre-teens had a section for skateboarding. Mill Valley's elites discussed business or where to eat dinner that night. It was a lively scene. I enjoyed the diverse energy, the sunshine, the varying voices. I was all alone, but I was free. I felt good at work. I wanted to take in the freedom without fearing it. Something good would come from that. Something bad would come from running.

Karma.

Progress.

My co-worker Maggie was quintessential Northern California. She was a female Xeno. Life is altogether too ironic at times. There's got to be some celestial connect the dots at work. The universe had to be the grand master puppeteer. She was a poet and her live-in boyfriend was a painter/surfer. She was the embodiment of the fog. She was Imagine Incarnate. I wanted to tell Xeno I had a member for his mad club. She would contribute to the journal and probably hop on board the dreamy dream of his art house. Telling Xeno would have to wait.

For now, Maggie was good distraction for me.

Once a week, I would set up a podium and microphone for a reading in the café. Maggie would set up the speaker's books at the counter and she would introduce the writer. She didn't like this part of her job. While the writer spoke, she would try to convince me to join her distraction.

"Dixson, why don't you bring your paintings Sunday night?" she'd ask.

"They're not ready."

"So what. This isn't a reading. It's friends sharing creativity."

"I don't know."

"What don't you know?"

217

"A lot."

"How long are we going in riddles?" she asked, smiling. Maggie was always upbeat even when she was frustrated during readings.

"I like riddles," I said.

"So do I."

"You know any?"

"No. Just you."

"I'm no riddle. I'm transparent."

"True. Maybe not a riddle, just ridiculous," she said.

"Just like everyone in this floating state."

"I'd rather float than sink." Maggie hit my shoulder. "Hey, I'm serious. It'll do you some good. You've been kind of moping. You could stand to float a little. Loosen that long body of yours. Put a dent in the Reichian armor."

"Don't tell me you built an Orgone Box."

"I should and put your tight, east coast ass in there."

I laughed and she winked at me. "Maybe you should. I don't know. It's a transition to California thing. You guys are a strange lot here. It takes time to get off the ground."

"Yeah, you're way too grounded."

I shook my head, dumbfounded. "That's what I love about this place. Here, I'm grounded, back east I'm a fruit loop."

"You know, you talk like Rocky Balboa."

I laughed.

"Yo Paulie," she said, imitating Stallone. "I love the part when he tells Adrian he doesn't have a phone, but he can call her brother. Then he screams out the window, 'Yo, Paulie, your sister's with me. She's fine. I'll call ya later.'"

"Great scene," I said.

"So. What do you say?"

"Who's coming this week?"

"My boyfriend completed a new painting. He's showing that. Phyllis says she's coming, but she usually doesn't show up. She thinks she's too good for us. She's got the Columbia MFA and New York agent and novel that might be picked up by the big boys. She thinks she should be reading at the podium not hunkering down with us salt of the earth artists. So, she's always a question mark. I don't know, a few others. What does it matter?"

"Just curious."

"You know the point is to breathe life into art. It doesn't have to be a lonely activity. And it doesn't have to be a business deal like Phyllis's writing. It can be down to earth, even in the kooky, flighty Bay Area. It's about the group anyway. Maintaining a family of friends. A coterie. Real families being so screwed up, an art family can help. There's a real connection. More real than blood. Creativity is better than blood. I mean, why else did you come out here?"

"What do you mean?"

"I mean, why did you come here? Family, right? Yours had to be messy or you wouldn't be here."

"You're oversimplifying it."

"No, you're overcomplicating it. I never met an east coast émigré out here who didn't have a messy wake."

"I think I'd be here either way. Maybe not. Whatever."

"Sweetie, truth unravels over time. Can't rush time."

"Maggie, when you going to get rid of surfer guy?"

"Can't rush time, Dixson. Besides, Dixson you don't want me that way. You want a sister. I'd say mother, but I don't want to age myself. Just come Sunday night. You'll start to get what you want."

"We'll see."

After about two weeks, there was a knock on my door around midnight. I was up. I was reading in bed. I was reading an Arshile Gorky biography. It was terribly depressing. He was shitting into a bag attached to the side of his abdomen. He had rectal cancer. His art was ignored. He was losing his mind and beating his wife. I believe it would end with him hanging in the foyer, his death greeted by his wife and kids. Christ, what damage done, handed down, generation to doomed generation? Why was I reading this? I should have been reading Louis L'Amour or Archie comics or something.

I answered the door.

"Fuck you!" Xeno said.

"What?" I said stupidly.

"You're kidding me, right."

"About what?"

"That you don't know what I'm talking about. You shouldn't be surprised, asshole. You have the audacity to say 'what?' Fuck you, Asshole!"

"No. I mean, I know what you mean. It was an instinctual answer to a midnight fuck you."

"Why?"

"It's a surprise."

"No, no, follow me here, shithead, why did you do it?"

"I don't have a good answer."

"Of course, there is no good answer. Give me a bad one. It's your only choice."

I'd actually had this one running through my twisted brain lately.

"A brief chemical attraction that got the better of us."

He pondered it for a few moments. His face was crimson and hands were clenched, his knuckles whitening from the excessively tightened fist.

"Dixson, you did a lot of horrific damage."

"I know. Let's talk about it," I said. "Let's lay the cards out."

"You already laid the cards. Nice choice of words. Bastard! Girlfriend fucking bastard! There's nothing you can say. You know, the first week I wanted to come over with a baseball bat and beat the living shit out of you."

I nodded.

"Hannah stopped me. She said she was just as much to blame. She said it was some temporary madness. A moment. Same asshole shit you just said. She had no feelings for you then. Has none now. Do you hear that?"

"Yes. It was a mistake. I'm just glad we didn't follow through."

"You followed through pretty fucking good."

"Yeah, but not completely."

"What the hell do you mean? Fucking my girlfriend is not following through. Is that your justification, you sick bastard?"

"No, Xeno, no. It's coming out wrong, but I guess the only thing I can take as consolation is that we didn't sneak into hotels and screw for weeks. That I didn't steal her from you. Instead—"

"You're a hero. Shut the hell up! So you let me have my girlfriend after you screwed her. Can you actually hear yourself? Can you picture in your insane brain what you've done? What the hell is wrong with you? What happened to you?!"

"That's not what I meant. I mean…Forget it. I know she loves you. I didn't mean anything I said, did, or am saying. I don't know what I mean. I deserve the anger. I deserve the baseball bat."

"Oh, poor Armenian victim. Woe is you."

"I'm sorry, Xeno."

"Consequences, Dixson."

"I know."

"Every action has a consequence. Next time think before you destroy!"

I nodded. My heart was beating rapidly and my mouth and spirit desiccate. I couldn't believe what I had done.

"We're leaving. We're going to Oregon. This was a sign. A giant, screaming red flag of a sign. We need to get out of this insane city. We need distance from you and San Francisco."

I nodded.

"You know, and you knew, she has giant emotional issues. Deep childhood shit. You fucking knew that. Incest and painful shit. She has trouble with boundaries with friends 'cause her family caved in on her as a goddamn kid. Her world crumbled and she's just repeating the same perverse drama of her crumbled childhood. You're just a role in a sad play and you played it perfectly. This happened before in her last relationship. She told me all about it. It has nothing to do with you. There was no fucking attraction between you two. She has no feelings for you. You got

221

that! You are anybody that would have been in that place. You are nothing. Just the male at the moment."

"Yeah." I said.

"You just filled a fucking role from her past pain. You were a pawn to her psychic pain. You got it! We're going away and she's going back into therapy. I'm going into therapy. We are. I've forgiven her. Not you, Dixson! Never!!"

Xeno turned to leave.

Stupidly I said, "And the journal?"

"It's dead. Like our friendship. Fucking dead! Got it! You murdered it just to get your dick wet. Sorry ass bastard. You are out of my foxhole forever. No trust. Hannah and I will survive. I hope you crash and burn!"

I was devastated. I stayed in for a while simultaneously feeling sorry for myself and hating myself. I took some days off from work. Eventually, I convinced myself that it was good that Xeno unloaded on me. He snapped me out of a numbness that I'd covered myself in. Protection. Perverse protection. I needed cataclysm. I had fallen into spiritual hypoplasia. I think I wanted it. Sought it. What we do we must seek on deep, unseen levels. Their relationship was intact. They were going forward.

I would too.

In the meantime, I felt an aloneness I had never felt before. An abandonment. Perhaps, I had felt it before when the family had splintered so often, but each period of aloneness in life must carry all the previous pains into the present. Makes it exponentially more potent. A storm gathering wind and rain along the way until it strikes with full fury. The moment is never truly the moment, but a vicious convergence of many.

I knew I would survive. It was my modus operandi. Seek disaster and seek solution. I believed this disaster would prevent me from falling into another one.

The last drink for the alcoholic.

The last line of coke.

The last break up.

Foolish hubris.

I found faith in the knowledge that in time things would get better. I started taking some yoga classes. I visited an herbal store and got some relaxation herbal remedies; Kava, Valerium, some type of flower oil that you put on your tongue. San Francisco alive. I stopped reading biographies of mad, deeply tortured artists. I began reading some Buddhism. Tao. My heart eventually stopped trying to crash through its ribbed cage. The aloneness went from typhoon to steady winds.

Manageable.

Of course, all the lonely, individual methods could never truly work. We need others or the walls close in. Maggie was there for me. Maggie was very impressed with my method of self-therapy. She was unforgettably supportive through the process.

She read my palm, did my astrological chart, showed me the ridiculous I Ching. I still don't understand that. Sticks falling into patterns and answers. Ridiculous. Buddhism was already a stretch. I even started to laugh.

At myself.

"Dixson, my friend, you're turning Californian." she would say.

"Just a temporary fix, my dear."

"Maybe, this was all about your attraction to Xeno."

"Here we go. Give me your theory, Anna Freud."

"It's obvious. Hannah was just your way of sleeping with Xeno."

"Hmmm. Only one problem."

"What?" She was smiling.

"I'm not attracted to big, burly red heads," I said.

"Not physically."

"Therefore, it's not sexual."

"Sexuality is only connected to physical appearance? Dixson darling, you surprise me."

"Well, be surprised."

"Part of you is gay. Does that bother you so much?"

"Maggie, my dear, I have come to the conclusion that all of life is not gay, but gray. One mass of chaos theory, clouds, mysteries, sphinxes, riddles, questions, stalemate chess games."

"I get the point. There is none."

"Precisely, except for one."

"And that is."

"I love women. Just about the only thing I'm certain."

"Well, Dixson, I'm glad you've got something straight."

I stayed in California through the summer. In total I lasted about four months. I was getting more peaceful and my aloneness was getting less poignant. It was becoming everyday, existential loneliness. Regular. Everyone's. I could breathe. I did miss Xeno and Hannah, but I knew all I could do to fix my deviance was stay away.

When I wasn't missing them or thinking of the tragic flow that I let myself get pulled into, I saw myself as a dime-a-dozen San Francisco transient. Just another runaway youth sipping some silly western, spiritual mirage. Clueless. Nevertheless, I had an east coast work ethic ingrained. I needed to show something for this venture. I worked hard on the paintings. I did turn all the sketches into completed works. I had quite a few. I didn't know what the hell to do with them, but I was happy about having them, clichéd youth or not. The mirage had moments of true delusion. We must accumulate some form of currency. Some forum. I liked them on a Maggie Gaines level. Art for art's sake. Creativity as religion. New prayer.

Xeno's level, too.

Their construction helped offset the destruction of a friendship. I gladly would have traded them in for the missteps with Hannah. But I had a feeling something good would come from them. I don't know why. The negative energy just got tired and heeded to a positive flow.

When I was completely done with the collection, which I called *Gone West*, I was done with San Francisco. I had come west to create my own moment in time as if I'd never have that possibility again. I did it. I said my goodbyes. I would really miss Maggie, but it was time to go. I had a true family of one in Providence. It was time to return home to the east. My grandfather needed me.

I needed him.

I put the *Gone West* collection in my hatchback and drove east early one September morning. I didn't paint or sketch at all during the trip. I saw America like a good tourist.

Art was finished for me. The escape was over. It was time to try life.

I was just another California casualty.

I lived in North Providence with my grandfather. I didn't have much of a relationship with my parents after their divorce. I saw them once in a while, but my father had moved to New York years back and had a new family. He kept in touch. My mother lived in New Hampshire in the house I grew up in. I wasn't close to my siblings at all. We talked at holidays and exchanged gifts.

My grandfather was a different story. We were close. I admired him more than anyone in the world. I'd been living with him since I was fifteen when the family finally, officially, thankfully disintegrated. Roles and repressions eventually implode. When they did, I told my mother I wanted out. My grandmother had recently passed away. My grandfather was in his late eighties. We didn't know his exact age. I reasoned he needed me as much as I needed him, but that wasn't true. He was in great shape, physically and mentally.

I was the mess stumbling along erratic rhythms, seeking large canvases with dark colors.

Kegham, my grandfather, lived through the Armenian genocide of 1915. His life put my self-absorbed plight in its proper perspective. Patriarchal madness didn't parallel national slaughter. He often told stories of his escape. The stories varied over the years and he got creative with them.

He was from a village named Van. The Vanetsis were known for their toughness and unwillingness to go down without a monumental fight. He said he had witnessed his father hold off attacking Turks with kitchen utensils. When word spread that the Turks were going to send in a sizable army to exterminate the stubborn Vanetsis,

Kegham's father sent him on the run to an orphanage near Russia.

Young Kegham left, but decided to turn back and help his father. He returned during the carnage. As he searched for his father, he was bayoneted by a Turk. He was injured, but conscious. He crawled into a pile of dead bodies and hid beneath the carcasses. His life instinct somehow allowed him to remain silent as the Turks reviewed the pile of death for any living Armenians. He could hear the sounds of bayonets puncturing skin and organs and slicing the bones of barely breathing or already dead bodies.

They didn't find Kegham. He was deep beneath the death.

He eventually passed out from the horror and stench of the carcasses. A gypsy woman, who was looking for any remaining jewelry, valuables, or clothing, came across Kegham. She rescued my grandfather and took care of him for weeks.

She told him the only way for him to survive was to leave. Even though they stayed in the remote nether regions of Armenia, he would be found. She told him that she had heard about a new government in Russia that would save the poor. Perhaps, he could find sanctuary there.

During his journey to Bolshevik Russia, Kegham sneaked onto a farm in the middle of the night. He was picking and eating grapes as fast as he could. He was caught by the owner of the farm and put to work to pay off the grapes. He worked so hard that the owner took him in. Kegham got a room to sleep in and meals in exchange for work. He did this for a couple of years.

Kegham knew of an uncle that had escaped to America prior to the genocide. Eventually, the owner of the farm was able to make contact with this uncle. The uncle wired money to Kegham to pay for the passage. He boarded a ship, sailed to Tiflis, Marseilles and then arrived in America in about 1921. He was a teenager. Dates and ages are all approximate. He doesn't even know his birthday.

It wasn't a priority.

My grandfather gave me balance. He had lived through death and still smiled his way through life. He was

226

Buddhist without even knowing what Buddhism was. The best kind. Authentic. The messy, selfish world of my parents was offset by Kegham's simple life. He was married to my grandmother for fifty loyal years. Life resembled what normal might be. They ate meals together. They watched the news. She read and sewed. She handled the money because he couldn't read. My grandmother had finished 6th grade and was a voracious reader of mysteries and romance novels. No heavy literary artifice. Just damn good stories. He made the money. She managed it. They discussed all the decisions.

Normal.

However, every version has an alternate, especially those versions glorified by those who seek to frame a story to their needs. I needed to see Kegham in a certain light. I refused to see him in any other way. Color my glasses rose, but don't take them off.

My grandfather had two children. My mother and her older brother, Haig. Haig liked to set the record straight about his father. He didn't visit much and when he did he usually had conversations with me while my grandfather occupied space in the room. I tried to include Kegham in our talks, but Haig focused on exclusion. It was awkward.

During summer breaks from college, when my grandfather wasn't home and Haig popped in, we would often have conversations about him. We didn't have these conversations when I was in high school. Apparently, Haig thought I wasn't old enough at that time. During the college years, though, he didn't hold anything back. The conversations were usually the same. Haig would attack. I would defend.

"So how's it going living with my father?" Haig would say, smoking a Lucky Strike.

"Going well. Peaceful. No chaos. He lets me do what I want."

"Funny. He didn't let me. He used to drag me to the races with him all the time."

"What do you mean all the time? He was working so much."

"At night. I spent my teenage years at the dog track. Can you believe that? He couldn't read, so he had me read

227

the racing forms to him. I thought it was fun at the time. Fun comes back to haunt sometimes. He's a lot more selfish than you think."

"I don't see it that way, Uncle Haig."

"Of course, you don't. Do you know the garage door story?"

"You've told me."

"Your grandmother was complaining to him to fix the garage door. It was jammed and wouldn't open and winter was coming. So what did my dad do? He went to the garage and ripped the garage door off its hinges. He came back in and told my mother, 'Now you can park the car in the garage.' We had no garage door the rest of the time we lived on Chauncy Street, unless you count the large piece of wood with broken hinges leaning up against the side of the garage."

"It's kind of funny."

"Now, it is. You know why he had no time to fix the garage or no money to pay someone."

"Gambling." I said.

"Dogs and horses were his life. His family was always secondary."

"I know."

"Your grandmother carried the family on her shoulders. He doesn't deserve the pedestal you put him on."

"It's my pedestal, Haig."

"He doesn't deserve it."

"Can we talk about something else? Why are you dumping all this shit on me? I have a different relationship. He's been a savior to me. You ought to cut him some slack. You weren't a perfect son, I imagine."

"I tried, but I didn't have odds next to my name."

"You ought to treat him better. You just ignore him. Do you enjoy the revenge as he's in his eighties?"

"I don't disrespect him."

"You should just make some small talk once in a while."

"And you treat your parents well? You reach out to your father?"

"Different situation. Whatever, let's talk about something else."

"I'm just setting the record straight, Dixson. You don't have a father that can't even read or write. An illiterate with all the services in this country. It's a shame. You'd think he'd have gone to school instead of the races. What does he do all day besides look at the numbers of the racing pages? What kind of life is that?"

It was true about the racing. However, it didn't bother me like it did Uncle Haig. I couldn't understand his bitterness and he couldn't understand my peace. Human walls. In fact, I enjoyed my grandfather's hobby. I'd read the horse's weights, gender, jockey, and recent record before the night's race. He had some system that would pick a winner and we'd watch the races on cable TV to see how he did. We'd figure out how much he would have won or lost. Amazingly, he seemed to win very often. I'd also take him to the track once every week or two. He had a connection at the track that would call him and give him a tip or two. Whenever we got the call, I'd take him. He used to go a lot to the track like Haig said, but that had changed after my grandmother died. He was worried about his money without her. He always knew she would make sure they had enough money. Without her, he was more careful. Sometimes, when I suggested we go to the track without a tip, he would point to the sky and say, "Frida's watching."

When I got back home, I spent a couple weeks decompressing from the long drive and the experiences of my western days. I watched Red Sox games and the races with him. He used his system and we checked the results imagining how much he would have won or lost. We went to the track a couple of times. He hadn't gone once during the four months I was gone. The first time we went we didn't have a tip. He pointed skyward and, "Sorry Frida, it's been a while." Heavenly invocations aside, time with my grandfather always grounded me. I digested my time west, my mistakes, the drama and damage of it all while being in his routine. He never changed a thing. Instant coffee, cigarettes, two eggs and toast for breakfast, ham sandwich for lunch and dinner at the church with other older Armenians. He had no use for church unless it offered food.

229

Life in his steady, status quo orbit was just what I needed. He was the flip side of California. California was just the flip side. One giant lost soul of a state.

It was September and I was too late to start a graduate program in education, but I went to the University of Rhode Island and applied for an education degree with a focus on teaching art. I considered going for an MFA with a concentration in education, but I decided to put art on the periphery rather than the center. Art was trouble. I had bad memories associated with creativity. My western tryst of deceit left a bad taste in my mouth about art. My temporary philosophy of regretting what you did rather than didn't do was finished. I had had a momentary, Rimbaudian derangement of the senses. Being home with my grandfather would arrange the senses normal. I put the California paintings in the basement. The basement was their origin. I used paint and sketch myself into an exit from the lacerating screams from above. The paintings were home, but this time tranquility was above. I covered them with some old sheets. Art was on hold for me. The best laid plans...

I got an internship through URI as an assistant teacher at an elementary school. Every week I had to go to URI to fill out some paper work about the internship and I'd also check on upcoming spring semester classes. While I was in the Art department one October afternoon, about four weeks after returning East, I saw an interesting advertisement crammed in amidst many ads. It was partially hidden, but I pulled it into light.

CEREBELLUM
7:30 PM
OCTOBER 30
COME SEE THE WORKS OF THE NEWEST
AMERICAN ART MOVEMENT UNRAVELED
NEW ARTISTS STILL NEEDED

There was a phone number listed. I thought about it for a while as I took the train home. I had put the *Gone West* collection to rest, but apparently it wouldn't die easily in my mind. The basement, the sheets, hiding it wasn't enough. It still lingered internally. It was no easy escape from the escape of art. It teased and whispered. Proffered grand horizons and infinite eternities. Extended the tiny orbit of one. In an instant the pendulum that had steadied began to swing.

Life simply seemed insufficient without it.

I got home and immediately dialed the number.

"Hello."

"Yes, Hi. I'm calling in response to the ad for new artists that was posted at URI."

"Good, good. Yes. Who are you?" the voice said.

"Dixson Naturian."

"Who's that?"

"Me."

"Good, good. I mean who's me or rather who's you? What's behind the name?"

"What do you want to know?"

"Are you an artist?"

"I have some paintings."

"Then you are an artist. Don't hide. Tell me more."

"I traveled the California coast this year. I painted a series of abstracts along the way from San Diego to San Francisco."

"Abstracts. Hmmmm. In what vein?"

"Gorky, Johns. Colorful drips and—"

"And psychic automatism. Hmmm, kind of a throwback style, a bit dead and dated, but I've always loved the first half of the century dream of culling the subconscious into art. Yes, good ole fashion Andre Breton with a paintbrush. Better than that Campbell soup detour in the 60's. Warhol screwed up the flow. They just acquiesced. Joined the game. No, no. Gorky, Pollock, they were fighters. Vigilantes. Yes, yes, but, well, all our stuff is quite modern, post-modern, post post-modern, but this could propel the movement with an homage to its once radical origins. We owe a debt to Freud's artistic sons. Yes. Good. Good."

"So?" I stopped not knowing what to say.

"What's the name again?"

"Dixson."

"Dixson what?"

"Naturian."

"You're Armenian?"

"Yes."

"Gorky was too. Yes, you Armenians are tremendous folk. Caucus madmen. You'd bring an ancient, viable will to the evenings. Armenians are survivors. Rubber bands. Like Jews. Never give in to the death instinct, but flirt with it. Juggling thanatos and eros and feeding off the tension. Born artists. Bards or businessmen, but nothing in between. Good, good. Bring your work to my place."

"When?" I asked.

"Now, of course, we don't have time. Why wait? Waiting is a sin. I hate waiting almost as much as I hate time. Right bloody now," he said, in a really bad British accent.

"Ok."

He gave me the address and hung up.

I went into the basement and exhumed the covered paintings. I put them in the back of the car like I had 3,000 miles away and two months ago. I headed to North Providence where this guy lived. I never got his name.

He lived in a rather seedy part of the city. There were several spas that were really Thai massage sex shops along the strip where he lived. His apartment was just across the street from a nondescript building that had 'spa' written in small, red electric lights. There was a pawnshop nearby and a decaying steakhouse next door to his building.

I rang the buzzer.

"Mr. Naturian?"

"Yes."

A buzzer sounded and I entered through the big, metal door that was painted maroon, but was now chipped and cracking. It was an old warehouse. It looked like a printing press at some point. There were old printing machines. There were other machines that I didn't recognize cluttering a giant room.

"Over here," I heard from the back of the room. I looked up and saw a loft in the rear of the room behind the

232

machines. There was a ladder made of wood that led to the loft whose floor was also made of wood. I climbed up.

It was a big loft overlooking the aging warehouse. There was a kitchen, a large bed, couches, a TV, a stereo, all the necessities without any separation. Everything had an area, but there were no rooms. Makeshift Manhattan art loft in North Providence. In the far right corner there was a heavy velvet curtain that must have hidden the toilet and shower. It was the only area of privacy.

"No walls." He said reading my mind from a swivel chair in front of his large, paper-scattered desk.

"I noticed."

"I hate walls. All kinds. The regular, but most of all the invisible ones. Still can't rid myself of those, but that's a discourse for another day. I digress, especially during digressions. They beget each other like Genesis. Everyone begets everything. Whole lot of begetting in the old days." He stood up and walked towards me.

He was short and rotund with disheveled, light brown hair. He had on an oversized beige sports, covering a wrinkled, white collared shirt, and baggy black khakis held too high above his ankles by maroon suspenders. It was a mismatched, unhip zoot suit. He put his hand forth to shake and I gripped his big, fleshy, sweaty paw. My hand disappeared within his, but he had barely any grip. He just effeminately enveloped me like a giant, thick cloth draped over my hand.

"My father owned this place. He was a lithographer. My whole family worked here. We had a successful business until lithography went by the wayside. Then my father built this loft and we all moved in so we could sell our house. Soon after, he had a heart attack and my mother died of a cardiac disease. Both before 55."

He looked at my eyes briefly and then looked away.

"I'm 45. The clock's ticking."

I didn't know what to say except for an assortment of bullshit clichés. I chose one. "You'll outlive them."

"No, I like my curse. It's a good curse. Impending death breeds life. I'm going to live the next ten years like a hundred. Lots of living. Lots of plank walking, you know.

No fears. No planning ahead. Just great leaps, lunar leaps, not earthly steps. Life without the constraints of faith."

I nodded to provide a response during the silence.

He pounded his chest on the heart side with his fist.

"Like Sammy Sosa. I like when athletes do that. It's big now. They pound their heart to tell themselves their heart got them to gladiator level. I'm not so keen on the pointing skyward to God for every little success. He hit the home run, not God, but hell, God's pretty tempting when you start out dirt poor in the Third World and end up larger than life in the kingdom of America, but that's another story. Lots of stories, but let's focus on ours. Focus. We're going to shake the kingdom a little. A few ripples in the moat. Maybe a wave. Topple the castle. Yeah, a big wave. Tremors. Earthquakes." He opened his eyes wide and made extended eye contact with me for the first time. "Cerebellum."

I must have looked incredulous.

"The reason you're here. The art movement. The next seminal movement in art that will be studied for years to come, just like your Andre Breton stuff. Cerebellum's modern sails need the winds of surrealism. The legacy of Gorky. You know I knew something was missing from the show and then you called. I love the destiny of it. The chance, the randomness. The surrealism."

"Gorky wasn't really a surrealist," I said.

"Everyone's a surrealist."

"You haven't even seen my stuff."

"All the better. We leave it to fate. I don't want to see it. Less thought, more trust."

"I have them in my car."

"No, no, no. I don't want to see it. We put it in on instinct. Like a book with no words in it. No, no. I don't mean that. Like a novel manicured and formulaically written like all of them now. The dreaded MFA novel. Then we take the words and throw them up like confetti and wherever they land is the new novel. The real novel. The inner truth exposed. Chaos theory realized. I'd rather read confetti, than the nicely constructed lies posing as art today. The written word must be exhumed."

234

As he babbled on, I was thinking how San Francisco suddenly seemed mundane. I had to come home to find some veritable madness.

"You know, I really liked Louis Aragon. *The Defense of Infinity*. What a title! What a book. Hasn't been translated 'cause the New World couldn't handle it. We have yet to defend infinity and that is what we all need to achieve. Aragon doesn't get much credit, but he was the true surrealist. Madly visionary. I think he succumbed to the bourgeois impulse, though. He lost it and went normal. Should have stayed so-called lost, which of course, is found."

"Never heard of him."

"What kind of surrealist are you?"

"I'm not."

"What?"

"I never said I was. You did. I like the abstract expressionists. My grandmother had some Gorky prints. Got me hooked on that style early on. I liked Johns and Pollock, but I'm no expert."

"They're all scions of the surrealists."

"Like us," I said smiling.

"Yes, now you get it. Everyone's a surrealist. Don't care much for Pollock, though. Wannabe eccentric and a mean chap. I'll take De Kooning anyday, both husband and wife. You want some coffee? Wine? Beer?"

"Coffee sounds good."

He had a pot already brewed. We sat at an octagon shaped table. He poured coffee for both of us."

"I want you in the show. You'll have your own room. There will be eight rooms, but no walls. No walls, just curtains. I hate walls, fences, tall shrubs, partitions. You know that. It's the ruination of this damn western world. All of us sniveling inside like turtles under attack. Sick. Pervasive sickness. Like the loneliest character in the world. You know the loneliest character in the great world of the imagination?"

"No."

"Every character has loneliness as his core. It's why we create, but the loneliness of the lonely has got to be the demented, religious fool in *Midnight Cowboy*. You know, the guy who invites ole Joe Buck into his apartment to turn a trick. Just flat out keeps repeating lonely, lonely, lonely. No minimalism there. Maximalism loneliness. That guy or even the red-headed teen, that Buck blows in the theatre. That's one hell of a lonely film."

I was thinking of getting the hell out of here, then burning my paintings and becoming a math teacher or an accountant. The world of art always seems to lead me to the madly astray.

"Yeah, it's a lonely film. Ratso and Joe were lonely as hell too." I said.

"Yes. Loneliness spawns art spawns loneliness. How's that for a phrasal palindrome?"

"So, the..."

"The show?"

"Yeah, the show."

"Cerebellum will birth the next great lonely art movement. I've been living my whole life for this show. All roads of my life, all the historical forces of my spirit have led me to Cerebellum. This show will collect the uncollected energy lingering about today's youth and galvanize it into creativity's full potency. We lead impotent lives. Quiet desperation, as Henry said. Cerebellum will return potency to the world of art, which has been castrated. Yes, it will bust open the aged and rusted hinges with the half-baked hunger of lustful, youthful youth. We don't want anything polished and formed and refined. We want it raw and fresh like your work."

"You haven't seen it."

"I don't need to. One can feel the kindred, collective unconscious when it's put before you."

I didn't say anything. I realized I was standing before the Elmer Fudd of American Art and I very well could be making a mockery of my paintings by putting them in this exhibition, but I knew I would. Mockery didn't seem all that disturbing. Just maybe this guy was...

"You know we get tired after a while. It's been one opiate after another. God, egalitarianism, the American Dream, whatever. Same wolf in sheep's clothing. The car and the black paved driveway is the booby prize. That's Springsteen. *Darkness on the edge of town.* This show will toss some light into the darkness. And this darkness is particularly haunting because we just don't know it's there. Scary, Mr. Naturian. Scary, surly lurking evil. We have opiate fatigue. We need a taste of the truth. Cerebellum will be the appetizer. The meal is coming."

"Where's the appetizer?"

"Where's the truth?"

I shrugged my shoulders.

"That's the question. The eternal labrynth. Children of an invisible God."

"Where's the show is what I want to know and I don't know your name?"

"Right now it's Veris."

"Right now?"

"Yes, I change it often. It's more truthful. Paves the way to the great truth hunt. Keeps me fresh. More alive. Gives rebirth."

"So Veris? Is it still Veris?" I asked, smiling.

"Armenians always have a sense of humor. Good for the art, too. The artist should seriously take himself not too seriously."

He gave me a piece of paper with directions.

"See you tomorrow." He turned and walked to a desk. He sat down, spinning a Rolodex. I climbed down the ladder and began walking through the lithography museum. I heard the spinning sound of the Rolodex. I got to the steel door, opened it, and spotted the thin, neon lights of Spa across the street. An image of a naked, faceless Asian woman kneading an old man's back leapt into my head. I could still hear the Rolodex faintly in the background. I thought of returning and asking why he was spinning addresses relentlessly.

Instead, I left.

The night of the show I had all my paintings ready to go. I had framed them in black metal. Minimalism. I had cards for each one. There would be an auction at the end of the show, and for a few moments I had delusions of discovery. Delusions of the superficial salvation of fame, artistic triumph, of being hailed heroic, a Renaissance man, groundbreaking. Delusions of fellatio by alive and artsy women.

Delusion can be very gratifying in the short run.

Until the truth gun is cocked, aimed and fired.

The show was on the 2nd floor of a strip of stores. Below Cerebellum and the next revolution and renaissance in American art, were a pizza place, an adult video store, and a CVS. The mockery was palpable.

I saw some others setting up their rooms. It was quiet. I saw an empty room with the words 'Gone West' above the threshold. There were easels ready for me. I placed the paintings clockwise from San Diego to San Francisco. The last one had the whispering image of the Golden Gate. I was done. What does an artist do at an exhibition? I guess, pretend to be an artist. Feign importance, perhaps. I decided to walk around and see what the others were doing.

The room next door was titled 'Linguistics.' Hanging from the ceiling were long strips of paper. They were the width of toilet paper and hung all the way down to the floor. You had to move the paper out of the way to walk. I looked around for something else. There was nothing else. I looked at the paper and noticed one column of letters. I read the column up and down, but it was not legible. Words weren't formed. It was just a column of random letters.

"You might find a word," said a voice.

A form appeared through the paper maze. It was the quintessential, dark artist. She had pale skin, black hair, and a long, shapeless, black cotton dress draped over her body. There was no hint of breasts, hips, curves of any kind. An upright rectangle covered in black cotton. I noticed tattoos on her neck. Flowers. Black dandelions. Red roses. Intertwined.

"You might."

I nodded.

"But you don't have to look for one. That might be too neurotic, but it's up to you. Who's not neurotic anyway?"

She left.

I let out a deep breath and left the neurosis.

238

The next room was titled 'Tent.' The artist's name was Jack Gallagher. There was a tent inside and nothing else. A simple, triangular tent that would sleep two. I could see a TV monitor inside. I bent down and went into the tent. There was a VCR and TV and two sleeping bags with the heads of stuffed animals sticking out. One was a deer. One was monkey. The TV was showing various images of nature. A stream. The forest. Squirrels jumping and frolicking.

What the hell was I doing here?

I tried one more room. There were tables and chairs with newspapers on each table. It was like a waiting room. I noticed the Boston Globe on one table. The Washington Post, The New York Times. Foreign newspapers, as well. There was a giant, Plexiglas box in the center. It was maybe ten feet wide and four feet high. Inside there was an enormous pile of shredded newspaper. I walked out of the room and looked at the title.

'YESTERDAY'S NEWS' by Charlene Meadow.

I liked this room.

I went back to my room. My room seemed so boring. Easels and abstract-type paintings. Everything was concept art and here I was with ole fashioned paint. Colors. My stuff was dated mid-century and the others were post-modern art school madness. I couldn't wait until this was over. I was nervous and felt foolish. I thought how I felt out of place with suits and equally so with avant-garde.

Middle ground's hard to find.

I sat at a chair near the entrance. A few people came in and looked at the work. They were young hipsters on the pose. They smiled on their way out. Nobody asked any questions. Nobody was going to buy anything. I heard some banter in the other rooms. I heard some commotion. Questions. Discussions of art.

Veris walked into my room. He looked at the paintings.

"You feel it?"

"No," I said.

"Momentum."

"No."

"You will. It's building."

239

I rolled my eyes.

He winked at me. "It's happening. Let it. No rain, amigo, on the parade."

He left.

I felt like going home and watching a baseball game with my grandfather. I was getting ready to leave and forget the whole stupid California mistake again, burn the paintings, and be free. As that momentum was building, a woman entered my room alone. Now, some real momentum. She was beautiful. My knees trembled. My libido and heart surged confluent energies into my body. My legs turned rubber. I actually closed my eyes. Tightly. I wondered if this were really happening. I shook my head. I reached down to grab my knees. I wanted to prevent my kneecaps from liquefying and running down my legs spilling all over the floor.

How would I explain that?

I bent down and held my knees, but I could still see her face. The Mediterranean skin, soft mahogany hair falling along her shoulders, sensual lips. She had a sleeveless, light blue shirt on and white Capri pants. A cerulean, summer sky with white, cotton clouds. No one part of her monopolized my eyes. It was her entire being that captured me.

I told myself this was not male lust wanting to copulate any beauty presented before the indiscriminate, lupine libido. This was delirium. Glorious delusion. The Glorious Revolution. The truth gun. No, not delirium, but the ultra-lucidity one feels upon seeing the one partner we have framed in our head and buried in our thoughts, but have never actually seen. There is a one. There has to be. It must be her. She was here right before my eyes causing chemical anarchy within. Seize the moment. There has never been a moment like this. I started to calm down out of absolute necessity. I stood up.

She smiled at me, seemingly undisturbed by my crouching tomfoolery. She looked back at my paintings. Was this the purpose of my art? Was this purpose of going to the west and painting? Was it to bring it to this moment and this person?

I didn't say anything for a while. I feared a volcanic, verbal explosion if I uttered one word. I feared getting down on a knee and proposing if she recognized my existence. Marriage might be rushing it before getting her name. I gave her some time and calmed my thumping heart.

When she finished, she turned to me.

"I like them."

"I'm glad."

"You are the painting."

"Painter." I smiled and relaxed that she was more human than the Helen of Troy perfection I was concocting.

"Yes, yes, my English makes me fool sometime."

"It's beautiful."

"What?"

"My English."

"No, not really. Almost one year here and I do silly mistake yet."

"No, it is. Your accent is also beautiful. Everything about you is."

"*Gracias.*"

"*De nada.*"

She turned a little red. I believe I did too, though I was feeling more relaxed. I wasn't going to let this woman leave this room without her knowing she was the one. Those stories you hear where people say they meet someone and know they are going to marry that person. I didn't know if she wanted me, but I knew she was right for me instantly. I refused to lose her to diffidence.

"So, Spain or Latin America?"

"Spain," she said.

"What part?"

"Barcelona. Just outside Barcelona. Can I make you a question?"

"Anything."

"What happened in California? I love your paintings. Yes, you are the painter. I love your paintings. They have a power, a energy. Sad and sweet mixed. Like life. Can you tell about them? I'm curiosity."

"You are curiosity."

"Another mistake?"

"No. Never a mistake."

"You too kind. My English will never improve with you."

"It's perfect to me. It doesn't need to improve."

She smiled again.

I was silent.

"Will you tell me about California? About the origin of painting?"

"I'll tell you everything you want to know about everything."

"That takes a long time."

"The longer, the better," I said. "Are you hungry? I know a twenty-four hour Chinese restaurant nearby. We can eat and drink and talk as long as you want."

"That is perfect."

"Let me gather the paintings and put them in my car."

"What about this exhibition? It's finished?"

I laughed. "Exhibition. Hmm, I don't know if I would call it that. It is finished for me. I don't belong here. You know, I was thinking of burning the paintings and now because of you I will save them."

"It would be a lost if you burned them. Why are you such anger on them?"

"It's a long story."

"We will have time."

"Did you drive?"

"No. I don't have a car."

"Then we take my car. By the way, how did you find about this crazy show?"

"I saw an advertisement at my school. I take English classes at Brown."

I nodded. Veris was right. Cerebellum would alter momentum, change the flow of history. Revolutionize the staid moment.

Mine.

I was the happiest man alive at that moment. That was the 38th Parallel of my life. Everything before seemed an irrelevant prelude. Everything in that moment seemed utopian harmony. Everything after, I projected, would be all the meaning any searcher would want. We are monogamous with the right person. We need a mate to get across the bridge.

"I don't know your name," I said.

"Sangiella."

"More beauty."

"And you?"

"Dixson. Less beauty."

"No, I like. I like the sound of Dixson and Sangiella."

"So do I."

We were both smiling fools, falling fast and hard. I could see she was in the same place as me. Gravity unshackled.

We took the paintings down and Sangiella helped me take them out to my car.

Veris stopped us.

"Dixson, what are you doing?"

"I'm leaving, Veris. I wish you luck with Cerebellum and I want to thank you."

"For what?"

"For her," I said, looking at Sangiella.

"The power of art can draw the fates in. Cerebellum has power, Dixson. Doth not mock this movement, for look what it hath brought thou."

"You are right."

"Do not forsake the muse, my friend. You will not be forgiven for wasting the dawn. Do not let go of the perimeter. Do not waste the dawn."

"Never."

Veris put both his hands to his mouth and blew a kiss at us. "Open the castle doors," he said, disappearing into another room.

We looked at each other and laughed.

"To the Chinese castle," I said.

We went to the aptly-named Summer Palace and sat in a maroon vinyl booth surrounded by tacky Chinese paintings, plastic plants, and many red tasseled decorations that the owner, Hung, once told me were supposed to bring good luck. There were many beautiful photos of the Great

Wall scattered about. Hung had traveled extensively in China. He was, however, Taiwanese.

We sat and talked all night. We ate dinner and drank Tsing-Tao beer until three or four in the morning. We laughed and joked and talked about America and Spain and all the things we wanted to show each other from our countries. Then we switched to coffee to get us into dawn. We couldn't waste the dawn. We toasted out coffee mugs to Veris. Then we began to share the pains of our life stories. Alcohol, caffeine, the moment loosened the hinges on veracity. She told me her story.

Sangiella came to America to change her life. She had left Barcelona to escape her family and her last relationship. She had foreseen bad patterns if she stayed and she thought changing continents and a new language would change her destiny. Her last boyfriend was a pilot for Iberian Air. He was very handsome, and in uniform was every young Catalan girl's dream. She felt so lucky to be at his side. However, he treated her horribly after a few months of bliss. He flaunted other women in front of her and she was so hurt and so angry at him, but she didn't leave him. She stayed. Their arguments escalated into abuse. He began striking her. Finally, Sangiella's brother sat her down and said she had to do something. He knew she had been lying about black eyes and bruises. If she didn't, he would go to the pilot's home and destroy him. She told me she felt suicidal. Empty. She felt she had lost her identity to this man because she had failed to carve her identity out for herself before entering the relationship. She had taken on his interests rather than discover her own. She had allowed him to shape her and hurt her. She felt like fallen clay on a pottery wheel. She went into therapy and over a few months was finally able to leave him. She spent one year with a therapist, who Sangiella said had changed her life. She recognized her unformed identity. She connected the present to the past. She got in touch with the tragedy that had befallen her home. Her older sister had died in a car crash with her father driving. Her father had survived, but the family was draped in trauma and melancholy for her entire childhood. Sangiella had been conceived just months after the death of her eight year old sister. Her parents never grieved or coped. They just leapt into headfirst solution. Sangiella. She felt guilty to be alive. She felt she was a replacement. She was thrown into a world with parents too numb to love again. Too afraid. Too guilty. After she removed herself from the abusive relationship with the pilot, she began to find inner strength. She began "to parent myself because my parents were never able to do it." The death of their daughter had permanently damaged them. Her mother never got over it and a pendant of her deceased daughter hung from her neck to remind everyone and herself of her agony. The pendant was never hidden by clothing. It was omnipresent.

 Sangiella wanted out. She didn't want to blame her parents. She wanted to understand them and the effect it had upon her. She felt she needed to leave them for a while to understand and process all of the past. Self-awareness unspoiled by anger. She wanted to continue to grow inside and gain strength. She decided to challenge herself by living overseas. She didn't know anyone in America. She knew almost no English upon her arrival. She had studied some in high school, but she was a poor student because of her insecurity and shyness. She wanted to prove herself as a student. After learning English, she would return home and look for work in tourism because her great passion was travel. She had traveled every year since she was sixteen. She traveled European style. Four weeks at a time, not a weekend or one week in Orlando. She had traveled to almost every European country as well as Thailand, Kenya, India, Cuba, and now the U.S. Her four weeks of traveling were the happiest times of every year.

 "And America? Do you like it?" I asked.

 "Not too much."

 "Why not?"

 "I don't like food, people are all such busy and no time for friends. The family I live with never see people. Just work and watch TV at night with the kids. Very bored life. In Barcelona we spend hours each day with friends. We stay late and talk, but we don't have so much money or job there. I miss home. I miss my family. They damaged me, but are my family and we yet have fun moments. I love them. I feel ready to be with them now. I feel ready to forgive. I'm stronger. I understand what they are now with the look outside. Make sense?"

"Yes, completely. When do you leave?"

"One month."

There was some silence.

"There is one thing I like about America?"

"Twenty-four hour Chinese restaurants?"

"Yes. And you."

The castle doors were wide open.

We went back to my grandfather's after watching the sunrise on Federal Hill. We didn't waste the dawn. She had told me so much about herself and I shared my demons as well. I told her about my family and the Xeno and Hannah madness. She told me about an affair she had had with a married man. There was no judging each other. The forgiveness only strangers can give. We accepted each other and respected our honesty and contrition. We put everything out in the first hours of knowing each other. Our connection felt invincible. I had never felt anything like I felt then.

She met my grandfather and immediately fell for him. She knew what he meant for me and this made him heroic for her, too. We spent everyday together. We had no privacy in either home to make love. The relationship was born and grew without sex. We kissed and talked and spent time with some of my friends. Eventually, we succumbed to desire. We took weekend getaways in New England and made love with wild abandon from the pent up energies. It felt just as right in bed as out of bed.

Chemistry.

In Boston we walked around Harvard University. She had always wanted to see Harvard. We went to Provincetown and she said it was like Sigis in Spain. The last weekend we went to New York City. Walking around Central Park, we made a vow. I would come to Spain and spend one month just like we had here. She would teach me some Spanish. I would meet her family, friends, live her life like she had lived mine. We wanted to make another vow after that month.

We had no doubts.

We had a dramatic, romantic goodbye at the airport.
I would leave in two weeks. My grandfather supported my
decision. He told me I was crazy with all this traveling and
worried about money, but he liked Sangiella. He nodded at
me and said, "She's a good girl." Simplicity. He gave me
$500 to help me in Spain. "One month, only?" He asked.
"One month and I'll be back."

Those were the longest two weeks of my life. I tried
to read about Barcelona. I tried to learn some Spanish from
a book. My head was not in it. I couldn't stand being away
from Sangiella. We spoke a couple of times a week. Those
were the only times I felt alive. I understood, finally, the
concept of having another half. Truly understood.

During those eternal couple weeks, I remembered an
old friend, Remy Serenghetti, who had been in a similar
position as me. Remy was five years older than I. I had met
him one summer during college when we both worked at a
restaurant waiting tables. He had met a woman from
Portugual. Another Iberian beauty. When I went back for
my junior year, he moved to Lisbon. I had heard he recently
moved back to the States with the Portuguese woman. They
had married and settled in Providence. I found his number
through information and called him up. He didn't say much
when I had asked about his wife. Remy was the shrouded-
in-mystery type. I never truly got to know him, but I had
always wanted to. I told him I was in a similar situation and
maybe he could share some of his experience in an
international relationship and living overseas. He invited me
over.

Most of all I just wanted to talk about Sangiella.
Tell someone about it. Hear her name coming from my
mouth. The separation was unbearable. The longing ached
in my chest. Deep, profound ache. Gorgeous, meaningful
pain. Pure longing. When I shared it with some friends, I
sounded pathetic. I'd see her in a couple weeks. Friends got
tired of hearing about it. I understood.

I was pathetic. I was euphoric.

I had my ticket to leave in two weeks. I'd never
make it. It felt like I had to wait a year.

Perhaps, Remy would understand my state of being.

I hadn't seen Remy since that summer a few years ago. He and his wife, Selina, were living in Providence when I knew him. They hadn't married yet and were planning the move to Portugal. He was waiting tables and taking classes in teaching English as a foreign language so he could find work in Lisbon. Remy was also a writer. He had written one novel that he was sending out to publishers during that summer. He told me he planned on writing a second novel in Portugal. "I'd write my European, ex-pat novel." He was quietly on top of the world. He was aloof, but friendly at work. He never socialized or engaged in the post-work antics of restaurant folk. He did his job and was focused on his art and his woman.

When I knew Remy, he had red hair that was buzzed short. He was muscular thin, and his short hair made his face more bony and angular. He had bright, azure eyes set deep below a protruding brow that cast a dark shadow over his eyes and nose. Light and shadow. Remy was intense. Striking. Swirling thought energy. He seemed on the verge of saying a lot, but he rarely did.

I had just gotten off the phone with Sangiella when I headed over to his place. Our conversations always left me in a state of orbit. I never expected love could be so potent. So consuming. I couldn't imagine a life without Sangiella, even though all but one month of my life had been without her.

Conversely, I now understood the truth of loneliness. The Hannah/Xeno mess seemed tiny, juvenile. This was real.

Remy lived in a two-family house. I rang the top bell. I heard him yell to come on up. We shook hands. "Come on in, Dixson." Remy looked the same. I sat down on the couch. CNN financial was on the TV. I could see the stock ticker tape going by below. "You want some coffee?" He asked. "Sure." He went into the kitchen. It was Monday, late morning. In ten days I would be in Barcelona.

His apartment was large and sparsely decorated. Bigger than I expected and simply furnished. It was all hard wood floors and no rugs. There was a greyhound lying in the corner on a puffy dog mattress. His long, skinny snout was aimed at me and his dull eyes rested apathetically towards me. I turned my attention to a photo on the wall. It was a red boat docked in a harbor surrounded by many other colorful boats.

"The Portuguese coast, Dixson."

"Lisbon?"

"Near. Cascais. It's pronounced Cash-caish. That's where we got married."

"Where is she?"

"She's still in Cascais."

I nodded.

Remy watched the TV for a bit and then jotted something down in a notebook.

"I left her," he said

"Your wife?"

"Art."

"Art?" I asked.

"Yeah, it's a myth. All skies and seas and suns and silhouettes. That's how I think of it. It was trapdoors and trampolines. How's that for alliteration and bullshit poetry?"

"You stopped writing?"

"I chose Dale Carnegie over Andre Breton. I chose real estate over surrealism. So obvious. One's real. One's shadowy abstract. Took me to long too realize that."

More surrealism, I thought. "What happened?"

He gave the greyhound a treat. The dog ate it without much interest and then plopped his face back down, still staring at me. I looked away.

"You play the game or the game plays you," Remy said.

I furrowed my brow.

"You know, I've always thought the greatest American of the 20th century was Malcolm X. He fought the game and then he realized he had to play. Constant evolution. Self-taught behind bars. Not some silver spoon stuck up his rectum, Ivy League phony. Constant evolution rather than permanent revolution. Learn and unlearn at the same time. Molt and then motion."

"You're losing me a little, Remy." I looked at the TV and back at him. "You buying stocks now?"

"Yeah. Stocks and property."

"Really?"

"Really."

"You've changed."

"You have to. One has to, that is. Or you get caught in a status-quo quagmire. Quagmires are bad places. One way tickets too often."

"Yeah, I got caught in one."

"You out?"

I nodded. I looked around the place. "I like it. Can I ask the rent?

"I charge $800."

"You own it?"

"Change. Evolution. Screw art. I got off the trampoline and walked around the trapdoor. You don't have to go through. You just take the easy way."

"Congrats on the house."

"Thanks. I rent out the first floor. Always take the high ground when given the choice. Just link Bunker Hill. Normandy. War 101."

"That's great, Remy, congratulations."

He nodded. "A little luck in the market and I should have another two-family house this year."

"Wow! You have changed. You hit it big with your novel or something?" I asked.

"No, I told you I left her. No more art. No more beards. No more Halloween."

"Did you ever get it published?"

"Yeah, Selina got a friend to translate it into Portuguese. Couldn't even get it read in America. So, we found a publisher in Lisbon. Little thing, but it went to my head. I thought I had my own little, neo-Lost Generation going. About 1,000 copies sold. Then, because of the European publication, we got some small American publisher to do it, too. He thought we had the next *Tropic of Cancer* and I fell for it. Delusions of grandeur. I leapt into my own circus. There are a few copies floating around somewhere. The book made enough money for a few meals for Ray, but it wasn't about the money, right, Ray. It's about truth. It's about art for art's sake."

He looked over at the Greyhound and laughed.

"Art for my ass's sake," Remy said.

"What's the title?" I asked.

"What?" He was jotting down more figures from the TV.

"Your book."

"Cascais." He pointed to the photo on the wall.

"The place you got married."

"Little hip, fishing town outside Lisbon. Last train stop. Swanky nostalgia on Costa Do Sol. We had our salad days. Days of wine and roses."

"You got a copy? I'd like to read it."

"Somewhere."

"What's the long and short of it?"

"The long and short of it?" he smiled. "Don't know really. Breton would have said any novel that has a long and short of it is no novel. Might have said. Arrogant Parisian that he was."

He drank some coffee and ran the back of his hand along Ray's jaw. Ray's tail wagged slowly.

"It's standard ex-pat stuff. Love story overseas. Innocent abroad. Lots of stuff about the place. I loved Portugual, Dixson. I want to die there. I wanted to die there. The coast of Portugal is like no other. Mystical, mad, transcendent. I spent hours sitting on the edge of cliffs north of Cascais. No people, just the sea. I'd close my eyes and breathe in the briny air and listen to the howling wind and the Atlantic raging into the jagged, rocky coast and then gently settle into foamy, white peace until it would do it all over again. Serene Sisyphus. Anger and peace flowing. I'd just sit on the edge of the old world. That's what it was, Dixson. The damn edge of the world."

I nodded. I didn't think he noticed as he inhaled. I was surprised at how talkative Remy had become. Perhaps, he was just quiet in groups and more free in intimate situations. Perhaps, it was part of his evolution, I presumed.

People change.

"You look out into the sea at dusk along Costa do Sol and you know why they thought it was the end of the world. Why they thought there were demons and beasts prowling the horizons. We don't have that external mystery now. All that's left now is the inside – chemical mind frontiers, neurons have replaced land and space. We're trapped in claustrophobia."

"Well, I'd like to read it. I remember reading some of your stuff back in our Grill 84 days. It was good stuff."

"Was. I'm done. Making money, my friend. Playing the game. Once I buy the 2nd house, I'll have 4 apartments to rent. I'll head back to Lisbon and have a friend manage the properties. Draw a salary on the rent and be able to work less over there. Have a civilized, normal life. Have a family."

"With Seline?"

"That's the plan. My plan."

"Her plan, too?"

He pondered that question.

"You know, I've been working like a dog. Work like Ray used to at the track. Ray used to run up in New Hampshire at Rockingham. I've been teaching English classes over at URI full-time and waiting tables full-time over Esposito's downtown."

"Shit, Remy, that's a lot of work." I looked closely at him. He did look tired. He had dark circles under his shadowed blue eyes.

"Yeah, I got no time except now. Monday daytime. My only free time and I've got to manage my investments. Got my money flowing into stocks and funds. Time to buy now, Dixson. Buy low, sell high. The bulls will be running soon and I'm gonna ride 'em right out of Pamplona. Get the hell out of town."

"Back to Cascais?"

"Yeah, the place, not the novel."

I nodded.

"You, my friend? Still painting. Still dreaming art?"

"No, I'm kind of like you. Went out west with Xeno. Remember him?"

"Vaguely. From what I remember he belongs out there."

"Oh yeah. I painted some stuff and it didn't go anywhere. I was planning to go back to school. Ran into a quagmire."

"Relationship quagmire?"

"More or less."

"Still want to be an art teacher? Kids, right?"

"Yeah, but I've been sidetracked."

"A woman?"

"Of course," I smiled.

"Yes, of course."

"She's Spanish. We fell instantly. I'm heading over there in ten days to spend a month with her. I'm going to ask to her to marry me."

"How long have you known her?"

"One month."

He nodded and looked down. He started to say something and stopped.

"I know, Remy, it's only a month. When you know, you know."

"What do you know, my friend?"

"I know I love her. I know my life changed the moment I saw her. I know what I feel."

"How do you know what you feel?"

"What the hell do you mean? I feel it. I know it."

"You think, therefore you are."

"Something happen to you and Selina?"

"Time can wreak havoc, Dixson. I don't know. Whole bunch of therapy has done good. Opened me up. Raw as sushi for a while. Never mind. One month doesn't give you legs for eternity."

"I know. It'll take work. It won't always be this dreamy, but it should start this way."

"Maybe not."

"Why not."

"I don't have any answers."

"You seem to think you do," I said in a piqued voice.

"When it starts out so dreamy, so perfect, maybe there are things going on inside. Things we run from more so than we are going to. Things that make us go headfirst."

"Remy, I don't know what happened to you and Selina. I'm sorry, though."

Remy looked away from me when he spoke. "Things can change. If only everyday could be the wedding day. Had no doubts. I fell in love a hundred times in one day on my wedding day. Every time I looked at her I fell in love again. I was marrying that moment. A thousand times

253

in a moment. You fall in love with an image, a hope. Puts a lot of pressure on the spouse. Kind of like Gatsby old sport and the tuning fork to the sky…the kiss of the dream woman Daisy ended the dream of love…slipped into the cracks of the old, dry earth soul…Time is powerful. Potent. Lethal panacea. Daisy didn't have a chance."

"Are you guys separated?" I asked.

"Yeah, but we'll work it out. I've changed. I told you I left art. Thankless lie. Adults parading around as children. Can't even stand to be in the same room as another artist. I lost my way a bit after the book got published. Thought I was something, but I realized I was nothing without my mate."

"Remy, I really hope you guys work it out."

He was still looking away. "We will. We have to. Shit happens so suddenly in hindsight. Can't explain so much. Black ink has spilled quickly. Everything got triggered so easily. Tangled. A pronoun. A syllable. A look. The tiniest event of the present can exhume the internal dead."

He looked over at me. "Mendacity," he said in a heavy voice and laughed.

"What she doing now?"

"I don't know. Where's you lady from again?"

"Spain."

He smiled. "Selina and I made love in La Sagrada Familia. Gaudi would have been proud." He was silent for a bit and then he began to sing. "Farewell and adieu your Spanish ladies. Farewell and adieu your ladies of Spain. Best damn movie ever. 'Not like chasing blue gills and Tommy cats at the pond. It' a big fish. Swallow you whole.'" Remy said in gravelly, cigarette Quint voice. "You wanna ante up, I'll catch the head, the tail, the whole damn fish. Or you wanna play it cheap and be on welfare all winter…Best character ever. Eating saltines. Peeling apples and eating the insides with a Bowie knife, too. Wasn't he?"

"Don't remember that."

"Maybe it was his sidekick. Little guy with flannel hat. Didn't say a word. Just followed ole Quint around. Loved him. Whatever. Anyway."

I didn't know what to say anymore. This wasn't going according to plan.

"Surfing Dixson. It's all surfing. You ride the waves, the flow and when the ebb rears up from behind. Stay calm until the next wave comes in. Don't lose your way, amigo mio. Beware of impulses."

"I'll remember that."

"The world is bipolar, amigo. We ought to plant some Prozak in mother earth. Get her back into the right spin. Axis must be all out of joint."

"I've met some crazy folk lately, Remy. You're right. California's full of them." I wanted to include him, but I didn't.

"The Humpty Dumpty state. Ole Humpty sat on a wall, Humpty Dumpty had a great fall. All the king's horses and all the king's men, couldn't put Humpty together again."

I wanted to leave. I was tired of his nonsense. Everything has been nonsense in my life except my grandfather and Sangiella. Remy was a mess.

"Let's cut to the chase, Dixson. You want your cards read?"

"Tarot cards?"

"The future. Your life with the Spanish lady."

"Sangiella's her name."

"How's her relationship with her parents? Her mother in particular."

"Not too good. She had some shit go down in childhood."

"And you and your parents?"

"Shitty, but I don't see them much, so it doesn't affect me."

He laughed condescendingly. A smug, insulting laugh.

"Remy I didn't come for your bleakness. All apologies, but—"

"Amigo, *Vaia con dios*. You are going to need him. You got yourself a subconscious war in the offing. Yellow sun and blue sky time ain't gonna last. The demons will start playing chess with you two. Collisions you won't understand. Moment is never about the moment. Pawns make their move quietly and then it's all bishops and rooks

255

until the queen strikes. When the shit hits the fan, it's open season for the soldiers marching below. A subconscious Stalingrad."

"You're like a typhoon on my parade, Remy. Thanks for nothing."

"I'm just giving you a caveat emptor. Ancient rhythms seek music, amigo. Heads up is all."

"I'm so goddamn happy about Sangiella and so confident, nothing bothers me. Remy, I wish you luck getting Selina back. I presume she left you."

He nodded. "I would have left me. I don't blame her now."

He got up and opened a closet. He grabbed a leash that was hanging on the inside of the door. "You want a take a walk with Ray and me?"

"No, I got to go. I got to get my passport," I lied.

"*Vaia con Dios, amigo mio.*"

"I don't need him. Good luck Remy."

We shook hands.

"Come here, Ray boy." Ray slowly got up, stretched out his front legs out and then his hind legs. He moaned as he limbered up for his walk. He walked really slowly toward Remy and then sat next to him. His tail was moving a bit as Remy showed him the leash.

"I wish you luck. Dixson. Say hello to Iberia."

Remy went one way. I went the other. I saw my bus pulling up to the stop. I ran really hard to catch it. Just as I got to the end of the bus, it began to leave. I ran faster and hit the glass on the backdoor. The driver heard me and stopped.

"Thanks," I said, as I put some change in the machine. The driver nodded.

I sat at the back of the bus and looked back. I could see Remy and Ray watching. He waved at me and I returned it. He and Ray turned and walked on. The bus rumbled forward.

I finally caught my breath. Once I did, I realized I was really tired. Tired from the past six months. So much had happened. I didn't want anything else to happen. Nothing aside from being with Sangiella. Remy was right.

It's all trapdoors and trampolines out there. Various offerings of anesthesia. It was all bipolar until Sangiella. The wide open road had narrowed and all its seductive exits had disappeared.

California, Hannah, Imagine Incarnate, Cerebellum, Veris, *Gone West*, art—it had all been exits. They dripped away one by one, but led me to the path.

I was thankful for the madness. Thankful for its conclusion.

I would decompress overseas and start life in Spain. I couldn't wait. I knew what I wanted and it wasn't about games of now or the moment. It was about the future.

Tomorrow I would take the $500 my grandfather gave me and buy a diamond.

No more false escapes.

Just the great and true entrance.

About the Author

Ken Janjigian earned a BA from Clark University in 1988 and MA from Lesley University in 1998. This is his first novel. He lives and teaches in the Boston area. Janjigian is currently working on a second novel.